Praise for *The Bones of You*

"Suspenseful and poignant debut . . . the increasingly tense storytelling and astute observations on mother-daughter relationships will keep readers turning the pages."—*Publishers Weekly*

"Has been compared to Alice Sebold's *The Lovely Bones*, as they both feature young murdered females as narrators. Indeed, Rosie's voice offers a dynamic narrative. Her disembodied perspective, tempered with other points of view—chiefly Kate's—adds an unusual and haunting layer to the novel."—*Library Journal*

"A dazzling debut from a writer who looks to me to have an exceptional future. Howells's novel has a rare freshness and depth that set her apart."—*The Daily Mail*

"This summer's hottest read."—*The Guardian*

"Skillfully plotted . . . keeps readers from guessing who was really responsible for Rosie's death until the strangely satisfying truth is revealed."—BookPage

The Bones of you

DEBBIE HOWELLS

PINNACLE BOOKS
Kensington Publishing Corp.
www.kensingtonbooks.com

PINNACLE BOOKS are published by

Kensington Publishing Corp.
119 West 40th Street
New York, NY 10018

All Kensington titles, imprints, and distributed lines are available at special quantity discounts for bulk purchases for sales promotions, premiums, fund-raising, educational, or institutional use. Special book excerpts or customized printings can also be created to fit specific needs. For details, write or phone the office of the Kensington sales manager: Kensington Publishing Corp., 119 West 40th Street, New York, NY 10018, attn: Sales Department; phone 1-800-221-2647.

This book is a work of fiction. Names, characters, businesses, organizations, places, events, and incidents either are the product of the author's imagination or are used fictitiously. Any resemblance to actual persons, living or dead, events, or locales is entirely coincidental.

PINNACLE BOOKS and the Pinnacle logo are Reg. U.S. Pat. & TM Off.

ISBN-13: 978-0-7860-3914-2
ISBN-10: 0-7860-3914-0

First mass market paperback printing: June 2016

10 9 8 7 6 5 4 3 2 1

Printed in the United States of America

First electronic edition: June 2016

ISBN-13: 978-0-7860-4110-7
ISBN-10: 0-7860-4110-2

Thank you . . .

To my friends who have supported me unreservedly: Ali, Candy, Clare, Giselle, Hazel, Heather, Natasha, Sarah, thank you, all of you—you're the best x

To Lis, for your help and generosity in more ways than you know x

To my sisters, Sarah, Anna and Freddie, for sharing the highs and lows along the way—and there've been some!

And to Annette Clayton, Steve Page and Terry Skelton for taking the time to share your inside view of a murder investigation—I hope I've done your thoughtful answers justice—any inaccuracies are all mine.

So many people have helped shape this book into what it is today, and especial thanks are due to my two brilliant and astute editors, Trisha Jackson at Pan Macmillan in the UK and Alicia Condon at Kensington in the US.

Huge thanks also to Juliet Mushens, super-agent, for making my dream happen, and to Sasha Raskin in the US.

Finally, to my parents for being my parents—dear Dad, you had more faith in me than I did! Mum, I wish you were here to share this.

And to Bob, Georgie and Tom, with love. This was always for you.

Stars are the souls of dead poets,
but to become a star, you have to die.

—*Vincent van Gogh*

Rosie

August

It's true, what they say about when you die. In the final, terrible seconds of my life, eighteen years flash before my eyes.

It's when I understand the difference between life and death. It's time. Did you know it takes 0.0045 seconds for an input to reach the brain and a further 0.002 for a reaction to happen? How long it takes to gasp with shock? How long, from when the knife first rips into me, before the agony starts? That seconds can stretch into eternity?

I feel myself leave my body, breaking free of the invisible threads that join me to it, until I'm floating, looking down at the blood, a thick, dark pool seeping under the leaves into the earth. And though my brain is starved of oxygen, flooded with endorphins, I'm hanging on, waiting for an unknown something.

And then it starts, in freeze-frames, moments of time caught like small plastic snow globes without the snow. I see my parents—too young to be my parents—but I know my mother's pale hair and the smile that doesn't reach her eyes, my father's firm hand pressed on her shoulder.

They're holding a baby in front of a small redbrick house I don't recognize.

It fades and blurs into another image, then another. Then, when I'm five years old, my pictures become motion pictures, and I'm in them. Living, hoping, dreaming, all over again—only this time, it's different.

The wonderful childhood I had, the toys, far-flung holidays, the TV in my bedroom, which I was so proud of, all still there, only shattered into a million pieces, blood-stained, dust-covered, shrouded in inky blackness.

Then the voices start. The secrets no one must ever know, which aren't secrets anymore, because I can hear them. The face that was always watching me, that knows the truth.

I'm looking at the movie of my life.

1

August

I put down the phone and just stand there, completely still.

"Mum? What is it?"

Everything in this house is Grace's business. At eighteen, she's allowed secrets, but no one else. When I don't reply instantly, it's not good enough.

"*Mother,* who were you talking to?"

"Sorry." You know those moments when your head is bursting with too many thoughts to form the words? My eyes fix blankly on something—a spot on the wall, an empty mug—not seeing them. "That was Jo. Something really odd's happened. Rosie's gone missing."

Living at opposite ends of a small village, with daughters at the same school, Jo and I belong to a group of mothers who meet now and then. I know that she's married to Neal, a renowned journalist, whose handsome face I've seen looking out of our TV screen more times than I've actually met him, reporting from the middle of war zones. That they have two daughters, drive new cars—her black Range Rover and Neal's BMW X5—and live in this big, architect-designed house, which I've been inside only once or twice. It's a friendship that extends to the occasional coffee or gossipy lunch, but it's Rosie to whom I've found myself drawn. They're the same age, Grace and Rosie, A levels behind them, the start of hard-won university places a few short weeks away, but the similarities end there. I know Rosie as a shy girl, quieter than Grace's crowd and who shares my love of horses.

Grace rolls her eyes. "She's probably just hanging out with Poppy and hasn't told Jo, because she wouldn't let her. Poppy's a slut."

She says it good-naturedly, like *idiot* or *moron,* but it's an ugly word on my daughter's lips. The reprimand's out before I can stop it.

"Gracie . . ."

And then my mind's wandering, as I try to imagine what's happened to her, seeing the clear eyes she hides behind the fair hair that falls across her face.

"Seriously, Mum. You haven't met Poppy. Her skirt's so short, you can see her panties. And she snogs any-thing—even Ryan Francis."

Ryan Francis is the worst male specimen on the planet, according to Grace, who's yet to explain exactly why.

"But Rosie's not like that, surely?" I struggle to imagine the Rosie I know snogging an indiscriminate anyone. She has a gentleness I've seen with my horses, which comes from her own instincts. They mooch peacefully around her through the long grass, like she's one of them.

"Duh. I'm talking about Poppy, Mother. But, you know, peer pressure and all that . . . I wouldn't be sur-prised. . . ."

Alarm bells start ringing. What if she's right and Rosie's got in with a bad crowd or, worse, been persuaded to run off with some less-than-desirable boy? Should I say something to Jo? Then I see Grace's face. She's winding me up.

"Well, whatever," I say, annoyed, because this isn't something to joke about. "If you hear anything, let me know. Jo's really worried. She hasn't seen Rosie since yesterday, and her mobile goes straight to voice mail. If it was you, Grace, I'd be out of my mind."

Grace hesitates. "I can get Poppy's number, if you like." Flicking her long red hair over her shoulder as she busies herself texting.

Thanks to the interconnectedness of today's teenagers, in a few seconds she has it. "I'll send it to your phone."

Half an hour later, I get through to Jo. She's jittery, not surprisingly, only half listening, her mind jumping all over the place.

"Not Poppy Elwood?" I can hear from her voice, she's shocked. "Oh, Kate, Rosanna wouldn't be friends with *her.* . . ."

"Well, according to Grace, she is."

"Oh my God . . ." I can hear her imagining her worst nightmare, that her daughter's run off or eloped. Jo's inclined to fuss over her daughters, even though Rosie's eighteen and about to leave home. "The police will find her, won't they? You hear about this kind of thing happening . . . but they always do find them, don't they?"

"Try not to worry, Jo." Sounding far more confident than I feel. "I'm sure they will—if it comes to that. She'll probably walk in any moment with a perfectly reasonable explanation. But why don't you call Poppy?" I remind her. "You never know. She might be able to tell you something."

"Yes, I suppose I should." She's quiet. "I still can't believe she's friends with that girl."

I know how she feels. All mothers have them. The friends who threaten everything we've ever wanted for our daughters with another way to live, another set of standards, which we're terrified they'll prefer to ours.

"She can't be all bad, or Rosie wouldn't be friends with her," I point out. "And at the end of the day, she's *your daughter*. She knows what's right. She's not stupid."

Jo's silence echoes my own hesitation, because it's not something Rosie's even hinted at, but I'm curious.

"I was thinking. . . . Does she have a boyfriend, Jo? Only if she does, he might know something."

"No. She doesn't. She's put all her time into studying. Not like . . ." She leaves the sentence open-ended.

"I'll get off the phone," I say hastily, ignoring her gibe at the students who work hard but play hard, too. Like Grace. "She might be trying to call you. Will you let me know when she comes home?"

Rosie will turn up. I'm sure of it. I have a gardener's inherent belief in the natural order of things. Soft-petaled flowers that go to seed. The resolute passage of the seasons. Swallows that fly thousands of miles to follow the eternal summer.

Children who don't die before their parents.

2

After I've spoken to Jo, I call upstairs, "I'm going riding, Grace. . . . Want to come?"

"Going out," comes the muffled reply from behind her closed door. "Sorry."

Another day, her indifference might irritate me, but not today. Grace likes to ride out early, when the air's still cool and the landscape quiet. Thinking time, she calls it. And it means I can set my own pace, instead of being swept along full tilt on teenage time, when the entire day happens randomly and at speed—until you arrive at the social-life part, which is what it's all about. And today I need time to clear my head.

It's hot for late afternoon, a heavy, muggy kind of heat that goes with the clouds bubbling up in the unstable air. As I walk across the field, the horses are lethargic, lazily flicking tails against the flies, momentarily interrupting their grazing to lift their heads when they hear me coming.

Apart from my own semiretired Reba and Grace's almost outgrown Oz, the horses here arrive with problems, according to their owners, who pay me well to reschool them. It fits around my work designing gardens, and, anyway, horses are my lifeblood.

Whatever else is happening in my life, they keep me grounded. It's their beauty, their spirit, matched by no other creature. The way they move, the warm, velvet softness of a muzzle against my cheek. There's no pretending with a horse. They read your body language. Know what you're thinking before you do.

Today I'm riding Zappa, a large gray I've been warned is unpredictable and dangerous. *Whatever,* as Grace would say, rolling her eyes. He's one of the most beautiful horses I've ever seen, with straight, elevated paces and dark, intelligent eyes. The kind of horse that hears your every whisper, responds to the smallest shift of balance. A dream.

This supposedly dangerous horse stands sleepily while I tack him up, then, once I'm on him, strides calmly up the lane, his pale coat contrasting with the rapidly darkening sky, ears twitching back and forth as he peers over walls and hedges. Not for the first time, I contemplate how long I can keep him here before I tell his owner there's absolutely nothing wrong with him.

At the top of the hill, we reach the bridle path through the woods just as the first, heavy drops of rain fall. The breeze is picking up, and Zappa jumps as a field away, a gust of wind slams a gate shut. I glance up at the sky, which is growing blacker by the second, then toward the woods, where beneath the trees, it's darker still.

Scenting the coming storm, Zappa takes the decision out of my hands and jogs into the woods. I press him forward just as the heavens open and the drops become a deluge.

Underneath the leafy canopy, the path is dry. The sudden cry of a pheasant startles him, and I touch his neck, steady him, as one of his hooves catches a tree root. As he breaks into a canter, out of nowhere Rosie's in my mind.

The other night, the last time anyone saw her, she could have been here.

My heart quickens with the intensity of the raindrops as I shake off the sense of disquiet that fills me. Rosie could have been anywhere.

But what if something has happened to her?

And then another, far more chilling thought.

What if something happened to her here?

I'm ice-cold all of a sudden, as if a stranger has walked over my grave, and it strikes me that there are no dog walkers, no other riders out here. I'm alone.

A feeling of foreboding hits me. Then fear, looming everywhere I look, except *fear* is too mild a word for the raw panic that engulfs me. I'm too terrified to think, as a single word screams inaudibly from deep inside me.

Run.

Zappa hears me, springing forward, even though the path narrows, and suddenly we're galloping, fear keeping pace with us, thunder crashing above us, wind whipping the branches at my face. A bolt of lightning sends him even faster, just as ahead of me I imagine a flash of pale hair. *Rosie's hair.* Then her voice—or is it the wind?— screaming my name.

Zappa's head comes up, and I try to slow him, but he's not listening anymore. All I can do is hold on, stay with him. Then, just when I think he's going to fall, up ahead the gloom lifts and there's brightness.

Zappa turns toward it as twigs snag at my clothes, and thorns rip my skin. Missing his stride, he scrambles up the chalky slope in front of us, then at the top, stops dead, pitching me headlong into darkness.

Rosie

As the image forms in front of me, instantly I know three things. I'm four years old; it's the first day of term and my first day at Abbey Green Primary, a small village school with a picket fence round its neatly mown grass.

My uniform is scratchy, and my braids pull on my scalp. I'm frightened, and I don't want to leave my mother.

"Come along, Rosanna. We don't want to be late." Taking my hand firmly in hers.

I am that little girl again, being pulled along, with a pit of dread in my stomach.

When we get to my classroom, Mummy remains at the door. I want to stay with her, but I have to walk in on my own, staring at the floor as everyone turns round to look at me. My face is very hot, and I want to cry again.

"Good morning, Rosanna."

Jeez. I'd forgotten Mrs. Bell. At the time, I liked how she smiled and was kind. Now I see a weary middle-aged lady with endless patience and too much love, worrying about her pupils, watching me when I'm not aware of her *kindly glances, reassuring my mother that I'll settle quickly, then, after her last pupil leaves, tired, gray from the heart complaint no one knows about, sitting for five minutes before she prepares the classroom for another day.*

I wonder how many children have passed through her care. I look around the room, at the little wooden tables that seat six, the book on her desk that she's read to countless children, just as she reads to us every afternoon without fail. Then the memories start, one or two at first, then a whole flood of them. The musty smell in the cloakroom where we hung our coats and shoe bags. How disgusting lunch was. The climbing bars in the playground, under the horse chestnut tree, where we fought over conkers. How when my mother collected me, I bawled.

I make a friend. Becky Thomas. She's small, with sharp eyes and dark brown hair cut in bangs. Now I see how her uniform is a hand-me-down, her sleeves too short, her skirt fastened with a pin. She wears scuffed shoes and squints at the pages of her book, because no one's taken her to get her eyes checked.

I remember I wanted bangs just like hers. I remember Becky's house, too, how it's squeezed between others that are the same, with long, thin gardens and lots of cats. Her mum smokes and says, "God," all the time, and her eyelashes are very long.

We play in Becky's room. Then Becky says we can dress up in her mum's clothes, so we put on pretty dresses that smell of perfume. Then we get necklaces, and I hear her mum coming up the stairs, and I'm frightened.

But she isn't cross. She laughs at us. "God, you're right glamour pusses, you two are," she says. Then she fetches one of her lipsticks, and we put it on.

I've never heard of glamour pusses. I wonder if it's to do with all her cats. We have fries with ketchup, which *she lets us eat in front of the television, and then Mummy comes. I hear her talking to Becky's mum. Then she comes inside and has that worried look that makes my tummy slide around inside me.*

"Get your things, Rosanna darling."

It's in her voice, too.

"Lovely name," coos Becky's mum, breathing cigarette smoke into the air behind her. "Ever so classy."

On the way home, even though I know she's cross about something, I'm so happy to have a friend, it bursts out of me.

"We had a nice time, Mummy. It was fun. We dressed up as glamour pusses."

"Rosanna . . ."

The ring of her voice makes me stop. I don't know what I've done, only that it's wrong. It must be, because I can tell she doesn't want me to talk about it. It's what that shocked, annoyed, worried voice always means.

Mummy drives much faster than usual and, when she's parked the car, tells me to hurry inside.

After she's washed my face, I hear my father's car. He revs it the way he always does before he parks, then slams the door. Mummy hears it, too. I see the deep line on her forehead. Then she crouches down, her hands resting on my shoulders.

"I don't want you to be friends with that girl, Rosanna. They're not like us."

I don't understand. I look at Mummy. I want to be Becky's friend, but Mummy must be right. I remember my happiness swirling down the basin with the running water. Feeling stupid for not knowing, and the taste of soap as I bite my lip.

"And please, Rosanna, don't tell Daddy what you did tonight. He won't understand."

She says it in a nice way, stroking my hair behind my ears. Then she kisses me as his key turns in the door.

"Quick," she whispers, standing up, placing a finger to her lips. "Remember what I said. Not a word."

And because I love my mummy, I do as she says.

3

Zappa's unscathed, but I'm not pretty. My face is scratched, and I've the beginnings of a black eye when Angus comes home that evening. He's suitably horrified.

"Christ, Kate. What happened to you?"

"The storm spooked Zappa in the woods. I had a fall."

I decide not to tell him about blacking out. Even after twenty years of marriage, Angus still thinks horses are dangerous.

I don't tell him about the fear, either, about my strange certainty that something terrible had happened there to Rosie.

I'd struggled to my feet to find myself in a small clearing at the top of a chalky slope, at the center of a ring of ancient beech trees.

A snorting sound had startled me, and I'd looked up to see Zappa standing there, reins hanging over his head, looking sheepish. One foot at a time, he ventured toward me, nostrils flared, clearly still on alert.

"Hey, boy." I reached for his reins. "It's okay." I patted his neck, reassuring him, before we slowly made our way back.

"You look a mess," says Angus.

"Thanks. You're full of compliments," I tell him.

"I didn't mean it like that, Kate." He comes over and gently touches my bruised cheek, which alone is enough to make me wince. Taking his hand away, he frowns. "Are you quite sure you're not concussed?"

"I'm fine, Angus. It looks much worse than it is."

"Maybe you should get yourself checked out."

I shake my head. I've been through enough for one day. Anyway, there's nothing more certain to make you feel terrible than spending hours hanging around an emergency room.

"Really. I'm okay." I manage a smile for all of about a second, as it comes back to me what was in my head out there. And then I realize.

"Oh my God. You don't know."

"Grace is probably right," he says when I've finished telling him. "Teenagers do the daftest things—even the best-behaved ones. And Rosie would have known her mother wouldn't like her going to Poppy's."

"I know." I sigh.

I want to believe him. And any other time, I'd just agree, pushing it to the back of my mind, while I waited for Jo's call to tell me Rosie had come home. But after what happened earlier today, illogical though it is, I have this unshakable feeling something's happened to her.

* * *

We eat inside. The air still feels charged, with the muted gossip spreading through the village, with more thunderstorms rumbling in the distance. It's just me and Angus. Grace went out before I came back. She's with friends, who are tightening ranks, holding their own vigil as they wait for news about Rosie.

"You're miles away," Angus remarks. "Stop worrying, Kate. She'll be fine."

"I know." I put down my knife and fork. "But what if she isn't? I'm sorry, but I'm really worried. Okay, so if it was Sophie, you could imagine it, couldn't you?" Sophie's a close friend of Grace's, with a mind of her own and an independent, rebellious streak that my daughter finds at once enviable and infuriating. Mostly the former, though. They're thick as thieves. "But not Rosie. It's just not the kind of thing she'd do."

I stare at my plate, the poached salmon and salad leaves, my appetite gone, wishing I knew where she was.

As another day begins, a day in which so far there is no news, it seems unbelievable that we must wait. I know the majority of missing teenagers return home. I know, also, out of those who want to, most come back unscathed.

But what about those who don't? If each passing second removes them further, blunting memories, hiding tracks, until no one can tell where they've gone?

Terrible possibilities crowd my mind, kidnapping, rape, trafficking, and worse, until unable to endure my own company, I drive over to Rachael's.

She's outside when I get there, unloading shopping

from the pickup she uses for the school run—Alan's, for use on their farm.

"Animals, small boys . . . there's not much in it," she's told me many times. Rachael and Alan have a thousand or so sheep and four sons.

"Here. I brought you these." I hand her a homegrown lettuce and a bag of potatoes, still covered in earth.

"Oh God, I wish you hadn't. Alan will start banging on about the garden again, and I really don't have time."

I've known Rachael too long to take offense at her bluntness. She was the first friend I made when Angus and I moved here twenty years ago. She's also completely turned the traditional role of the farmer's wife on its head, firstly by not marrying Alan, then refusing to give up her city job, even though these days, some of the time at least, she works from home.

"I know you don't—that's why I brought them. I'll wash them. He'll never know." I pick up some of her shopping bags.

"You're an angel. Put the kettle on, will you? I'm desperate for coffee."

I follow her inside through the riot of wirehaired terriers that rush to greet us, through to her kitchen. "Have you heard? About Rosie Anderson?"

"What about her?" Rachael's voice echoes through the cool vastness of her cavernous farmhouse.

"She's missing."

"Probably a boy, or else she's partying," Rachael calls back. "I remember doing that once. I was gone for three days. I think I shacked up with this boy I fancied. . . . God, I can't believe I did that. My poor mother—she never said a word, or perhaps she thought she'd got rid of me!"

"Jo's out of her mind. Rosie's not your typical teen-ager."

"The quiet ones are often the worst! Seriously, though, I'll watch out for her. Jo must be desperate." Rachael comes into the kitchen, and I hand her a mug. "I've got this phone meeting at half past. . . ." She glances at the time—just twenty past. "Where has this morning gone? How's your lovely Grace? Enjoying her summer? You've no idea how lucky you are, having a daughter. This entire house practically oozes testosterone. . . ."

It's how Rachael talks, in a series of questions to which answers are not mandatory. But before I can get a word in, her phone rings.

"Bollocks. He's early. I have to get this, Kate. Sorry. But let me know if you hear anything."

I let myself out while Rachael takes the call, her strident voice following me outside, as I'm thinking, *Is it just me?*

Apart from Jo, isn't anyone else worried about Rosie?

When I get home, Grace is in the kitchen, Sophie at her side, grazing, the way teenagers do, stripping the fridge, the larder, before moving on to the fruit bowl. Her current fad isn't so much low carb as no carb, destined to end as it always does in a feast of nothing but carbs.

"Hi, girls. Have you heard anything?"

Taking another bite of her apple, Grace shakes her head. "No one has. It's really weird."

"Could you speak to Poppy?" I know they're not friends, but doesn't something like this unite people? "She might know something. Gracie, I was thinking. . . . Do you know if Rosie has a boyfriend?"

Even after Jo's told me she hasn't, I'm still wondering, because all teenagers have their secrets.

Grace hunts around in the fridge. "She might, but Poppy won't say. Not to me. And I don't understand why the police aren't looking for her. I mean, what if something's happened?"

"I'm sure they must be by now." Words intended to re-assure—myself, as well as Grace—my unease heightened as I get that she, too, is thinking the unthinkable.

I leave it as late as is reasonable before calling Jo.

"Hello?" Her voice is breathless, as though she's just run up a flight of stairs; her tone desperate, which tells me nothing's changed.

"Sorry, Jo. It's only me. Kate," I add. "I won't keep you. I just wondered if you'd heard anything."

"Kate . . . no . . . Every time the phone rings, I think . . ." Her thoughts are scattered; her speech disjointed. "I'm so worried. I can't talk. The police have just arrived."

"Of course." My stomach lurches. "You go. We'll speak soon."

And though I know that the police need to be there, that questions should be asked, no stone left unturned, suddenly I'm cold.

"Mum, we're going out." Grace appears in tiny shorts and a Beatles T-shirt, followed by Sophie, who, by virtue of her long legs and lanky frame, manages somehow to be wearing even less.

"Where are you off to, girls?"

"Josh's," they answer in unison.

Josh is a friend from school who has parents with a breathtaking tolerance for teenage gatherings and a summerhouse—Josh's den—across the garden.

"Gracie? Be careful, sweetie. And ask everyone about Rosie, won't you?"

Silencing the part of me aching to keep her here, at home, watching her every step, keeping her safe, until we know.

"*Mum* . . . of course I'll be careful. We're only going about two miles." She catches Sophie's eye, and I see the familiar code flicker between them.

Sophie gives me a hug. "Don't worry, Kate. We'll be fine—and we'll make sure everyone's looking for her."

I watch them walk out to Grace's car, shiny haired and long limbed. Laughing at something Sophie says, filled with that unshakable belief that teenagers have.

That nothing bad will ever happen to them.

"It's routine," my pragmatic husband says when I tell him the police have arrived at the Andersons'. "It's what they're paid for, Kate. You'd expect them to be there."

"I know. But it means Rosie's still missing, doesn't it?"

"Well, perhaps now they'll get on with finding her. I'm starving. What's for supper?"

"Salad." Food's the last thing on my mind.

"Again?" Angus wrinkles up his nose. "I didn't have lunch, Kate." He sounds disappointed.

"Maybe chicken. I'll look in the fridge. I was going to go shopping, but I forgot." I hesitate. "You know Grace has gone out again. . . . It worries me, Angus, while Rosie's missing. . . . I mean, we don't know what's happened, do we?"

Angus comes over, puts his arms around me, reading between the blurred lines that have crept in and are suddenly everywhere I look.

"I'd like to see you stop her," he says softly. "Grace will be fine—as I'm sure Rosie will be, too. Stop worrying. More than likely, she'll turn up."

Rosie

Where light falls on my childhood, I know happiness, fleetingly. Enough to know when it's gone.

I remember a day in London. Mummy's eyes bright as she does up my shoes and brushes my hair. Telling me we'll have the best day. "Ever," she says, crouching down, taking my hands in hers, her eyes sparkling, their brightness catching mine.

Like all the best days, it's just us.

I love the train, with its big seats and movie-screen windows. The being on the inside looking out. The split-second watching of other people's lives, full screen in front of me, then slipping past, then gone.

When we get there, Mummy takes my hand.

"I'll show you something special," she tells me in that voice that makes my heart burst with excitement. "It's new, Rosanna. You're so lucky to do this."

I hear people talking about it as we join the back of a long queue. London Eye. Not knowing what it is until I see it, reaching all the way to the sky.

To start with, I'm scared, but as we're slowly lifted

higher, as the city gets smaller, the view gets bigger, I feel myself slip into another world. I wonder if all cities are like this. Full of other worlds. I glance at Mummy, her hair so pretty, her eyes so far away, knowing that she's found one, too.

I have ice cream, and Mummy drinks coffee. We go shopping, but then Mummy says we have to go somewhere. Meet someone. A good friend.

I don't want to meet Mummy's friend. I want to keep this day just for us, but she says we have to.

"Now, Rosanna. I can't be late." And I remember thinking it can't be a good friend, because good friends don't mind if you're a tiny bit late.

Mummy's friend lives in a grand white house, up wide steps, with a shiny bell and brass plate on the door. When she rings the bell, a lady in a white coat and red lipstick lets us in.

"Come in, Mrs. Anderson. Mr. Pinard won't be long."

We wait in a room, on a velvet sofa opposite a tank full of tiny fish that ripple it with color, looking at the pictures on the walls, of beautiful women who don't smile. Who are perfect. Until the man comes in.

I hide behind her. I don't like how he sounds. "He's not from England," Mummy whispers. And he's her friend. I can tell from how he kisses her cheek. Smiles into her eyes. Tells her how beautiful she looks. How she calls him Jean. He calls her Joanna. Tells her the scars have healed so well, are so small, he can't see them. How he leans down, shakes my hand. Says how pleased he is to meet me.

Only, when his eyes wander over my face, down my body, I curl up inside. Stare up into cold blue eyes. I don't know why we're here. Then Mummy goes with him into another room, telling me to wait, on my own, with the fish—"They're so pretty, Rosanna"—closing the door.

And I'm frightened. I don't like it here.

I don't like him.

Suddenly, the day is spoilt.

I want to go home.

And I can't see the fish through my tears.

4

In just two days, gossip and speculation morph into something much darker. Even as I feel my way in this new landscape, I'm not prepared when the police come here. The young, fresh-faced policeman, barely older than Grace and whose lack of any sense of gravity makes him somehow inappropriate, with the older policewoman, who introduces herself.

"Sergeant Beauman, Sussex Police."

From her manner, the way she speaks, I know instantly, she has done this too many times before.

They talk to Grace first, alone, after I've butted in, insisting I want to sit in with her, while Grace assures me that I don't need to and it's fine. But it's not fine. I know she's not guilty of anything, but irrational fear seizes me, that she'll accidentally say the wrong thing and somehow incriminate herself.

"We'd prefer it," Sergeant Beauman says to me as Grace disappears into my study. "Sometimes teenagers say more without their parents present."

"I don't think she knows any more than she's said already," I tell her. "She doesn't keep secrets from me."

Sergeant Beauman gives me the knowing kind of nod that goes with having a teenage daughter of her own, then follows Grace in and closes the door.

I sit for what feels like ages, uncomfortable, the palms of my hands clammy, before it's my turn, and as I take Grace's place, even though it's my chair in my house, under their scrutiny I'm reminded of being back in school.

Sergeant Beauman asks the questions, the young policeman listening intently, occasionally chipping in. They ask me how I know Rosie, writing it down, as though everything I say has hidden meaning.

"She comes to see my horses. Helps out a bit. She's sweet—and she's really good with them. I don't think her parents know. At least, I haven't told them. She's never said as much, but I've always felt she didn't want me to." I gabble the words incoherently, inadequately. "I mean, she's eighteen. . . . Parents don't have to know everything, do they?"

Aware of my own duplicity, because if it were Grace riding someone else's horse, keeping secrets from me, wouldn't I want to know?

Sergeant Beauman chooses not to comment. "So, recently, has there been anything different about her?"

"I've asked myself exactly that. I can't think of anything," I tell them, watching them scribble. "Only the necklace. She wore it all the time—only I expect you know about that. It's probably not even relevant."

Sergeant Beauman looks up. "Can you describe it?"

"It was unusual. Really beautiful. Made of red, purple, and green glass beads linked with these delicate swirls of silver. It was a present, but she didn't say who gave it to her."

A thoughtful look crosses her face. "How well do you know the family, Mrs. McKay?"

"I know Jo through school. . . . Grace and Rosie were in the same sixth form. That's how we met. A few of us mothers get together for lunch sometimes. They're a really nice family." I shrug, trying to think of what there is to say. "I've met Neal a few times—in passing. I don't know what else to tell you."

"Is there a Mr. McKay?"

"Angus works in London. He's a finance manager. He doesn't know Rosie. He isn't into horses."

The Sergeant Beauman's pen hovers over her pad, then scribbles again. "Thank you. That's all—for now." She gets up. "If we need to talk to you again, can we call you at this number?"

She reads back the number I've given her, and I nod. Then she hands me a card.

"If you think of anything else, or hear anything, could you call me?"

Strangely quiet, Grace and I watch them drive away.

"It's weird," says Grace. "Only, I was thinking . . . You know when Rosie comes to see the horses? She never comes when I'm around, does she? It's as if it's not just the horses she wants. It's you."

Over the days that follow, painstakingly, methodically, the police work their way through the village, asking questions, making us see each other through a stranger's eyes. Infecting us with a bacterial kind of fear.

"Do you think they know, Mum?" For once, Grace is actually home longer than just to wash her hair or collapse into sleep. Needing the safe familiarity of home ground.

"Know what, sweetie?"

She's hesitant. "There were these guys hanging out in the woods."

I spin round. "Did you tell the police when they were here?"

Grace shakes her head, slightly embarrassed, give-away pink washing her cheeks.

"*Grace* . . . who were they?"

She shrugs. "I don't really know. Just . . . friends of Sophie's."

"You have to tell Sophie they really should talk to the police."

"Mum! I can't! It's up to her! Anyway, I don't even know where they are."

"Well, if they're Sophie's friends, she will, won't she?" There's a waspish tone in my voice, because from Grace's flushed cheeks and evasive answers, I'd say there's more to this than she's telling.

She says nothing. From an early age, Grace has known that silent defiance is impossible to argue with.

I fold my arms. "Okay. I'll talk to Sophie, then. Or I could always call Lorraine." Sophie's most unmaternal of mothers, called Lorraine by her offspring, too.

Grace's eyes widen. "Just don't, Mum, okay?"

"So, you tell me. This isn't funny, Grace. Rosie's been gone four days now. She might have been kidnapped or hurt or anything."

Grace looks apologetic, but then she leaps up, alarmed. "Mum! I forgot to tell you. It's going to be on the news. Josh told me. Quick . . . We may have missed it. . . ."

She runs to turn on the TV. I follow.

Sophie's friends forgotten, we catch the national news mid-broadcast. It's left to the last minutes of the program. In case anything more important, more newsworthy crops up? Is there anything more important than someone's missing child? My head fills with unanswerable questions as Neal appears on the screen.

I watch him, drained, tense, his pain clearly drawn on his face, as he makes a heartfelt plea. To all of us, whoever we are, wherever, to imagine if this were our daughter. To anyone who knows anything, no matter how irrelevant, how trivial it may seem, to please, *please* come forward.

His eloquent, desperate words are the soundtrack to a photo of Rosie, flashed onto the screen, showing her beauty, her pale hair, that faraway look in her eyes. I glance at Grace, who has tears streaming down her face. On the second "please," his voice cracks, and my heart breaks for them.

Like a fallen, unseasonal Christmas tree, our village lights up with phone calls. My heart tells me to call Jo, but my head cautions me. *At such a time, is it right?* I decide not calling doesn't feel right, either, and I dial her number, imagining her home alone while Neal's still in the TV studio, ashamed of my relief when no one answers.

As soon as I put down the phone, Rachael calls me.

"You did see that, didn't you? Neal on the lunchtime news? Just so bloody awful, isn't it? That poor family . . . And someone must know something. Come over tomorrow, Kate. Ten-ish. Oh God, Norman's cut himself. . . ."

Only pausing for breath after she's gone.

* * *

I catch it in my words to Beth Van Sutton in the village shop. Here, too, among the locally farmed meat and boxes of vegetables, her trays of homemade cakes, fear lingers.

"Terrible, isn't it, Kate? That lovely young girl . . . that poor family. The police have been in. They're talking to everyone, you know."

It's no surprise the police have spoken to her. A human inventory of village comings and goings, Beth and her husband, Johnny, have run the shop for as long as anyone can remember. Know everything and everyone—almost.

"Johnny's talked to the police about organizing a search," she adds. "People round here need to do something."

It's the obvious next step, to turn fear into action, gather our numbers and seek out the most hidden places—but no less shocking.

"It's unbearable, isn't it? The not knowing." It rolls off my tongue almost without me noticing. To a point, it's true, until my mind inevitably fills with the many possibilities that are each a million times worse than just *not knowing*.

Beth looks shocked. "No news is good news." Then she adds, "Have you seen the strawberries? Second crop, they are. Really tasty."

Her eyes meeting mine as the cliché passes between us silently.

Life goes on.

When I get to Rachael's, she's in her habitual state of chaos.

"Kate! God, I'm pleased to see you. The police were

here yesterday. . . . Have they been to you yet? Of course
they have—you told me. Do you know if they have any
leads? Someone must know something, don't you think?
Let's go out for lunch. The kids have eaten everything,
and I haven't had time to shop."

"Pub?" I suggest.

"Pub." Rachael sounds relieved.

"I tried calling Jo last night," I tell her as, pausing for
breath, she grabs her bag and hunts around for her keys,
before giving up and leaving the door unlocked, as she
often does. By her own admission, they have nothing
worth stealing. "Just after Neal's appeal. She didn't answer."

"I'm not surprised. I can't imagine what they're going
through. There was a reporter snooping around the farm
this morning. Alan set the dogs on him."

"Your dogs? That's hilarious." Rachael's dogs may be
multiple, but they're harmless.

"He didn't know that, though, did he?"

The pub is busy for midweek. Like a car crash on the
opposite side of a motorway, is a missing girl suddenly a
spectator sport? We opt for inside, a table near an open
window.

"Has Alan noticed a group of boys hanging around?"
I'm thinking of Sophie's friends. I must ask Grace if she's
talked to her.

"I don't think so. Though on all those acres, anyone
could be there. He'd never know." She raises her eyes to
mine. "That's the trouble round here, isn't it? There are
too many places to hide."

I've thought that myself, but if Rosie has run off with
someone, the same someone who gave her that beautiful
necklace, she could be safely camped out in one of tens of
hiding places. No one would know.

Perusing the menu, Rachael sighs. "Would it be incredibly greedy to have the steak, d'you think?"

We're halfway through our lunch when across the bar, I see a face I'd recognize anywhere. One I haven't seen in years. The last person I'd expect to see *here*.

"Laura?" Incredulously, shaking my head in disbelief. Is it her? But as I say her name out loud, she turns toward me, and I see her face light up.

5

"I don't believe this!" Laura comes over and hugs me.

"Me neither! Rachael, this is Laura. We were at school together," I explain. "Went on our first teenagers' holiday together, fell for the same boy. Then she went away, and I never saw her again. Until now! I can't believe it!"

"Partners in crime," Laura says, pulling out a chair. "Are you sure you don't mind?" Aimed at Rachael.

"God, no. Help yourself. Join us for coffee. I'll go and order."

As Rachael gets up and heads over to the bar, I glance at Laura, wondering where the frizzy hair and the soft plumpness have gone. This Laura is sleek and honed—and her clothes incredibly fashionable.

"So what brings you here? I'd heard you moved to the States. Are you back?"

"I live in New York." She pauses. "I'm a journalist, Kate." Speaking slowly, gauging my reaction, her eyes rooted to mine, as I start to get a sense of where she's going with this.

"You've heard about Rosie." It's a statement rather

than a question. My pleasure at seeing her dissipates, because I'm not sure how that makes me feel. Disappointment that my old friend makes her living out of other people's suffering? "It's a long way to come, Laura. And no one knows what, if anything, has happened to her."

Laura nods. "I know. And I really hope, as much as all of you do, that she just walks back in, unharmed. But it's a big story. Neal Anderson's a household name. There's more to it, though. Before this happened, we'd planned a series of articles on the hidden victims of war zones. Including Afghanistan. Human stories about what happens when towns and families are decimated, and about those who remain—the elderly, the maimed. The orphans." She pauses. "He's already agreed to an interview with me. You see, he's connected with an orphanage in Afghanistan."

It's the first I've heard of this; suddenly, she has my attention.

She goes on. "Seeing as I'm here, anyway, my editor's agreed to let me cover this, too. Half the country is following this—and it's been a while, hasn't it? You must all be terribly worried."

Thinking of Jo again, I'm not sure. There are more than enough rumors circulating, and it feels disloyal to discuss her family like this. They're too close to my heart.

"I don't know, Laura. Jo's a friend. It might be better if you talk to someone else."

Laura sits back, still watching me. "Will you give me a chance to explain how we work? I can understand what you're thinking, because right now, if I were you, I'd feel the same. But I'm really not one of those horrible, ruthless reporters who twist facts and who'll do anything for a story. I promise you, cross my heart. Obviously, it's awful that Rosanna—or Rosie, you say she's called—is missing. There's a story to write, sure, but accurately. And sympathetically, because awful though it is, this happens to people. The papers will print it, Kate, regardless. And not always the facts, either. You know that."

"She's right." Rachael reappears with a tray of coffee. "So who do you work for?"

"An American magazine called *Lifetime*. . . . It's a monthly journal—mostly about family and the kind of real-life issues facing women. I'll give you a copy. I've got some upstairs."

"You're staying here?" Rachael places cups in front of us.

Laura nods. "For a couple of days."

Until Rosie comes back, is what she means.

Or doesn't.

However bright the sun, however warm and soft the air on my skin, I discover you can't unlearn fear. It's there, all around us, as we gather to search for Rosie. I wonder if Jo knows just how much support there is. But after a long day yields nothing of any significance, as daylight fades, numbers fall away, leaving the police to continue with a dog.

It's there again, fear, my instant split-second response, that evening, when my phone rings. I'm in my pajamas, tidying the last of dinner away before I go to bed, meaning it's late enough that it's important.

Grace's number flashing up on the screen.

"Mum, they've found her. . . ." Her voice is small and shocked.

Oh God.

"Is she all right, Grace?"

"She was in the woods. . . ."

My heart misses a beat, because it's not what I want to hear, nor is the rushing sound in my ears as it comes back to me. *The storm, Zappa, my fall . . .*

Clamping the phone to my ear as my heart leaps wildly, pointlessly with hope, because I know already from her hesitation, from the tremble in her voice, long before she speaks the words.

"Mum . . ." Her voice breaks. "Rosie's dead."

Rosie

I'm ricocheted forward through two elastic years. Another bigger, noisier car, which my father drives too fast. I'm slumped in the back, on the soft, low-slung seat, and can't see out, so sickness rushes over me in waves. Mummy's sick, too, all the time, but she says hers is different.

When we get to the new house, I shiver under a streetlight while my father stands in the drive, just staring at it. Then steps back, still staring, before a smug look spreads across his face. It's not like our old one. It's too big and dark.

As we go inside and can't find the light switch, my father says, "Really, Joanna, this is your fault."

It's when I notice how he always calls her Joanna, not Jo, like other people do. I wait for them to find the lights, listening to the echo of their footsteps, wishing we were back in our old house. But when it's warm and lit and the furniture is set out, and after about five days, when the windows have curtains and the rooms look a bit like our old rooms, and I have new toys and my own brand-new pink TV, I decide I like it here.

I start my new school under a lavender sky just before a hailstorm, small, in a too-big overcoat, carrying my schoolbag, following other children across the playground just as the hail starts. I remember its icy sting against my hands and face, the drumming sound as it falls on the pavement. I don't see my mother bolt for the car or the lavender sky darken to a steely gray. I never look up.

I'm nervous all morning, staring out through the window at the gloom lightened only by an ice carpet, imagining I'm caught in a gray hinterland where the sun never rises, until break time, when a girl asks me to play. That's when I meet Lucy Mayes, and then a little while later, the sun comes out and the ice melts away. I find out Lucy's clever and lives in a nice house quite near ours and plays the violin. As Mummy says, she really is the perfect friend.

And then, just before Christmas, our house made beautiful with a tree that glitters and presents tied with ribbons piled underneath, Delphine comes to us, another perfect daughter in the random world that isn't random.

I look at my sister, who has my pale hair and eyes that stare into mine as if there are secrets there. She's someone who needs me. A gift.

When we're alone, I call her Della, liking its sound and how it flows off my tongue.

As I watch, the feeling comes back. The same excitement, mixed with happiness and gratitude for Christmas, my new sister, and my perfect childhood. I whisper to Della about the things we'll do together and how I'm her big sister. I'll always look after her.

It's a bubble that lasts until the night before Christmas Eve. My father comes home late, shouting at Mummy, who has crystal tears that hurt her. She goes upstairs to comfort Della, because she's crying, but he pulls her back and locks Della's door.

I cry then, and the baby behind the locked door cries because of the noise, and because all she wants is a warm body to cuddle against. But my father's shouting at Mummy, and wherever I look, I can't find the key. So while my six-year-old self talks through the door to her baby sister, I stand above her cot, whispering to her.

"It's okay, Della. You're not alone."

6

Death casts its shadow, leaving our hearts sad and tainting our world with fear. Have I reached that point in life where from here on it will always be there, lurking, just out of sight, but waiting in the background for its next victim?

And while our questions go unanswered, life goes on, the sun rising over grass sparkling with dew and the dawn chorus as loud and sweet as any morning, just as Ella, my neighbor, walks past with her black Labrador and the post arrives and Angus goes to work. He has an important meeting with the head of an American company, who's flown over from Boston just to see him.

Early morning, with the sun rising through the trees, is a time of day I love. Not just the quiet, but the low, clear light, which gives color depth, each petal and leaf freshened by the cool of the night and the dew. But this morning, I don't see the rose that's bursting into bloom, just as I breathe the lavender without savoring its warm fragrance and pick the last of the raspberries without tasting them.

Yesterday I'd have called Jo—to see if she'd heard anything. But in this changed world, I don't. It feels too intrusive. Instead, my thoughts turn to Grace and her friends, reeling from the realization that even this close to home, no one's invincible.

"I should have done something, Mummy. . . . I should have been nicer, been her friend. . . ."

Her childhood name for me, her hysteria—partly tiredness but heartfelt—is completely understandable. But not her guilt.

"It's not your fault, Grace. Even if you'd been friends, it doesn't mean you could have stopped it."

"She doesn't deserve this, Mum. . . . She never did anything wrong. . . ." Past and present are muddled as she navigates unfamiliar territory.

"I know she didn't."

All I can do is hold my daughter's sobbing body, grateful with every fiber of my being that I still have her, can still touch her, hear her voice. That it wasn't Grace who disappeared, that I'm not Jo, whose world has been decimated.

"I have to go to the funeral . . . even if it means missing class, Mum. I can't not go."

"I understand, Grace. We'll work something out. It's okay."

"Everyone says they're going," she says. Her eyes are bloodshot; her face is stained with tears. "I know we weren't best friends, but it doesn't mean we can't, does it?"

I discover, too, that grief is different things to different people. Comes in many guises. In shocked silences and closed doors around our village, as people try to shut it out. That a blank face or fleeting smile can hide the worst, most private kind of agony.

I leave it several days longer than I planned before I call round to see Jo, expecting drawn curtains, locked doors, and no one to answer. It would be easier, too, because I can leave the flowers I've picked from the garden in the shade of her porch. Post Grace's card. Not have to look at her and see from the pain in her eyes how real this is.

As I pull up outside, there are several parked cars on a road that is usually empty. The press? But though I feel eyes watching, they don't approach me, even as I raise my hand to knock and the door opens.

"Jo . . ." I look at her, then hold out my arms, suddenly unable to speak. For all the time I've spent thinking about this, prepared what I'd say if I actually saw her, there are no words.

She lets me hold her, and I think, *She's still Rosie's mother. She'll always be Rosie's mother. Nothing and no one can change that.*

"I'm so sorry, Jo. I didn't want to disturb you. I just wanted to leave these."

"Oh. They're lovely. . . ." She barely looks at the flowers I hand her. Her eyes are glassy; her words thick with medically induced evenness. "Will you come in?"

"I won't, Jo. I don't want to intrude." I step back.

"Please . . ." There's a pleading note in her voice as she glances up the road to see who's watching her. "Please come and have a cup of tea."

I follow her inside, awkward, because I don't know her well enough to be here, dimly recalling how tea and grief are as synonymous as fish and chips. Then, as we pass from the hallway into her sitting room, I stop to gaze in astonishment. There are flowers and cards covering every surface, so many and so beautiful, it's almost wrong.

She doesn't pause, just walks down the steps into the huge live-in kitchen. I can't help thinking that if we were closer, I'd gently bully her into sitting down while I made the tea, perhaps sneak a drop of medicinal brandy into it. But we're not close. And Jo's private—if not about the shops she buys her designer clothes from, or the gala balls and charity events she and Neal go to, then about the real stuff. The nuts and bolts, the nitty-gritty of cherished hopes and dreams, and how her family, like anyone's, is everything to her.

Today even the kettle looks too heavy for Jo. She's so thin, so brittle, ethereal in her grief, with huge eyes and pale skin. I notice her hair, the same shade as Rosie's, only fractionally shorter, so that from behind, you could almost—but not quite—mistake them.

"Is Neal here?"

"He's with the police. . . ." The mug in her hand shakes. "I should have gone. . . . Couldn't face it. . . . They're tracing calls to her phone. . . ." Her voice wobbles.

"Can I do anything? Anything at all?" I ask quietly.

She shakes her head, then gathers herself and pours boiling water into the mugs, while I look around at the spotless white and steel units, the massive range-style oven. Immaculately clean and tidy. *And expensive,* I can't help thinking, hating that I even notice.

She brings the mugs over and pulls out a chair opposite me.

"It's nice of you to come, Kate. I appreciate it. People send things. . . . They don't come here. It's like it's contagious."

Her voice is flat, her eyes bright with unshed tears, as

incredibly, she maintains her composure. I shiver inwardly at the thought that you can catch death like a virus.

"They probably don't want to disturb you," I say gently. "That's all, Jo."

"So many cards," she says, sounding blank. "I can't believe how many. Even from people we don't know."

Does it help? Is it in any small way a comfort to know you're in the thoughts of so many people? It prompts me to pull Grace's card from my pocket and place it on the table.

"Grace asked me to give you this."

She reaches out slowly and takes it. I wonder if she's thinking the unthinkable as she thinks of Grace, knowing I would be if it were my most precious, most loved person whom someone had taken from me.

Why my daughter? Why not someone else's?

"Can you tell her . . . thank you?"

I sip my tea, but Jo's remains untouched. Then a quiet sound from behind makes me turn round.

Perhaps because Jo rarely mentions her, I always forget Delphine. I know from the way Rosie talked, the way her face would light up when she mentioned her sister's name, they were close. As she stands there, I take in the same pale hair, the familiar look of uncertainty. So like Rosie—until I notice her eyes. In place of Rosie's quiet friendliness, her watchful look unnerves me.

"Hello. I'm Kate, Grace's mum," I tell her, remembering too late that because they're school years apart, she may not even know Grace.

"Hello." Her voice is quiet, but like her sister, she is well spoken. "Mummy, please may I have lunch?"

"In a minute, Delphine. When Kate has gone. Why don't you go and watch the television?"

Delphine goes without a murmur, but I take it as my cue. Swallowing the last of my tea, I get up. "Really, I should be getting back."

Jo doesn't protest, just puts her undrunk mug down and leads the way to the door. Then, as she opens it, raising pain-filled eyes to meet mine, she says quietly, "They found her in the woods."

Suddenly, I can't move, my mind struggling for words of comfort that don't exist, but Jo goes on.

"She was buried . . . under leaves and moss. Someone saw her hair. . . ."

Her voice is suddenly high-pitched, jogging my mind back to the present; then, as she says "hair," it cracks, and she crumples, sobbing in my arms.

Two hours later, hours in which I do my best to console her, knowing that nothing I do can ease her loss, I make lunch for her and Delphine, lunch that Jo doesn't touch and Delphine only picks at.

"You've been ages," Grace says when at last I get home. "Did you see them?"

"Yes. It was awful, Gracie. Just so, so sad. For all of them. I saw Delphine, too. And the press was hanging around." I'm exhausted. The weight of grief—even someone else's—is exacting, draining.

From the look on Grace's face, I know she feels it, too, that she's trying on Delphine's shoes for size, as I have Jo's.

"Some of us want to go to the woods later. To take flowers . . ." Grace looks at me, half seeking my approval, though if she's made up her mind, she'll do it, anyway.

"You may not be able to, sweetie. The police are probably all over the place, searching for any clues as to what happened."

She looks aghast. "It's a public place, isn't it? They can't really stop us."

"They probably can. Until they know how Rosie died." I pause. "Gracie? Why not leave it—just for now? Wait till the police have finished up there. Why don't you ask Sophie round instead?"

"I'm not staying in, Mum. We're all meeting up. It's already organized. Anyway, nothing else is going to happen, is it?"

Her question hangs there, daring me to tell her otherwise, as we look at each other, as I stifle my inner voice, which is shouting silently, *We don't know that. We can't be sure about anything.*

"Is it, Mum? Not with the police everywhere." Repeating the question, eyes bright with tears, asking me to tell her nothing will happen to her, to make it all right. And I can't, because with Rosie dead, I don't know how to.

"Of course not." There's nothing else I can say. "But I really think you should put off going—just until the police have finished, that's all."

"I was in those woods," I tell Angus, as we lie in bed later that night.

His presence is reassuringly normal. It's late—he had a dinner that dragged on—but he's taken tomorrow off. That he didn't know Rosie means he's more detached than I am.

"When I had that fall, I didn't tell you, but the weirdest thing happened."

Now I think about it, and in the light of everything I've found out since, it isn't just weird, it's creepy.

"I'm not mad, Angus, but it was like I could feel that something terrible had happened there. I've never known anything like it. Zappa felt it, too, I'm sure. It's why he bolted."

He glances at me over the top of his glasses.

"Sorry. I don't know what I mean."

I hedge then, because Angus likes his world scientifically verifiable, and much as I adore my husband, his total inflexibility and pigheadedness, which can be strengths elsewhere, have caused many a heated row between us. So much so I wonder why I've even mentioned this.

But for once, wisely, he doesn't push me.

"How was Jo?" he asks instead.

I shrug. "Fragile. Devastated. I didn't see Neal. He was with the police."

Angus shakes his head. "God. You read about these things happening to someone else, somewhere else. Not to someone you know on your own doorstep."

"I know."

"I suppose they'll do a postmortem."

"I suppose they'll have to." I sit up. "She could have been murdered, Angus."

"Unlikely," he says. "It was probably just an accident. I'm sure the police will get to the bottom of it."

"But it's not like she fell off a horse, is it? How can a young, healthy person just have an accident that kills them?" I persist, unconvinced. "In the woods, of all places? And Jo said she was covered with leaves."

·Dozens of us walk, run, ride our horses through there every day—the worst that ever happens is a bruised knee or sprained ankle.

Angus puts down his book. "Anything could have happened, Kate. She might have fallen or even had a heart attack. It's rare but not impossible. It can happen. To anyone, whatever their age."

Maybe I'm wrong and he's right. He carries on reading, but my head fills with unwanted images. Of Rosie, alone in the dark. Rosie in the woods. Rosie with an unseen, unknown person who wishes her harm. In a morgue. Only now it isn't Rosie anymore; it's just her gray, empty body, with the pale hair that someone spotted in the leaves. Her ghost still out there, haunting the woods. And what if the police don't get to the bottom of it? If there's a murderer loose in our village? What if it happens to someone else?

I'm awake for hours that night, eventually dozing off in Angus's arms, but not before I've made a pact with God, or whoever's out there, that I'll do anything, absolutely anything, to keep my family safe. I don't care what happens to me.

Then, when my eyes finally close, I'm back in the woods. At the same clearing where I fell off Zappa, hearing the leaves and the wind. This time, there is no rain, just birds singing and a sun that's unnaturally bright, and as I look down, I see Rosie lying beside me, as if it's the most normal thing in the world.

Her hair, longer than I remember, is spread around her, a rippling carpet of pale silk. She reminds me of a beautiful painting, her body covered by an intricately woven blanket of green moss and golden leaves.

I try again and again to stir her. *Rosie. Rosie. Wake up. You must wake up. . . .*

But she doesn't move. Then the trees fall silent, and the woods darken. The fear is back. *I have to run.*

I pull at Rosie's arm. I can't leave her here, but she won't move. I pull harder, hear myself scream at her.

Wake up, Rosie. You have to run. . . .

Her eyes open, and for a moment, she looks at me. Then I'm losing her. Her mouth opens, but no sound comes from it.

The scream is mine.

I open my eyes, aware of my face wet with tears. I'm shaking and shaken to the core. The image of Rosie is still sharp, down to the sweep of her lashes against her cheeks and those pale eyes, riveted to mine, telling me something, I'm certain of it.

Beside me, Angus mutters something unintelligible as I slip out of bed, glancing at the illuminated hands of my small alarm clock, far too agitated to sleep. After fumbling on the back of the door for my dressing gown, I creep downstairs.

When I have a large design project, the night's the best time to work, when the house is at its stillest, when the odd creak is comforting, the tick of the clock its heartbeat. But tonight is different. I'm on edge, seeing movements in every shadow, imprints of menacing faces outside pressed against the glass, silently watching me. Aware there's a murderer who could be anywhere.

I fill the kettle to make tea, then draw the curtains, shutting out my demons, before sitting down at the table, the mug cradled in my hands.

The last time Rosie came over to see my horses, I think she'd been here a while, hiding, watching out for me, then appearing to just turn up, as if by chance. I hadn't heard her open the gate; I'd just come out of the tack room, and there she was.

"Rosie! You made me jump!"

I watched uncertainty flicker over her face. She was like that. Never quite sure how to read me, just as she herself was unreadable.

"Sorry." She hesitated, twisting a lock of her hair round one of her fingers. "It was just . . . I wondered if you needed any help today. Is it okay?"

"Of course it is! Catch Reba if you like. She needs grooming." Semiretirement can sometimes be too quiet for her, and Reba enjoys being fussed over. I threw Rosie a head collar and watched the quiet way she moved among the horses, the gentle way they nuzzled her.

She always asked, always apologized. My answer was always the same. *Yes.* Like me, I guess she needed what only horses were able to give her.

One thing surprised me, though. Where Grace's friends would bypass stable chores in their impatience to get on and ride, Rosie never once asked to. On the one occasion I got her up on Reba, from her smile you'd think she'd conquered Everest. She was a natural rider, with the kind of light hands you can't teach and an innate feel for what the horse was thinking.

I wanted to teach her, but we never progressed further. When I offered to talk to Jo about giving her riding lessons, she looked worried.

"It would be better if you didn't tell her. I just like coming here to help," she said quite anxiously, repeating herself in that apologetic way she had. "Like now—if it's okay?"

It remained an unspoken, slightly awkward secret between us. One I never mentioned to Jo, though I considered it once or twice, but there was never any reason why I should.

Rosie kept herself to herself, not mentioning friends to me, but she was a sweet, pretty girl, and I often wondered if there was a boy in her life. The last time I saw her, I commented on the jewel-colored necklace.

"That's so pretty, Rosie."

I watched the tinge of faint pink in her cheeks as her hand went to her neck, touching it.

"Thanks," she said shyly. "It was a present."

I wondered then, but as always, she didn't say and I didn't ask, "Who from?" Not understanding her secrecy. Was she hiding something?

Then my mind wanders back to that afternoon in the woods. Was I spooked by the storm, or had something else been there with me? Is it possible? Do I really believe that? Then, as I sit there in the silence of the night, I feel a hand on my shoulder and my heart stops.

I jump up, spinning round, my tea going everywhere. "*Jesus!* Angus! Don't creep up on me like that."

My husband's bleary with sleep. "Who else would it have been?"

I shake my head at him. "I didn't hear you. You frightened the life out of me."

"I just wondered where you were. Come back to bed." His hair is pointing all ways; his pajamas are hanging off his lanky frame. He yawns.

"Okay. I'll be up in a minute."

I clear up my spilt tea but suddenly don't want to be alone. After turning out the light, I follow him.

7

Over disorientating days that merge seamlessly, we learn more. First disbelief, then shock ripples through our village. It wasn't an accident. Rosie was murdered.

Murder. Until now unspoken, a word that out loud triggers an aftershock.

As it reaches Grace, she gasps; her hand goes to her mouth. "Rosie was murdered? Oh, Mum, it's so horrible." She's in tears, her eighteen-year-old world tumbled sideways into an ugly parallel universe that's sprung out of nowhere overnight.

A visceral, wrenching loss fills me then, not for what's happened to Rosie, but for Grace and the safe, nurturing, loving world that she's grown up in, so full of promise, holding her dreams and the stars, and that's suddenly gone.

I put my arms around her and hold her close, hating what this is doing to us.

* * *

As facts slowly filter out, the first strands of a spider-web of something sinister appear. It was as Jo told me: her body was discovered in the woods. There was evidence of a struggle, during which she suffered several blows to her head, before she was stabbed viciously a number of times. And then follows the part that I struggle with, because they found her in the same clearing where I fell off Zappa.

And I didn't see her.

On Facebook, a public outpouring of grief is unleashed, unchecked and uncensored, spreading like wildfire, as buried amid the many tributes to Rosie are more sinister posts hinting at the reasons behind her murder.

Grace is horrified. "It's sick, Mum. Most of them don't even know her." All traces of teenage bravado gone, using "sick" in the old-fashioned sense.

"I'm sure they'll be removed, Gracie. And anyone who knew Rosie will ignore them."

As if that's not enough, the lowest echelons of the press show their true colors, too, with a front-page article on "acclaimed news reporter Neal Anderson and his wife" visiting the site where their daughter's body was found and featuring an intrusive, devastating photo of the family taken several years ago. It's followed by speculation about an unknown, unnamed boyfriend and hints at a secret life Rosie led, with another, more recent photo of her, those pale eyes seeming to look out of the pages into mine.

"They shouldn't be allowed to do this." Grace slams the paper on the table with the full force of her anger. "They're evil. It's so wrong, Mum, making up lies and printing her photo like that. She was just a normal girl. Her poor family . . ."

"I know, Gracie. It's horrible. I feel the same."

"*Why* do they have to put her picture on the front?" Grace stands there, all formidable five feet four inches of her bristling. "Isn't just writing about it big enough for them? Isn't it bad enough that she's dead?"

"The trouble is, it's always the most scandalous news that sells papers," I say sadly. "And this is a big story."

She shakes her head, tears rolling down her cheeks. "If it were the last job on earth, I wouldn't work for them," she says. "They're lowlifes, the lot of them. Someone should sue them."

I agree with her but leave it to rest uneasily in the background along with everything else, unresolved, as the search for the murderer begins.

And I call round to see Jo.

Ten of the worst days have passed since I last saw her. Jo was always thin, but now she's skeletal, her chin a bony protrusion, her cheekbones defined far beyond the point of beauty. She's wearing a soft cream tunic that swamps her tiny frame and a voluminous scarf round her neck.

"I was driving past," I say, even though I wasn't, and I've come round just so she knows I'm thinking about her. To reassure myself they're somehow clinging on, inside their own private hell.

"Thank you, Kate. . . ." She looks haunted. I notice, too, that for the first time since I've known her, her roots need doing. That under the salon pale blond, she's quite gray.

A man's voice calls out, "Who is it, Joanna?"

A fleeting look crosses her face, and I'm reminded of Rosie's when she was caught off guard.

"He keeps thinking it's the press. They won't leave us alone," she says, then raises her voice. "It's Kate, darling."

"He's working from home," she says, glancing over her shoulder.

"That's good," I say, relieved she's not alone. "For all of you."

But before she can reply, Neal appears behind her.

Though I know his face from numerous TV appearances, I've met him only a handful of times, at local cocktail parties or parents' evenings at school. In the flesh, he's good-looking, a well-built man with a limp that's the legacy of his job—a sniper bullet in Afghanistan, according to local gossip. Apparently, he was lucky it wasn't worse.

He's weathering this better than Jo is—at least on the outside—but even in their combined grief, they're a striking couple, his healthy robustness contrasted with Jo's frailty.

"Hello, Kate. Are you coming in?"

Even now, I notice that quiet assurance in spades, the kind of charisma he has, which men can't learn but either have or don't have.

"Hello, Neal. I'm sorry. I didn't mean to disturb you all. I just wanted to tell Jo . . . well, nothing really. Just, if I can do anything, she knows where I am. . . ." I trail off, leave it open-ended, because it sounds so lame and so inadequate, like offering a Band-Aid for third-degree burns or a broken neck.

He nods just once.

"I'll see you soon." I kiss Jo's cheek, then glance at the clock on the wall behind her. "Sorry, I have to go. I've a meeting with a client. I've already postponed twice. . . ."

I babble the lie, but I don't want to say I'm taking Grace to see a movie. It's irrational, but such is my guilt that she's here and Rosie isn't that I can't even mention my daughter's name.

Is this how it is now? Are we all suspects? Behind the facade of constrained smiles and familiar exchanges, there's a shift in our village. That we could have a murderer in our midst is a thought none of us can ignore.

Remember that man who rented the Stokes's barn conversion a few months back, who allegedly commuted every day, who kept to himself? He could have been up to anything. Do you think the police know about him?

Those young men who camped on Dudley's farm this summer, helping out, so they said. They were illegal immigrants, you know. He didn't even have their real names.

"There were some boys camping in the woods. Friends of Sophie's . . ." I fall silent, wondering if the police have been told, berating myself for not reminding Grace.

"What about the boyfriend the press keeps on about? He's the obvious one to talk to, isn't he? He'd know if anything funny had been going on. I'm surprised she didn't mention him to you. . . ." Rachael sits at my kitchen table, stirring her coffee.

"I think all that's just gossip. You know what the pa-

pers are like. Jo told me she didn't have one. And Grace
didn't know anything."

"Really? Bloody scandalous, isn't it?"

I nod, feeling the lump in my throat. "She was so private, Rachael. And shy. And now she's everyone's business. . . ."

"I know. Awful, isn't it? Talking of the press . . ."
Rachael's thoughtful. "Have you seen your friend at all?"

"You mean Laura? No. To tell you the truth, I'm
avoiding her."

"Why?" Rachael frowns. "I liked her. Did you look at
her magazine? Only it's not trashy. It's intelligent. Did
you know she's a psychologist? She writes really well."

"I'll look. I just hate the idea of adding to all the gossip out there."

"Kate, look at it this way. You could help her tell the
actual true story—if you wanted to, that is. Fair enough if
you don't, though. I'm sure she won't be short of offers."

I keep coming back to Sophie's friends, knowing I
have to tackle Grace about them.

"Sweetie? Did you talk to Sophie? About going to the
police?"

She shakes her head, her eyes wide and serious. "I
have to, don't I?"

"Yes." I say it gently. "They may know nothing about
Rosie." I frown. "But what if they do? And I've never
really understood why you've kept so quiet about them."

Grace sighs; then the familiar defiant look is back. "If
you really have to know, they're not really Sophie's friends.
They were just these guys she got weed from, that's all. I
didn't touch it, Mum. I never do. Just so you know."

Knowing what my reaction will be, daring me to be furious with her, Grace stands her ground. Any other time, I probably would be, but while I wasn't looking, while a murder took place, the rules shifted imperceptibly.

"Sophie know how stupid that is? Buying weed from just anyone like that?"

My mind racing, because yes, they're probably harmless, but what if they're not? What if Rosie somehow got caught up with them?

"Mum! It's just weed!" Grace's outraged cry breaks into my thoughts. "Everyone does it—except me, of course." She says it resentfully, as if it's somehow my fault that she's missing out.

"Whatever, Grace. All that really matters is finding the murderer. I'm sorry, but Sophie talks to the police today, or I will."

Knowing she's in the wrong, Grace glowers at me, then turns and flounces away.

And then a thin veneer of normality filters in, sorely needed, as I busy myself with new clients' gardens, finding peace as I always do in the music of the seasons. The drone of insects and the harmonies of the birds, pitched against the backdrop of the wind. Perfect fleeting moments, until the Everest-sized mountain that's Grace's university shopping list rears its ugly head.

"You can't need all this!" I gasp in horror at her list. "You don't need new bedding, Grace. We have plenty. Or towels . . . and plates and mugs . . . Come and have a look in the kitchen."

And then we go shopping and buy new towels, new

china, new bedding, and new everything else, diverting ourselves from recent events with frivolity, soft fabrics, and prettiness, as the closer she gets to leaving, the more time picks up speed, the more precious each minute suddenly becomes.

8

September

The next time I see Jo is at Rosie's funeral, a sweet, gentle endurance test, with sunlight, tears, and too many people crowding into the small village church. The overflow mourners stand outside, forming a human tunnel, which, I'm told later, closes in as her coffin passes, and follows behind. Here at least, no side of her is left unguarded.

The service is far removed from the brutality that's brought us here, with flowers, familiar hymns, and the unbearable, overwhelming sadness that unites us. The only indication of the untimeliness of Rosie's death is the two uniformed officers standing at the back. At one point, Grace nudges me, mouthing, "Poppy," and across the church, I glimpse a pretty face flanked by two others, caked in thick makeup running with little rivers of black mascara.

Some classmates bravely deliver a eulogy through their tears, painting a picture of Rosie so bright, none of us will ever forget, while ugly, pointless thoughts filter into my head. *Is the giver of the necklace here? The murderer, even?*

There's relief afterward that it's over. I snatch the last days of our summer, cramming them with late nights and early mornings. Long rides with Grace, where we gallop recklessly, flat out across stubble fields, then let the horses wallow in the stream. With barbecues and friends and oversize plates of food, the house upside down but scented with cooking and the last of the roses from the garden. They're joyous, life-affirming gestures, where I concentrate enough love and laughter into sweet, precious memories to tide me over until Grace is back.

One evening, I find myself alone, and there's a window of daylight that's just wide enough to exercise Zappa. He's my sole remaining client, which at this time of year, with its shortening days, is a blessing.

As I walk across the fields, I see the three of them—Zappa; Grace's pony, Oz; and my old Reba—walking peacefully together as they used to follow Rosie. For a moment I fancy I catch a strand of pale hair, see Oz rub his head on an invisible shoulder, Zappa nuzzle a hand that isn't there, before suddenly, they throw up their heads seemingly at nothing, then wheel round and canter away.

As I ride up the lane, the sky is quiet, a veil of high cloud washing it a milky blue. There's also a chill in the air, and I jog Zappa to keep warm. Then at the top of the hill, on impulse, for the first time since the storm, I turn him into the woods.

I've known for some time that I have to do this. Lay Rosie's ghost, if that's what it was. Only, unlike the last time, we're not alone. As Zappa trots past dog walkers and someone running, he snorts gently, feeling the layers of freshly fallen leaves under his hooves, wanting to canter. When I touch his sides with my legs and lean slightly forward, he breaks into strong, rhythmic strides.

Here and there, sunlight brushes the trees, painting them burnished copper and gold. We keep going until up ahead, I see the slope where I fell last time. Boldly I point Zappa up there, and again he takes it in two long strides, only now I'm ready.

This time, at the top, I just listen. To Zappa's breathing gradually slowing, to the wind through the treetops, to crisp leaves floating, then landing on the ground. Here and there are the scattered remains of flowers people have left, nibbled at by rabbits or the deer that hide until dusk, when they can claim the woods as their own. And again, I can't help thinking, *Rosie? Are you here, too?*

Then all too soon, Grace goes.

I always knew it would be difficult, but in the aftermath of what's happened, illogically, I want to keep her close. It's a three-hour drive to the university in Bristol, and we manage to laugh most of the way there, but after, when the last of her possessions is unloaded and installed in the simple room that's to be her home, when it comes to good-bye, I fall apart.

"Please, Grace, be careful."

"Mum! I'll be fine! Don't! You'll set me off, too."

"And call me . . . anytime you like."

"I know! Of course I'll call you, Mum."

"And . . ." But I can't let her go.

Angus kisses her cheek, then firmly takes my hand. "Come on, Kate. It's time to go."

I can't speak at that point, just steel myself, indelibly scorching our hug into the fabric of my memory.

Rosie

I'm not sure where the wish comes from, but when I'm eight, more than anything in the world, I want a puppy. I can't know it's because my heart bursts just to love, that it craves to be loved in return, only that Lucy Mayes has a small spaniel that's old and doesn't play. She says he's boring and he smells bad, but his fur is soft and his eyes melt when he looks at me. When I ask my father, he says I have to wait until I'm older. So I do what he says. I use the time to learn about puppies. About training them, about walking them and feeding them, about how tail wagging can mean all these different things. Then, before my next birthday, I wait until Mummy's there, too, and Delphine is sleeping upstairs.

My father's sitting next to her, on the new white sofa, which Delphine and I aren't allowed on. I wait until he's finished telling Mummy about the assignment he's just come back from, where there was shooting and their hotel got blown up. How frightened everyone was, but how lucky we are he got out alive.

It's the perfect moment. He's survived. It should make

him the happiest man there is. Mummy looks at him, then kisses his cheek. But even before anything happens, I'm nervous. Snakes-in-my-insides nervous—which is what Lucy always says, because it feels like snakes curling and wriggling inside you. Or when I'm less nervous, maybe worms.

When I ask, my father looks at me crossly and says, "If you really want a puppy, you'll have to wait, Rosanna, until you're twelve," even though Mummy places her hand on his arm, says, "Please, Neal. A puppy would be really lovely for the girls. . . ."

But he pulls his arm away, gets up, stands there, his back to us, while Mummy catches my eye and shakes her head, looking worried, because his anger is like a storm cloud. We both know it's decided. And the room turns into a horrible, cold place that I don't want to be in, full of people I don't want to be with. But there's nothing I can do.

When. I'm. Twelve. Seems too far away to be real.

Soon after that, I remember my skin erupting into dry, scaly patches that itch. The doctor saying I have eczema. My mother saying it's in the family. How can they not see?

I know what it is. Not eczema, but disappointment, a parasite in my blood, circulating round my body, eating me away, gnawing at my skin first until it flakes off, then deeper inside, at my belief in people.

The next year, before my birthday, I know I shouldn't ask, but there's a picture in my head about how it would be, having a puppy. Cuddling it, feeding it, watching it grow. And I find an ember of hope. Ask again. Even though I know.

"How dare you?" says my father. "Don't you remember? I said twelve, Rosanna. Twelve."

Then he takes the ember, snuffs it out, tramples it under his boots, and buries it in ice until it's dead.

When it gets to my twelfth birthday, I don't ask. But the week before, even though I don't want to, my father makes me go to look at some puppies, a whole litter of them, squirming and wagging and whimpering. My wish comes back stronger than before, and I know if I can have one of these, I will never ask for anything again.

They are all beautiful, and it's hard, but I choose one—a little black and white girl puppy with a springy tail like a piece of rubber, who nibbles my chin, then washes my face with kisses.

All the way home, I think, The best things really are worth waiting for. *Even four years—that's how long it's been. But my father's kept his word. In my head, I have lists of names, then decide there really is just one name that's perfect for her.*

It's Hope.

The night before my birthday, I can't sleep. I'm wondering where my parents are hiding Hope, straining my ears for little whiny puppy sounds, imagining that small, wriggly body in my arms again, knowing it's my last night without her.

The next morning, when I open my presents, I ask where Hope is.

"Oh," says my father, "we changed our minds. We've bought you a guitar instead."

Then he laughs.

And the love that was waiting inside me, the huge, bubbling, bottomless well of it, leaks away until it's gone.

After that, I lose trust and faith, too, watching my face grow paler as in their place, disappointment breeds, spreading through my body like a network of veins. Then my eczema gets worse, and I get blinding, thumping headaches that make me sick, which Mummy gets, as well. She says I need to lie down and take pills. That I'm just like her, but she'll look after me. Not long after that, my father goes away for a long time. Then, when he comes back, I lose Lucy Mayes, too, because we move again. Another town, another house, another school. I start at Blackley Secondary School, a sprawl of concrete and glass under a midsummer sky.

It looks welcoming, the sunlight rebounding off the glass, making it sparkle. That's where I see the sky, in window-sized pieces of blue-black, with fluffy clouds reflected above mirror trees.

My teacher, Miss Wilson, is young, in high heels, and says she hopes it won't be difficult joining midterm, but if it is, I must tell her and she'll help me. Then she turns round and says to another teacher in a very quiet voice, "How strange, moving schools midterm. You'd have thought parents would think about that. Oh well . . ."

The work isn't difficult, but this time, making friends is. Not because the girls aren't nice here. They're really friendly and interesting. They ask where I live and what music I like. I could be friends with them, but I already have friends, friends I really like, in other schools, which I didn't ask to leave. And if I make new friends, they'll be taken away, too.

I miss Lucy, but it's not like before. It's like a nerve dying or a tooth being pulled out. When the pain fades, there's emptiness.

9

October

With the funeral behind us and our teenagers scattered around the country, as the wrench of separation gives way to relief that away from here, at least they're safe, as we adjust to new, quieter lives, I get together with other mothers to organize an informal rotation where we take turns calling on Jo. A good idea in principle, we agree, but being up close to Jo's grief, in the home in which Rosie's absence is so noticeable, is too much for most of them, and before long it dwindles, then stops altogether.

"You're so good to me," she says as she lets me in, beautifully dressed as she always is in a slim tunic and pale linen trousers, one of her trademark scarves looped round her neck. Touched up before Rosie's funeral, the roots are perfect again. "But you mustn't worry, Kate. I'm fine."

I know she isn't. How can she be? I wonder, too, how she ever will be.

"I brought a cake." Even though I know Jo won't eat it, but it's a gesture. "Chocolate. I thought Delphine might like it."

She takes it, says nothing. As I follow her down the steps into the kitchen, over on the table, her mobile buzzes. She glances across at it.

"Would you mind? It's probably about the work I'm doing for Neal."

"Of course. I'll put the kettle on." I'm gradually feeling my way around this pristine, ordered kitchen that's so unlike my own. I know to fill the polished steel kettle from the tap with the built-in filtration system. Once I used the other one. Only once.

I get out two of her coffee mugs, distinct from tea mugs—Jo has a separate shelf for each type—and notice some new additions in there, gleaming white with intricately designed handles. She's still deep in conversation, and absentmindedly, I pick one up, turn it, admiring the unusual shape, before it slips through my fingers onto the floor. Jo looks up from her phone, aghast.

"I'm really sorry," I tell her later, for about the tenth time, because she looks so upset. "Please can I replace it?"

"Oh, it's fine," she says, managing a laugh I know is forced. "Really. Don't worry, Kate. It's just a mug! It's my fault, anyway. I shouldn't have been chatting for so long."

Is she really taking responsibility for my clumsiness? It puts me in mind of the kind of thing I'd say to Grace—when she was four. *It's my fault you tipped the paint over. I should have been keeping an eye on you.*

We move on to small talk about the weather and how unseasonably warm it is. How gorgeous her kitchen is, which clearly pleases her, because she animatedly, bizarrely, tells me at length about the company that designed it for them, but how it isn't perfect and how next time, they're already planning something better.

Then I comment on her garden, designed by someone who really knows what they're doing. It has the structure and year-round interest that many lack. Something's changed, too, since I was last here. A small, evenly shaped apple tree has recently been planted—not by Jo, who has beautiful hands. Her unchipped nail polish is a dead giveaway.

"It's a lovely shape, Jo. Do you know which variety it is?"

She shakes her head. "I'm afraid I don't know the first thing about gardening."

"Does Neal look after it?" I gesture through the window. The long, neat lawn is flanked by elegantly planted borders. The new tree is dead center at the far end.

"Oh, no . . . We have this man who comes in every week. That reminds me—I must call him. He's missed the last two." She shakes her head. "Or maybe he's not coming anymore. I get so muddled, Kate." She looks at me beseechingly. "He and Neal didn't get on."

"Where is Neal?"

"He's gone away."

"How long for?" I can't believe he's left her alone so soon after Rosie's funeral.

"He wasn't going to," she adds, reading my face. "He's in Afghanistan, though not working this time. He and some colleagues started a charity. For children orphaned by the fighting."

"I had no idea." Laura had mentioned the orphanage, but she hadn't said he started it. Suddenly, Neal Anderson's joined my list of people who do great things in this world, who count. And just maybe, too, it gives him something else to think about and takes him away from what's here. "You must be so proud of him."

She nods. "It's the main reason I don't have a job. Oh, I know some of the mothers think that I do nothing with my life, but sometimes he's away for weeks. And anyway, I help him—do some of his paperwork, make calls, organize meetings."

As she speaks, I realize how little I know about her. About either of them.

"Why don't I help you with the garden? Just for now? I could fit in a couple of hours . . . if you wanted me to."

But Jo doesn't reply. She's gazing outside, beyond the trees, beyond the sky even, somewhere far away where I can't reach her.

I lean forward and touch her arm. "Jo? This must be so hard. . . ."

Feeling it with every fiber of my being.

Her gaze doesn't alter. "I wonder sometimes"—her voice seems to come from miles away—"what I did to deserve this, Kate. All I ever wanted, as long as I can remember, was a happy family. I thought it was one thing I could do really well. . . ."

There's a lump in my throat, because I share every word, every sentiment of what she's saying. To a mother, most of life can be reduced to the one thing that matters: family.

"I can't talk about it," she whispers, her eyes swinging round, catching mine and showing the full force of her agony. "I'm so sorry. . . ."

As I look at her, I see how little it would take for her to shatter into a thousand pieces—like the mug. Even taking her grief into account, she looks terrible. She gets up, pushing away her chair, struggling to hold herself together.

"Why don't you lie down for a bit, Jo? Try and get some rest."

Wishing with all my heart I could in some way ease the burden on her.

"It's just *so* bloody awful," I say to Angus that evening.

After the warmth of the day, the night is chilly, and he's lit the first fire of the season. We're slumped on the sofa, and I'm leaning against him, my feet up, with a glass of wine, watching the flames flickering against the heavy pattern of the fireback.

"Every time I go over there, it's the same. She holds it together—just. I've no idea how. You know, since the first time, she hasn't cried."

"It's probably just her way of coping. Different people react differently, don't they?" says Angus. "And God knows what it does to you, knowing someone killed your child."

"I know." I've thought of that, also. Still do, far too much, imagining pain that can only be an echo of what Jo feels.

We're quiet. I'm thinking of Grace. She's called a few times, bright exchanges that leave my eyes blurry and my heart bursting with pride. She's settling in, breaking away from us. Discovering beautiful, iridescent wings.

"Nice, this, isn't it?" Angus sits back happily, feet up on the coffee table. "Just you and me . . . There's actually food in the fridge, no teenagers tearing in and out. And Grace's doing what we always wanted her to do."

He's right. I snuggle against him, feeling his warmth,

my feet curled underneath me, trying but not able to savor the moment.

As Rosie's death blends into the backdrop of our lives, the petals drop on the last of Jo's flowers, which for weeks have kept arriving. But when I next visit, flowers aside, the sitting room's changed.

"New sofa?" My surprise must show in my voice, because Jo looks up sharply.

"We were going to redecorate . . . *before*. . . . I'd forgotten all about it until the sofa turned up yesterday."

"What a nuisance for you. I mean, right now, you could probably do without it."

"Oh, it's fine," she says briefly. "It's just a sofa. Would you like tea?"

"Please. Have you managed to track down your gardener?" I ask, following her into the kitchen, thinking how this normal, meaningless conversation about things that don't matter is somehow bizarre.

"He's not coming anymore," she says vaguely. "Neal's found a local boy to sweep up the leaves over the winter. To be honest, right now, it's the last thing I want to think about. We can find someone new in the spring."

She's right. There are more important matters than her garden to worry about. "Tell me, Jo . . . only, how's Delphine? She's always at school when I'm here. I never see her."

She considers her reply. "You know . . . she's quite surprising. She's not at all like Rosanna was. The police sent someone for her to talk to—a family liaison officer. But she's okay. For someone so young, she's strong."

It's a detached assessment rather than an affectionate

one, and I look at Jo, wondering if she's on something. Her tone is flat, her words are measured, and there's the same numbness about her I saw just after Rosie was found. The same blankness in her eyes. Unless, as Angus says, switching off is the only way she can function.

She turns away from me. "The police told me. How Rosanna used to go to see your horses."

There's the smallest edge of resentment in her voice.

"She did—if she was passing by. She'd just walk down across the field to talk to them. Not for very long," I assure Jo, feeling awkward that she heard about this from someone else. "She loved horses. I would have mentioned it before. I always assumed you knew."

It's easier to lie than to tell the truth. Even now, it would feel like a betrayal of Rosie's trust.

Jo nods very slowly. "I didn't," she says, adding tearfully, "I didn't know about her friendship with Poppy, either, did I? It makes me wonder what else I didn't know about."

Guilt washes over me for adding to her already backbreaking burden. "I should have told you—only there really wasn't anything to tell, Jo. It was never a planned thing. More like walking down the street and stopping to talk to someone you weren't expecting to see. That was all."

She dabs her face with a tissue. "I'm sorry, Kate. I overreact to everything. . . . I'm glad it was your horses she went to see. And you."

Slowly, she turns back to making the tea. Feeling awful, I try to change the subject to the daughter Jo still has, who must surely be suffering, too.

"Does Delphine have many friends?"

"One or two. There was this dreadful girl she was

friendly with, but we've discouraged that. It wasn't the right kind of friendship."

Another Poppy. It puts me in mind of the girl Grace befriended a few years ago. *Cleo.* Loud, in a too-short skirt, and reeking of cigarette smoke. I struggled with that one, wanting to steer Grace away from her. It was Angus who persuaded me not to and assured me that no harm would come to Grace if we watched her from the background, not too closely, but just closely enough. He was right.

"There's always one," I say sympathetically. "Only you have to let them make their own mistakes, don't you?"

"Neal isn't quite that forgiving," she says. "He has such high standards. He always wants the best for them, for . . . her."

She fumbles with the unfamiliarity of the singular. And we all want the best for our children. But whatever Jo says, Delphine can't be that strong if her parents decide who her friends are.

"She misses Rosanna dreadfully." Jo pours the tea and sits opposite me. "And the press coverage hasn't helped."

I shake my head. "It must be dreadful, for all of you. Especially—" I break off. I can't bring myself to mention the rumors that even now are still being whispered around our neighborhood.

"What were you going to say?" Jo looks up from her mug.

I'm awkward again, treading on eggshells. "Nothing, really."

Then I change my mind, because surely Jo should know.

"Actually, Jo, it's not nothing. I was thinking about

the rumors that paper printed. About Rosie . . . Rosanna having some kind of secret life. It was disgraceful."

She freezes. "She really didn't. She was a good girl who worked hard at school. They were just rumors, Kate. The papers are full of them." She stirs her tea before looking up again. "You know what they're like. Half the time, they print just for effect. You have to try not to let it get to you."

I'm not sure I could handle it as well as she appears to. "What about Neal? How is he coping?" Gently, not meaning to pry, but the loss of a child can destroy the closest of families. I watch as Jo's eyes fill with sorrow.

"He's heartbroken. He just throws himself into his work. It's what he does—to take his mind off things. We try to stay strong for each other, but underneath, he's like I am. He just hides it better. He's an amazing man, Kate."

"You all are, Jo. Strong. Amazing."

She shakes her head, but her eyes are shining. "Thank you. But I'm really not."

Two days later, just as I finish breakfast, there's a knock on the door.

Mildly irritated at the interruption when I'm rushing to get ready for work, I open it to find Laura standing there.

"Kate! I hope you don't mind me turning up like this, only I didn't take your number. Beth Van Sutton told me where you live."

"Hi! I'm sorry. I'd ask you in, but I'm about to go off to work." Aware it sounds like an excuse.

Laura looks uncertain, unsure whether I'm fobbing her off.

I pause. Rachael's right. I should at least talk to her

about this properly. "Why don't you come back? Say, one-ish? Have lunch?"

She looks relieved. "Thank you. That would be great."

But the few hours pruning and tidying a client's walled garden allow me to order my thoughts and step outside my rather blinkered view of journalists. I realize I want to know what's happened as much as any other parent around here. And just maybe, strangely, Laura has a place in all of this. By the time she arrives for lunch, I've come to a decision.

"Come on in. You'll have to excuse the mess. I haven't been back long."

"Please. You should see my house. And it's just me." She follows me in.

"Have a seat. I'll finish throwing this together, and we can eat outside."

"Great." Laura perches on one of the battered wooden chairs, tanned legs neatly arranged, skirt reaching just above her knees.

"So, how are you getting on? Are you finding out what you need?"

"Slowly . . . There are always people who want to talk for ages about nothing of relevance to Rosie. And others who don't want to know me."

Like me, I'm thinking.

"It isn't personal," she goes on. "But just by nature of being a reporter, some people think you're the devil's spawn."

The spoon I'm holding slips out of my hand, clattering to the floor.

But as we sit outside, lunch laid out on the table under the shade of our old oak tree, as the spark of our old friendship is rekindled, I start to relax. I'm curious, too, about Laura's life.

"So, tell me. Why did you move?"

"They offered me a job. Ten years ago." She helps herself to salad and slices of ham. "It was a job I couldn't refuse. You see, I went back to school and studied psychology. *Lifetime* wanted someone to write about mental health issues. At that point, I just wanted to get away from here. . . . It was the right job at the right time. I was lucky."

"No children?" I've already noticed the absence of a wedding ring.

She shakes her head. "There was a guy. It's a long story. . . . Anyway, as it turns out, I'm better off without him. I have great friends. And I love my work."

But as we eat, I have to ask. "So . . ." I hesitate, not sure how to put this. "How is what you write different from everyone else?"

"Well"—her voice becomes more businesslike—"forget everything you've ever thought about the gutter press. I'm not interested in hitting the headlines. There's always a story, but I want more than that. I guess, with Rosie, I'm looking from her parents' angle. Trying to find out not just what but why it happened. Was Rosie already a victim in some way even before her death? I suppose you could say it's what's behind the story that interests me."

As she speaks, suddenly I have goose bumps, realizing that aside from wanting to see a murderer caught, I, too, want to know. *Why?*

"Okay," I say quietly. "Ask me anything you like."

She looks surprised. "You're sure, Kate? I completely understand if you'd rather not."

"No. It's fine. I've thought about it. And I do trust you. It's not like it will hurt Jo. It might even help."

Laura looks grateful. "Thank you. Do you have time . . . if we make a start now?"

I nod as she reaches into her bag and pulls out a leather-bound notebook.

"Okay. So, why don't you tell me how you know the Andersons."

I tell Laura what I told the police, including about the necklace, while she takes notes, only at the end pausing to ask a question.

"Isn't your daughter a similar age?"

I nod. Laura's been doing her homework, but then, what did I expect?

"They weren't friends?"

"Not particularly. It wasn't that they didn't get on. They were just very different."

"And they didn't spend time together with the horses?"

"No."

"Did that surprise you?"

"I never used to think about it. It was a hot summer, and Grace used to ride out early in the morning. Her social life took up her evenings. It's just how it was."

An echo of Grace's words bounces back to me. *She never comes when I'm around, does she? It's as if it's not just the horses she wants. It's you.*

A frown wrinkles my forehead. "Grace commented on it, though. Just the once. That Rosie came over only when she wasn't around."

Laura writes it down, then sits thoughtfully, her head slightly tilted to one side.

"I've talked to a few people," she says quietly, "who,

in all honesty, probably didn't know her as well as you. I'm trying to build a picture of the people in her life. Her relationships. What she did, where she went, who might have seen her . . . One or two mentioned seeing her with a boy. No one has a bad word to say about her—or any of the Andersons. One or two bitchy comments about Jo, perhaps, but she's incredibly beautiful. People are jealous of that."

"Grace told me there were some boys hanging around. Druggies. One of her friends bought some weed from them."

Laura looks at me questioningly.

"I just keep thinking . . ." I hesitate.

"Kate, there will always be someone selling weed."

"It's not that so much. It's just, well, I keep wondering if maybe Rosie knew them. Or got caught up with them because of someone else. Like Poppy, her friend."

"That's the other thing. . . . There are all these rumors, Kate, about a boyfriend, but no one seems to have come up with who he is."

"Jo told me ages ago there wasn't one."

Laura frowns. "Maybe she didn't know. I should try and talk to Poppy. Do you know where she lives?"

"I can find out from Grace. But I wouldn't get your hopes up. And be careful. Her family is quite . . . intimidating, I guess you'd say."

"Oh. Okay."

Laura reaches into her bag and passes me a card. "If you think of anything else, could you call me?"

Shortly after she leaves, a knock at the door startles me. "Mrs. McKay?" It's Sergeant Beauman, and I notice another uniformed figure sitting in the police car that's parked outside. "Sorry to disturb you again, but would you mind if we had a look round your stable yard?"

"Of course not. What, now?"

She nods.

"Okay. I'll just get my boots."

I go to fetch them, wondering what they think they're going to find, deeply unsettled just at the thought.

As if that's not enough, that evening, before Angus gets home, I hear another car pull up, then footsteps running up the path and a loud hammering at the back door. Through the kitchen window I see it's Jo.

I hurry to the door and open it, horrified. She looks distraught. Her eyes are puffy and red; her hair is all over the place; her body shaking with huge, racking sobs.

"Jo . . . what is it? What's happened?"

I hold out my arms, and she falls into them, an awful animal sound coming from her as finally her grief vents itself.

Much later, when at last she quietens, I get her onto a chair, still clinging to me, then seize both her arms.

"I'm so sorry," she sobs. "I didn't know where else to go."

"It's okay, Jo. Really it is."

But she raises her tearstained face. "It isn't, Kate. It never will be."

"What is it? What's happened? Have the police found Rosie's murderer?"

She shakes her head, then whispers, "*Neal.*"

As she says his name, I'm struck by the chill of fear, because this family has suffered enough, too much. "Has something happened to him? Jo?"

Her face is stricken, her words blurring into each other. "Had a row. Neal said . . . I'm a bad mother. . . ."

I'm horrified. They're both suffering, both hurting. How can he be so cruel?

"Oh, Jo, that's an awful thing to say. Of course you're not. You loved her. She was your daughter."

But she wrenches herself back, away from me.

"You don't understand." Her eyes are wild, darting all around, as though she's looking for something. "I should have been able to protect her. . . ."

Delphine

Everyone has a destiny. Rosie told me that. A future that already exists—hidden from us but still there, in the future—and each thing that happens to us, each choice we make, each person in our life takes us closer to it.

Rosie told me she knows what hers is. She's known for a while.

She told me she's going to die.

Rosie

There are pictures of other towns, other houses, other schools—so many now I don't remember what order they came in or the names. The fact that I'm used to walking into strange classrooms, feeling twenty pairs of eyes on me, being the subject of teachers' questions doesn't make it easier, just predictable.

This time, the house is in Bath, a city of honey-colored stone and mellow light. Of music, art, and beauty on every street corner. Of warmth and life. The house is old, with three floors, close to the river, so that you don't hear traffic, just the water over the weir, endlessly flowing despite whatever happens around it, as it always has.

I work hard in school and get good grades, and Mummy says how happy she is. She has a friend, Amy, who has red hair and wears crazy clothes and makes us laugh; who hugs me tight so I can feel how soft she is and breathe in the scent of flowers she wears. My father is busy with his new job, and for fleeting seconds, the shadows lift, the dark patches fade, and our house is full of light.

It lasts a year, nearly. Long enough for one memorable Christmas, but not a second. A Christmas of garlands twisted up the stairs and a tall, sparkling tree under which presents are piled. Of people and laughter. It even snows. A Christmas that holds the promise of happiness.

At the end of the school term, I'm allowed a party. I have a soft velvet dress with silver buttons, and Amy curls my hair. For one afternoon, all my friends come over. We play games, sing carols while Amy plays her guitar. Then we have tea, and it's proper party food. Sausages on sticks, mini cheeseburgers, marshmallows dipped in chocolate, jelly and ice cream. "Because parties should be special," Mummy says. It is the most perfect, beautiful afternoon, and at the end, as they all leave, she gives everyone a tiny present tied with ribbon.

"Because you want people to like you, Rosanna, don't you? To remember how lovely your party was, how pretty our house looked," she says. "Now, when they look at your present, they will."

Then, when everyone's gone, Amy comes into my room and gives me a present, too. A tiny silver horse.

She places a finger to her lips, and her eyes sparkle with secrets. "I had a charm bracelet when I was your age," she tells me. "This was the very first one my mother gave me. And now I want it to be yours."

I hold it tight, feel the tiny hooves digging into my palm, the most precious thing anyone's ever given me. A piece of Amy.

"You better hide it. It's our secret." Then she winks.

A few days before Christmas, my parents throw their own party. From my room, the little horse on a ribbon round my neck, I listen to the music, the hum of voices, with Della. Then we spy from the top of the stairs, marveling at red-carpet dresses, diamonds, and dinner jack-

*ets. Only, of course, now I see there's more. That behind
the glamour and the opulence, the lacquered hair and
the fabulous clothes, there's the preening, the alcohol-
induced flirting, the dabbling on the edges of promis-
cuity.*

*And in their midst, reflected in the friends clustered
round her, Mummy shines, a beautiful jewel, attentive to
each person in turn, making sure they'll remember that
this is the best Christmas party ever. Remember her.*

*But even through the cluster of friends who love her,
Mummy sees her. Amy sees, too. Another moth to my father's flame, with her spun-gold hair and berry lips. Who
doesn't dabble but dives right in.*

*I remember watching from my window, seeing her
leave before everyone else, not aware of my father slipping out the back door, still buttoning his coat as he jogs
up the street, catching up to her.*

*"We can't," she tells him, her whisper-breath small
frosted clouds, when he pushes her under the shadow of a
tree. "Your wife is lovely. You have a family, Neal. . . ."*

*"It's just a kiss," he tells her, his face an inch from
hers so she can see how bright it is. "One kiss."*

*Even out here, in the cold, she wants him. I can tell
from how she looks at him sideways from under lowered
lashes, from how the scarlet lips are parted, how an visible hand pulls her to him. And this time, it is just a kiss.
But there'll be a next time, they both know that, planned
in secret, in low voices, in lies.*

*When he comes back, the party in full swing, do I
imagine the hum of voices stills for about 0.0005 seconds,
then restarts, brighter, decibels louder than before? Heads
turning, then turning back? Pretending nothing is different? Do they even care?*

But it is different. The sparkle is tarnished; the tree dying; the promise of happiness broken. Mummy isn't shining now. She's powder white.

First the shadows, then the packing boxes are back. Amy comes round, begging Mummy to let him go without her. To stay here.

"You can't go on like this." Amy's eyes are serious. "Please, Jo. I'll help you—you know I will. You and the girls can live with me. We'll get you a good lawyer. . . . It'll be a fresh start. You'll be fine, honey, I promise."

For a moment, for the only time, Mummy hesitates. Thinks about it for a nanosecond, imagines life without my father, having her own house, and a future that only she can see and I can only guess at. But I can see the words forming behind her eyes.

"You don't know him the way I do. He can't help the way he is. He needs me. I know you only see the worst of him, but really, he is an amazing man."

Not seeing the tears in Amy's beautiful green eyes as she walks away.

That's when I learn how fragile hearts are. That they can break only so many times. The living, breathing cells that hold them together turn to cold, dead scar tissue, which can't feel. Which isn't able to love.

We don't see Amy before the lorries come and we leave, again, for another town, another house, another school.

And when I unpack, the silver horse has gone.

10

Something's niggling in a corner of my mind. I don't remember what it is until the next time I'm sitting in Jo's kitchen, looking out at her garden.

"You know, that little apple tree, Jo . . . I've been thinking about it. That's probably not the best place for it. I think I'd move it before it gets too established."

She looks surprised. "Why? I like it there."

"Well, from a gardener's point of view, as it grows bigger, all the plants underneath will be in shade. And you won't be able to reach the apples without treading on the underplanting."

"To be honest, I'm not that bothered about the apples," Jo says. "I'm happy with it where it is. If the plants need replacing, I'll get someone to come and do it. You're probably right, but just now, I have so much to think about."

It's against my gardening ethics, but I shrug. It's her garden.

But in this post-normal world, something else doesn't add up. After her heartbreaking declaration of guilt the other night, when she spent the evening sobbing her heart out, telling me how if she'd been a better mother, known where her own daughter was, Rosie might still be alive, Jo's acting as though it never happened.

"Jo . . . since the other night, I've been really worried about you. Are things okay with you and Neal?"

I see from the way her shoulders tense, from the breath she takes in and holds, I've struck a nerve.

"Oh . . . yes." When she turns round, her face is calm. "We talked. He was angry. We all say things in anger, don't we? We were both upset. I'm so wrapped up in my-self, I forget sometimes that he misses Rosanna just as much as I do. How can I do that?" For a moment, she looks stricken. "I understand why he said it. He feels as guilty as I do. We should have been able to stop it from happening. He didn't mean to upset me. He's a remark-able man, Kate."

It's what she always says about him. And yes, he is, and he does many good things. And they're going through about the worst that can happen to any parent. But I can't help thinking, *What kind of man lets his wife walk out, distressed and tearful, the wife whose heart is broken and who's just lost their child?*

And just this once, I push her on the subject.

"I'm glad, Jo, because you were so upset. I know all this is a nightmare, but even so—"

She doesn't let me finish. "You know? You can't know," she flashes. "Grace's at school, and she'll come back. She'll always come back. Rosanna's gone. *Gone* . . . Do you really know how that feels?"

She stands there, her body trembling, her cheeks flushed pink, little knowing how agonizingly, painfully aware I am of this every time I see her.

Then the words rip out of her, a long, unbroken string of them.

"It's hell, Kate. You have no idea. . . . One minute I think I'm coping, and then the next it's like I'm falling into the deepest, darkest pit, and there's no way out. It's like part of me's been cut off. . . . It hurts. So much. She's my daughter. . . ."

I go toward her to offer comforting arms, a shoulder, but she pulls herself upright, and when she speaks again, it's the flat, cold voice of a total stranger.

"I know you mean well. But I know why you're here. You think by taking on *my* pain, you're safeguarding your own family."

I feel my cheeks cool as the blood drains from my face. Even though I know that this is her grief talking, that it's targeted at me only because I'm here . . . Is she right? Is what I perceive as supporting, bolstering, caring for her ultimately just selfish? .

"I'll go," I mumble, leaving the tea, picking up my bag. I know she's hurting, but I'm out of my depth. I can't reach her.

At the front door, I pause to look at her. "I'm so sorry if I've upset you, Jo. I only ever wanted to be a friend."

As I speak, her face seems to change, taking on a desperate, tormented look, as she clutches at her hands.

"*I'm sorry* . . . ," she whispers. "I just wish they'd find the person who did this. Please, Kate. I should never have said that to you. You've been . . . such a good friend. . . . Oh God, what have I done?"

I've never witnessed such an extreme swing of emotion. There are tears in her eyes as she begs, "Please, don't go. I need you."

Her onslaught leaves me battered, but I see it for what

it is. She's lashing out at me because the strain is taking its toll, because her agony's unbearable, because I'm here. What's happened to Rosie could have happened to any teenager. Even Grace.

Still could happen. The murderer's still out there.

"You've got too sucked in, Kate. Give her some space," says Angus that evening, when I tell him.

"How can you say that?" Still raw after Jo's outburst, I can't bear another stab at me. How can he, when he knows how hard I've taken this? And isn't it a measure of our friendship that Jo can say what she likes, be so honest? The truth can hurt; we all know that. And Jo's hurting more than anyone can imagine.

"Hey. Don't be mad. You've been a really good friend to her, Kate, but you can't change anything. It sounds like she's all over the place—not surprisingly, after what she's been through. And what she said is true. None of us can really understand how she feels—thank God."

I sigh. "I just feel so sorry for her."

I know he's right, but it's not that simple. Has Jo's grief become my grief? Have I somewhere along the way made myself responsible for her?

"Come here."

I let him pull me close, my head against his shoulder. Maybe I have got too sucked in. Too involved. Maybe, for my sanity, I should step back.

A week later, a week during which I avoid any contact with the Andersons, I visit the wholesale nursery where I buy my plants. They're holding one of their rare open days, displaying fabulous autumnal plants in rich earthy shades, with pots of bulbs and winter flowering shrubs stacked up behind, waiting to follow.

It's what I need, like visiting an exhibition or going to a musical, only instead of flooding your senses with art or music, it's about plants, their scents, colors, textures. Yes, I buy, but I enrich my soul and fire my imagination, taking away far more inside my head: images of sumptuousness, planting combinations, the endless possibilities of what time and the seasons can create.

"Morning, Dan." I wave at the familiar figure coming toward me. I've known Dan for about ten years, soaking up the snippets of knowledge he imparts when the mood takes him. "You've outdone yourselves again! I love all of it!"

"Cheers, Kate." He looks pleased. He and his team work tirelessly to put this on, but it's good for business, and over the years, word has spread, drawing designers from miles around. "I've got some new bulbs you might like. You got time to take a look?"

"Definitely." Excitement flickers inside me. In past seasons, Dan's new varieties have set trends. He keeps a close eye on changing fashions. They also sell out extremely quickly.

"They're in here."

I follow him into a polytunnel marked STAFF ONLY, honored to be one of his chosen few allowed behind the scenes on hallowed soil. Just then, his mobile rings.

"Sorry, Kate. Won't be a minute."

Breathing in the familiar earthy smell, I wander over and examine the large board where a picture of each flower is displayed. There are tulips, narcissi, amaryllis, hyacinths—in shades I've never seen before. My thrilled gardener's heart skips a beat.

"Sorry, love." Dan joins me. "I'm needed elsewhere. Take your time and have a look. If you want to order anything, talk to Alex over there."

He's looking at the young man at the far end of the tunnel, his back to us, methodically pricking out seedlings.

Then he turns to me and nods his head toward the door, gesturing me outside. Mystified, I follow him.

"Just so you know, he worked at that house where the young girl went missing. I'm only mentioning it because I know they're just up the road from you. Don't say anything, though. Hit him rather hard, I think." He says it quietly, clearly not wanting to be overheard.

Dan knows where I live. In the past, he's delivered to me. With every word, my curiosity builds, because I know, with certainty, I've found Jo's mysterious gardener, and no way can I leave without talking to him.

But I've work to do first. I'm taking my time, studying the plants, mentally constructing what I want to create and noting down quantities. It's not long before I hear footsteps coming toward me.

"Do you need any help?"

Looking up, I get my first close look at Alex. He's taller than me and, I'd guess, in his early twenties, dark haired, with a gardener's tan from days spent working outside. Striking looking, but with wary eyes and an aloofness in his manner, which means I don't warm to him.

"I think I'm done," I tell him. "Here."

I pass him my list, and he reads through it, then nods slowly. "They're good together," he says. "I sketched something earlier based on the same varieties. If you hang on, I'll try and find it."

I watch him rummage on the tabletop, from which he produces an A4 sheet, and I'm surprised to see that as well as designing gardens, he can draw, far better than I can. He's sketched a winter flower bed to die for, in a drawing that would look great in a frame, hung on a wall.

"White narcissi, with gaultheria in the foreground," he points out. "Then by the time the narcissi go over, you've got burnt-orange tulips and green viburnum taking center stage. I've put in other colors, too, just here and there. A bit of hot pink and that black one. Thought it looked better kept simple."

"It's stunning," I tell him.

Alex shrugs. "It's not groundbreaking. People think they like the unusual, but when it comes to their own garden, mostly they like things a bit traditional."

It's exactly what I find. There will always be the odd client with a taste for the avant-garde, but mostly people like English-garden flowers that they know the names of, the same ones that have been around for years.

"That's exactly it. But if you're a designer, what are you doing working for Dan?" Trying not to appear overly interested, but I can't help wondering if those dark, impassive eyes that tell me nothing might be hiding something.

Alex frowns, and I feel his eyes boring into me.

I'm suddenly uncomfortable. "Dan mentioned you used to work for the Andersons. But only because he knows I live nearby."

He just shrugs.

"Actually, I'm glad I've met you. I'm really impressed with their garden. I love the borders." Trying to defuse his obvious hostility and strike a more friendly tone, watching the expression on his face remain unchanged.

"It's always easy when your client throws money at it." He sounds bitter, as though he resents them. "They didn't mind what I spent as long as it looked 'impressive,' I think the brief was. 'Expensive' may have been in there, too."

I nod. *Impressive* and *expensive* describe everything about the Andersons' house, but then why not? They can clearly afford it.

"I think they miss you. Or the garden does. . . ." It's meant harmlessly. Humorously, even. I'm not expecting the look like thunder that crosses his face.

Rosie

A barreling surfer's wave drops me into a summer without my parents. The summer I discover what happiness means. A summer of uninhibited noisiness, with camping in homemade tents hung over washing lines and long nights under starlit skies, with toasted marshmallows and English beaches and freedom.

It's running wild with my cousins through cornfields speckled with poppies until we reach the beach, shrieking as we dive into the waves. It's the timeless shift of tides and blazing sunsets, lying on cool, damp grass and staring long enough until one by one you see the stars. It's homemade cakes and ice cream, Auntie Carol playing with Della's hair, her head full of invisible thoughts of her daughter, Isabel, who died.

Everyone says how sad it is that Isabel "went" so young. It's the wrong word. Isabel didn't "go" anywhere. She crossed an invisible line, just as I have. She's here now, her head on Carol's shoulder, her arms encircling Carol and Della, grinning over their shoulders at me.

It's a summer I wish I could live my entire life, while my own life floats like the fair-weather clouds above my head, until my mother arrives, holding out arms, chasing freedom away with her perfume.

"Darling! Come and give Mummy a hug! She's missed you so much."

While the last sweet, mouthwatering taste of happiness melts away like the strawberry ice creams on the sea-front, I walk toward her, holding out my arms, because I love her.

And then I feel guilt covering me from head to toe, because until now, I haven't missed her. Guilt because I love her, but I don't want her here. In her perfect, pale, uncreased clothes she belongs at home, not here in Auntie Carol's world. Because I want this summer to last forever.

I look at her. Have I really forgotten how she looks? Her face a flawlessly painted mask stretched over her bones? Where are the lines that hold love and laughter, like Auntie Carol has? But then, Mummy doesn't need them. She doesn't laugh.

11

November

Another week goes by, the tenth since Rosie went missing, a week in which autumn eventually takes a hold and, after the summer we've had, brings a year's worth of leaves down almost overnight. It's another week in which I don't see Jo, nor do I hear from her. It's only by chance, when I'm driving home after work one afternoon, that I see Delphine.

It's her hair that catches my eye. Rosie's hair, only longer and clipped back off her face. She's walking along the pavement in small, precise steps, looking straight ahead, until I slow down and pull over.

"Delphine? It's me. Kate. Your mum's friend. Would you like a lift?"

Alarm, then a flicker of recognition cross her face. Does she wonder at every passerby? If *that man* who looks like someone's father, or *that woman* with the fair hair, who looks completely innocent but might not be, could they have killed her sister?

She climbs into the passenger seat. "Thank you," is all she says.

I wait for the click of her seat belt, then drive on.

"How is school?"

"Fine, thank you." Her voice is girlish, but then she's twelve. So young—far too young to know this kind of grief.

"I haven't seen your mum for a while," I say. "How is she?"

"She's okay."

"Is she at home, do you know?" It's the perfect excuse to just pop in and say hello to her.

Delphine hesitates. "She might be. I don't know."

When I pull up outside their house, she doesn't meet my eyes, just gets out and picks up her bag.

"Thank you for giving me a lift."

"You're welcome." I frown. Both Neal and Jo's cars are parked in the drive. "You know, I haven't seen her for a while," I repeat. "I might just go in and say hello."

But Delphine says nothing as she walks toward the door, then pushes it open, leaving it ajar for me to follow.

I stop just inside. "Hello? Jo? It's me. Kate . . ."

I hesitate, thinking perhaps she's still mad at me, but as I turn to go, I hear a man's voice.

"Kate? Thank you for dropping Delphine back. It's good of you."

Neal's coming toward me, in jeans and an open-necked shirt.

"It was no problem. I was driving right by. I hoped I might see Jo."

"Ah." He glances away, slightly guarded. "When did you last see her?"

"A couple of weeks ago." I shrug, making light of it. "I just wondered how she was, that's all."

He nods. "It's good of you. Look, she has one or two

things going on at the moment. She's gone away. Just for a while."

"Is she all right?"

"She'll be fine." Then he studies me. "Actually, do you have a minute?"

When I come away half an hour later, I've learned that Neal cares deeply for his wife and that, not surprisingly, Jo is struggling more than she lets on, as he told me.

"She's gone away . . . to rest, mostly. She's been working too hard—for me, I'm afraid—as well as everything else. I'm hoping it'll do her good, just getting away from here."

We're sitting across the kitchen table from each other, Neal leaning on his elbows, hands clasped, his eyes trained on them.

"Poor Jo. I had no idea things were still so difficult." Realizing too late the crassness of my words, because how could they not be? Thinking, *If I'd lost Grace* . . .

He pauses, frowning at the table, considering something. Then he looks up. "Has she told you she's been ill?"

It's the first I've heard about an illness. I shake my head. "No. She hasn't."

"Joanna . . ." He hesitates. "Her life hasn't always been easy. She had a breakdown, Kate. A lot of stuff caught up with her. From the past. Stuff she'd buried for a long time. But that's what happens. And it's always just when you think life's going your way. . . ." He breaks off. "She's very good at hiding things. You must have noticed. Particularly since Rosanna *died* . . ."

His voice cracks, and then I get it, that every second of every day, for Neal and Jo, in this house, surrounded by their memories, there will never be any escape from what's happened.

"I didn't know, but she's surprised me," I say honestly. "Just the way she's kept going. If it was me, I don't think I'd be capable of anything."

"The thing is . . ." He trails off. "It's hard to put into words, but you keep going because you have to, but it's always there. Guilt. You can't stop thinking about it. . . . And as soon as you forget, even for a few seconds, you feel guilty, Kate. *So guilty* . . . Guilty that it happened and we couldn't do something. Guilty that we're here and she isn't." He slumps, defeated. "That's where we are, I guess. Both of us."

Wishing in some small way I could help them all, my heart reaches out to him, because he's clearly hurting just as much as Jo is, and to add to it, he has to prop her up, too. I feel an overwhelming sadness at how unfair it is that one person must bear so much alone.

I come away knowing that in spite of the blowup, his outburst at Jo, Neal's a good man.

It occurs to me only much later that I've forgotten to tell him I met Alex.

Rosie

It's the year I come top in my class, with As in every subject except math. You don't see how hard I've worked or how proud I feel, or the small part of me deep inside that glows. My teachers are happy, and so is Mummy. Only, because of the math, that evening, when my father gets home, he makes me fetch the little pink TV set from my bedroom, the one I've always had, then takes it outside.

As he places it on the low wall, I hear birds and faint strains of laughter from next door. It's a beautiful evening, the pale blue sky crisscrossed with vapor trails, sunlight flickering through the leaves, but my stomach is churning as he gets a chair for me to sit on. Then, not speaking, he picks up a brick.

"About your grades . . . ," he says. His voice is too loud as he stands in front of me, passing the brick to and fro between his hands, and I wonder what he's doing. Then he raises it and brings it down. I hear the splintering of the pretty pink plastic first, then my own gasp of

shock as the screen shatters into a million pieces. I'm thinking, Why? even as I lean forward and I'm sick.

He tells me to wash down the deck with the hose. Then says how stupid I am to be sick over a little girl's TV set. A TV set, for Christ's sake! That my math grade isn't good enough. I need to knuckle down and work harder. Then he hurls the brick into a bush.

I get the hose and wash down the deck, wanting to vomit the ugliest words I can think of in his face, tell him that it wasn't the TV set that made me sick. I'm not that stupid.

It's him.

I'm fifteen by then. I have a new friend called Emma Carnegie, who you know is happy just by looking at how her hair swings when she walks, how her eyes are lit from inside, and how she laughs at nearly everything. She has three older brothers and thinks it's cool that I've lived in so many places. She's lived in Winchester her whole life and says it's boring.

Winchester. I could like it here, but I already know I won't let myself. This is where our home is—for now. Another house in another town, where Delphine wants to stay forever. She doesn't understand yet that we won't.

When it's Emma's birthday, she has a party. Her house is messy but full of music and chatter and life, coming and going. Her parents and their friends. Her brothers and their friends. Others—always welcomed, like I am.

Before her party, Emma asks me to sleep over. My heart sinks because I know I have to tell her that my parents won't let me, which she says is really stupid.

"For F's sake, we're fifteen, Rosie. I said 'F'!" Then laughs at her own joke.

"You're so right!" I laugh with her, a hollow pretend laugh. "I'll ask them again!"

And I'm frightened then, feeling that worried look like my mother's that makes my head hurt, that if I don't go, Emma won't want me as a friend. Then I'm angry that my parents won't let me decide, when it's my life and Emma's friendship is important to me.

Now I see a dilemma that's my parents' doing. But I don't know that at the time. As I work out how to keep Emma's friendship, how to keep my parents happy, I have no choice. And so it starts.

The lie begins with two lies. To my mother, that I'm going to Emma's to watch a movie; to Emma, that it'll be great! I'm sleeping over!

I wear jeans and a T-shirt so my mother doesn't question me, just drives me over there and doesn't come in. Emma isn't a perfect friend, but because her father's in a famous orchestra, she's good enough. Already there's music. Food on foil-covered plates prepared by Emma's mum, generously and happily, and with love.

I get ready with Emma, curling our hair, putting on makeup—sweeping eyeliner and long layers of mascara, then soft pink lipstick—laughing with her, pretending I do this all the time.

I lie that I've forgotten my clothes—that was the third lie. How could she believe I'd forget my clothes? The thrill I feel when Emma says I look gorgeous in the short dress and pretty shoes she lends me. I look at myself, eyes sparkling. Alight, like Emma. I remember the reason for it, too.

His name is Adam, Emma's youngest brother, not quite two years older than us, kind of shy and sweet, the *first boy who holds my hand, dances with me as the sun goes down, then later, much later, when it's dark, under the oak tree at the end of the garden, when no one's watching us, the first boy whose soft, gentle lips touch mine.*

I remember him being just the right amount taller than me, so that when he leaned down and I turned my face up toward his, our lips met. The denim shirt he was wearing with the sleeves rolled up, his hair kind of messy and needing cutting. How when he kissed me, everyone else faded into the background, and how I floated, so high I nearly forgot the lie. How I remembered just in time, clasping a hand to my head, closing my eyes. Crashing down to earth.

"I'm sorry, Adam. I really don't feel well."

And I so don't want to do this, so want to stay here, with him and everyone else. It's the lie that kills me inside.

His look of concern. "Come and sit down. I'll get you a glass of water."

But I don't want him to leave me, even for the minutes it will take for him to walk to the kitchen and back. "It's okay. Really, I'll be fine. It's a migraine. I get them sometimes. It's probably best I go home."

Telling Emma, watching the disappointment spread over her face, followed by sympathy I don't deserve. I don't see the tear she sheds as she goes to get me a glass of water, how sad she is because I'm her friend and I've let her down. Or how she stands up to Leah Williams, who says I'm a weirdo and she doesn't understand why Emma even asked me here.

Adam's eyes, following me down the drive as I get into my father's car, which arrives dead on ten o'clock and waits, just as we agreed.

I don't see that when we drive away, the party mood goes quiet, then dies. I just sit as my father drives, hands clenched on the steering wheel, waiting.

And he knows I'm waiting.

After ten minutes like ten hours, when we're nearly home, as we turn into our drive, when he's spun it out as long as he possibly can, at the very last minute, when I'm holding my breath, he spits it out with contempt.

"Who was the boy?"

The boy.

"Emma's brother."

It isn't a lie, but if it was, I wouldn't care. One lie, fifty lies. What's the difference?

He hesitates, while I get out of the car and calmly walk inside, because whatever else he can do, however he looks at me, whatever questions he asks, he can't make me say things I don't want to say. The secret is hugged inside, where no one can get to it, no one except me, where I can say his name over and over and no one can hear it.

His name is Adam, *I say silently, looking at my father's back.* Adam. Adam. Adam.

Lies are like dough or malignant tumors. They get bigger. I meet Adam at lunchtimes. On Tuesday evenings, when I walk to the library with books that don't need changing, or Thursday evenings, at running club, only neither of us puts on the trainers we're carrying. We just walk.

It takes a few weeks, the shortest, sweetest time, to learn what it is to trust. To know he won't hurt me for no reason. That he'll be where he says he'll be. That nothing will change out of the blue, without warning.

Until it does.

One day, when I get to school, Emma is cool with me, then sits with Leah Williams, their backs to me. Adam isn't in school. Then on Thursday, he doesn't meet me at running club.

Next time I see him, it's between classes. He's walking along a corridor toward me; then about ten feet away, he looks up and sees me. Freezes. My heart does that flutter, but then I see his eyes. Cold, hurt, staring at mine, full of hostility and broken promises. Then he turns and walks away, and my friendship with Emma follows, like his shadow.

I never find out why. I just remind myself that no one's different. People are all the same. You can't trust any of them. You can't have faith in them, because eventually, they will always let you down.

Only now, as I watch myself, my head staring at the floor, filled with those black words, Adam's back disappearing down the corridor, I see how wrong I was. There are such good people. People worth taking a risk for. If I'd run after Adam, questioned Emma, made them tell me the truth: Adam walking back from the library that night. The car slowing, drawing up alongside, the window winding down. Adam stopping. His lovely, warm face friendly. Opening his mouth with a greeting that isn't uttered, instead forced to listen as foul threats and abusive words are hurled in his face. The car driving away.

My father's car.

12

Grace comes home, just briefly, a whirlwind of lightness and laughter. We go out riding, me on Zappa, her on Oz, in spite of the drizzle, which stubbornly refuses to let up. After a canter through the woods that leaves her cheeks pink and her eyes glowing, conversation inevitably turns to Rosie.

"Mum? Do you think they'll ever find who did it?"

"I don't know, Grace. I hope they do, because whoever it was deserves what's coming to them."

But it's more than that. It's too easy to forget as time passes, as the initial horror fades. Neal and Jo, all of us, our entire village in fact, still bearing the burden of Rosie's death, we all deserve to know the truth.

We're approaching the clearing where Rosie's body was found, when at the top of the slope, I see the back of a man. I frown, trying to make out who it is. He's too tall to be Neal. Then, as we get nearer, I see he's younger and clearly distressed, his arms tightly folded, his shoulders heaving.

"What is it?" Grace follows my gaze. "Who's that?"

"*Shh.* Come on. Don't stare."

We walk past, but as I glance over my shoulder, he turns enough for me to see his face, red from crying, and I draw a breath, not because he's a man who's inconsolably, unbearably in pain, but because I know him.

"That was Jo's gardener," I tell Grace when we're out of earshot. "Ex-gardener. His name's Alex."

"So what d'you think he's doing there?"

I shrug. "Probably just paying his respects."

Even though from what I saw, it was far more than that.

"Mum, it's been ages. People do that stuff in the first days, not over two months later."

"Not always." I hesitate, wondering whether to tell her what I'm thinking. "Unless . . . Do you think that maybe there was something between them?"

"Rosie wouldn't go for someone like him. Anyway, he's too old." Grace dismisses it with the air of someone who knows.

"There aren't rules, Grace. They could have been friends. And it might not be the first time he's been here. Or maybe he wanted to be sure he'd be alone."

When Grace goes this time, it's a bruise, as opposed to a ripped muscle, in part because it isn't long until Christmas, but also my mind is elsewhere.

The next day, I go to look for Alex. It's already raining when I reach Dan's nursery, icy needles rather than cats and dogs, but with a cold that's no less penetrating.

"You just can't stay away, can you, Kate?" Dan quips.

"Hi, Dan! I've come back for more of those tulip bulbs—if there are any left?"

"Because it's you, I'll go and have a look."

Dan strides off, and I wander up and down the rows of plants, somewhat depleted since I was last here, searching for hidden gems I missed the first time round. It's not long before I see Alex.

"Hello again."

He glances at me, then looks away. "Hi."

And then I realize I haven't really thought this through. How to say I saw him in the woods, or to ask about Rosie, without it sounding like I'm a nosy middle-aged woman with good intentions but who's essentially prying? In the end, I decide it is what it is.

"I thought you should know, I knew Rosie, too," I tell him. "She used to like being with my horses."

He's very still as he works out what I'm saying. That I'm a friend. Straightening up, he turns to face me. "She told me you were always kind to her. She felt safe with you."

Safe. A strange choice of word.

He goes on, his eyes full of his pain. "You should have said the other day, when you were in."

"I know. I should have. But I hadn't realized you were more than their gardener." Feeling my way, watching his face, how his jaw tightens. "I saw you in the woods. I was riding there the other day with my daughter."

He shifts uncomfortably.

"You and Rosie . . ." I hesitate, choose my words carefully, gently. "Was there something?"

I see him clench his fists at his sides as he raises his eyes heavenward. When he looks at me again, they're full of tears. "Yes. We were together. For a long time, no one knew. Then Joanna got suspicious, and, well, let's just say she wasn't taking any chances. Just the idea of her daughter with the hired help . . . Well, you can imagine, can't you?"

He speaks with so much bitterness, and while I don't agree with her, I get it about Jo's order of things. We're all different, and it's how her world is, with her cleaner, her gardener, even the teachers at school—all, quite firmly, good people she needs in her life, but on her terms.

I'm also stunned that she didn't tell me about Rosie and Alex. But confronted with his obvious distress, I forget that.

"I'm so sorry." I touch his arm very gently. "Sorry you've lost her. Sorry they treated you like that, too."

He stiffens, wrestling with himself. "I loved her. I can't bear what happened. What kind of monster would do that? *To someone like her* . . ."

"Have you talked to the police?" I ask.

"They came to see me just after she was found. Asked me how long I'd worked there. Stuff like that."

"So they do know? About you and Rosie?"

Alex stiffens. "I didn't do anything wrong. There was no reason for them to know. Anyway, it wouldn't do any good."

"What do you mean?"

He hesitates; then, when he speaks, his face is flushed, and his words resonate with anger. "You really want to know? It's people like those bloody Andersons. They love to blame other people, people like me, if they have the chance, because they're better than I am. That's what they think. . . ." He shakes his head. "The truth is, Neal's a nasty piece of work. Rosie hated him. Had as long as she could remember. He's the worst kind of control freak, Kate. You wouldn't believe the stories she told. I wouldn't be surprised if he had something to do with this."

His words shock me. Then it comes back to me, what Jo said, that he and Neal didn't get on. "God, Alex . . . that's some accusation. How can you even think that?"

"Rosie argued with her father. The day before she disappeared. He wanted to stop her from going out—from seeing anyone. She told him that she'd had enough of him treating her like this, and that if he didn't stop, she'd leave home and never speak to him again. He totally flipped."

"You need to tell the police, Alex. All of this. They *will* get to the bottom of it. But all parents row with their teenage children," I say, thinking of my own overprotective instincts, Grace's proclamations of independence and hotheaded acts of rebellion. "It's normal. Things get said in the heat of the moment—"

He interrupts me. "But Rosie didn't lose her cool. Not ever. She told me she'd never won an argument with him, unless he wanted her to, for perverted reasons of his own. That's the kind of guy he is. Pulls their strings like they're bloody puppets."

His eyes are menacing, his stance is almost threatening, and I take a step back, glancing over my shoulder for Dan, but he's nowhere to be seen, as Alex continues.

"He controls that family, Kate. Each one of them, even his wife, from their every move down to the ground they walk on. Even the air they breathe. The man's a psycho."

But I don't see it. "Arguing's one thing, Alex, but Neal a murderer . . . ?"

I'm filled with unease at both the strength of his outburst and what he's suggesting, because he's wrong about the Andersons. All the time I've spent there, I haven't seen a hint of what he's describing. I imagine Grace bringing a boyfriend home, and Angus taking a dislike to him, because that's clearly what's happened. Telling myself that Alex's emotions are raw because he's lost the girl he loved—anyone can see that. And, like the Andersons, he desperately needs someone to blame.

"Watch out for him," Alex mutters. "I mean it."

"Are you sure you're right about Neal? He's an amazing man." As I say it, I realize what I'm doing and that they're Jo's words, rolling off my tongue as if they're my own. "He's really worried about her. He'd do anything for his family."

"Yeah," says Alex darkly. "Exactly. Anything."

Rosie

Florida is big. Big beaches that stretch for miles, like the sky, which is big, too. And close enough that you can almost reach up and touch the clouds.

It's a once-in-a-lifetime holiday, Mummy tells us. One we'll always remember, because it's so much better than ordinary holidays. Not everyone travels first class, she tells us, as we walk onto the plane and turn left instead of right. I smile at the stewardesses and say, "Thank you," not seeing how behind my back, they glance at each other when my father boards. Whisper about that arsehole TV reporter who demanded a free upgrade and wouldn't take no for an answer.

I don't see any of that. All I remember is the flight being magical, like a dream, cocooning us in luxury, gently devouring the miles until we soar down, a huge Disney bird, into the adventure awaiting us.

The room Della and I share has two big beds and views of Cocoa Beach. We visit the Kennedy Space Center, Disney World, go shopping in malls, eat out at buzz-

ing, neon-lit diners. Della and I rent bodyboards, and I remember the waves, like horses, racing me to the shore.

And while the sun tans my skin and lightens my hair, I lighten inside. My mother is beautiful, my father handsome, my sister happy, and for this handful of days, removed from our ordinary lives, we can just be.

We watch my father water-ski. He's good at it. After, he chats with the boat driver, this guy called Ed, who winks at me, then gives him a card, which my father looks at and puts away in a pocket.

Imagine a monitor in a hospital showing a heart attack–sized blip, followed by a flat line. It comes at the end of the first week, though now I see it building up. My father's drinking, his restlessness, his boredom with his family, his need for danger. The dream is over.

Mercifully, then the monitor was turned away from me. I saw only my parents dressed up to go out, my mother in a new black evening dress, her hair put up in the hotel salon, her skin the color of soft toffee, my father in his bow tie and dinner jacket.

Della and I wave them away, filled with our own excitement at the movie channels and room service we can choose from, taking an hour to decide exactly what we want to order.

And while we sit there, eating huge pizzas, overlooking the Atlantic and watching the same waves we played in earlier, I see the expensive restaurant my parents go into. The bottles of wine, the best, chosen not because he loves good wine but for effect. Then, after, more whiskey. The casino upstairs, my father's reckless way with his family's holiday money and his extraordinary belief that the only way to recover his losses is to gamble more. Even if it empties his bank accounts.

I see my mother try to persuade him to leave, then give up and climb into a cab she can't pay for, which the hotel charges to their account. The sick, anxious look as she wonders how the hotel bill, the rest of the holiday, or any of this will be paid for in one week's time, when we leave.

I'm sleeping when my father comes back at dawn, his shirt rumpled and smudged with a stranger's lipstick, reeking of whiskey, then falls into the bed where my mother tossed and turned but hasn't slept, where he sleeps the guiltless sleep of the dead.

Della and I awake to our mother, freshly showered, her makeup perfect, opening our curtains.

"Let's have breakfast, girls. Then we'll go to the beach! We'll leave Daddy to have a lie-in."

"Can we bodyboard?" Della asks.

"Of course." Her eyes rest on each of us, as with stellar strength she forces her lips to smile and her eyes to warm, even though her husband is unfaithful and worry is crippling her.

"The sun's out, girls. It's another perfect day."

It is a perfect day, just the three of us. We don't see the hair of the dog, the pills my father takes to assuage his hangover, the agitated phone calls he makes, one after another, until shares are sold and his account is once again solvent, before joining us late in the afternoon, resting a firm hand on my mother's shoulder, saying we should all go out for dinner.

Nor do we see her ask in their room when they're alone, her face stricken with anxiety, the sick feeling that hasn't left her, "Neal, how are we going to pay for everything?"

He doesn't tell her, just shakes his head and laughs, a horrible, cruel sound.

She asks again later, after dinner, which she wasn't able to eat, because she's so worried.

This time, he doesn't laugh, just raises a hand and slaps her hard, then stands there, drinking more whiskey, as she staggers against the bathroom door and hits her head.

The next day, it's my father who opens our curtains.

"You can order room service," he tells us. "Then we'll go down to the pool."

Della and I fight over the menu and order strawberries and croissants and hot chocolate, then pull on swimsuits, ready to go.

In the lift, my father talks to another family in a fake American accent, which makes Della giggle. Then the doors open, and we're back out under that huge sky again, in that air that smells so different, in this world that's so different from our own.

I don't see upstairs. Mummy wincing as she painfully layers makeup over the marks on her face. The carefully arranged clothes, flimsy, loose-fitting, with long sleeves, which could be hiding sunburn rather than bruises. The sunglasses that hide the tears filling her eyes.

13

Alex preys on my mind. When I've thought about Rosie with a boyfriend, I've imagined warmth, strong arms, and kind eyes. Not unashamed hostility and bitterness.

"I'm sorry, but I didn't like him." Laura and I have gone to Rachael's, where I've filled them in on how I met him. Given the high male occupancy of her household, lunch at Rachael's is never guaranteed, but to my relief, she produces homemade soup and crusty bread, with a large wedge of cheese.

"Why ever not?" Rachael's spooning the soup into bowls.

"Yes. Why, Kate?" Laura's curious.

"He was angry, and I understand that. It was something else. He seemed really aggressive. I just couldn't see him with Rosie. It was like there was all this rage bottled up inside him. I got the feeling that if he was pushed, he could get quite nasty. Obviously, I don't know," I hedge. "It's just a hunch."

I backtrack then, not wanting my own subjective, biased impression of him to color cold, hard facts. "I mean, I would have liked to ask him about her necklace, but I didn't dare."

"Maybe next time," Rachael says cheerfully, placing bowls in front of us.

"I kind of hope there won't be one, if I'm honest. He warned me off Neal, too."

"Really?" Rachael's voice is sharp, as both pairs of eyes swing round toward me.

"He said Rosie hated him. You should have heard him. He can't stand Neal."

"The police do know, don't they? About him and Rosie?" Laura sounds alarmed.

"I think so. I tried to persuade him that it would be better if they heard it from him than from someone else." But I can't be sure. Alex hadn't looked convinced, and shortly after, I'd left.

Laura speaks. "It's really hard to tell, isn't it, just from one meeting, whose story to believe? The nicest people can have the darkest secrets."

Rachael and I look at her.

"Don't look so shocked! You both know it's true. We all judge based on first impressions, but in actual fact, a lot of the time they're wrong."

But no matter how often I play them back, Alex's comments unsettle me. Of course, there are always two sides to every story. Always. A few days later, I see Laura again. As the investigation continues to be drawn out, she's moved into one of Rachael and Alan's empty holiday cottages, just down the road from their farm.

"This is gorgeous." I've admired this cottage for years. It's the smallest, with flint walls and far-reaching views, too often sitting empty for long spells.

"I love it, but I'm a bit worried about the garden," she tells me. "If it grows, I won't be able to open the door."

"You're safe until spring. This has to be resolved by then, surely? And you'll be home."

"You'd think so. Come on. I'll show you round. It's very cute."

After giving me a guided tour of its five small rooms, she makes us tea, which we take through to the sitting room, hot from the log fire.

"I have to ask you something." She looks troubled.

I hear Angus's voice. *For God's sake, Kate. Don't get so sucked in.*

Think of Alex's raw anger.

Then Rosie's voice, screaming my name in the storm.

"The thing is, after you spoke to Alex and heard everything he suggested about Neal, I went to see the Andersons. Neal already knows why I'm here, and I explained that I wanted to help them get to the bottom of what happened to Rosie. I wasn't sure what they'd say, but they asked me in and we talked . . . about how isolating it was for them as a family, how frustrating that there are no leads. She was sad. He was sad, too, but still charming. They seem like a normal, quite close-knit family. Aren't they? Or am I missing something?"

"No. I don't think so. I think Alex is emotional and angry because the Andersons didn't treat him well. And because he's lost Rosie, obviously."

"I spoke to Joanna alone. She obviously thinks the world of her husband. She told me Neal's an amazing man. What is it?"

I'm shaking my head. "It's what she always says about him."

"Oh. Right. Well, he isn't your run-of-the-mill bloke, is he? And I spoke to Delphine. Strange girl, isn't she? I couldn't read her. But I asked her, in several different ways, about her family, and she kept saying how lucky she is to have such loving parents."

"She's hardly even spoken to me," I say.

"It was about the only thing she did say. So . . ." She takes a large glug of her tea. "The thing is, Kate, Joanna said that a week before she disappeared, Rosie told her it was over with Alex. There'd been a bit of a thing between them, nothing serious, but he'd got a touch obsessed. Alex came round, apparently. Joanna refused to let him in, because Rosie didn't want to see him again, only he wouldn't take no for an answer. He got angry, threatened her—that sort of thing. But then he left, and that was it. Over."

I frown. "I wish she'd told me. Having met him, it certainly sounds believable. Only it's not what he said to me. He told me Rosie had a row with Neal and threatened to move out."

Laura shakes her head. "How do you know who to believe? Of course, it doesn't necessarily mean Alex is the killer. Anyway, he has an alibi. He was with friends. There's no way he did it. So then I went to see their neighbors."

"I've never even met them," I tell her.

"Well, it was interesting. They said they hardly know the Andersons—other than to say hello, that sort of thing. But one morning, a few days before Rosie died, they heard an awful noise going on. Voices yelling. A man's voice and a woman. They think it was Joanna. The man shouted several times about how he wanted to see 'her.'

He didn't say a name. Apparently, the woman was scream-ing back at him. They couldn't make out her words."

Was it Neal's voice? Or Alex's? Is it even relevant?

"Neal was away." Laura reads my thoughts. "Which rather begs the question, was it Alex, which seems likely, or someone else? And I agree. It's strange how Joanna says nothing to you."

But knowing Jo as well as I do, I realize it isn't that strange at all. "I know the way she thinks. She hated the thought of her daughter and the gardener together. Alex told me that, too. Jo thought he was beneath her. And, anyway, as far as she was concerned, she didn't lie to me. By the time I spoke to her, it was over."

I remember the necklace. "There is one thing, though. If it was Alex who gave her the necklace, if he and Rosie had fallen out, or if he didn't matter to her, she'd hardly wear it all the time."

Laura's thoughtful. "The one she was wearing the night she died. It's never been found."

"The murder weapon hasn't been found, either, has it?" It's impossible to believe, after the detailed police searches and given the ongoing vigilance of the villagers.

Her eyes meet mine. "Curious, wouldn't you say?"

And while all this goes on, the fact remains. That ever since she exploded at me, I haven't actually seen Jo, more than to raise my hand across the street. Not that I hold it against her, but it was what Angus said that made me think.

None of us can really understand how she feels.

I know I can't. I don't want to be a constant reminder to her, either, of the daughter I still have and the one she's lost, though if she wants my friendship, I'll welcome her with open arms.

And as if reading my mind, that evening she calls me, full of remorse.

"Kate? I'm so sorry I haven't been in touch. I was awful to you before. It was a really bad day. Actually, it's been a bad few weeks. Can you forgive me?"

"Oh, Jo . . . really, there's nothing to forgive." And whatever she said to me, there isn't, because just getting through each day must take all the strength she can muster.

"But there is, Kate. I threw your kindness back at you. I'm truly sorry," she says humbly.

It comes back to me what Neal said about guilt. And such is my own guilt, however illogical, that I haven't shared her suffering, I can forgive her anything.

It's Jo's idea to meet on neutral ground at the Green Man, a pub that's just outside the village.

"It's so good to see you, Kate. You look so well." With a beaming smile, she hugs me, degrees more warmly than she usually does, which was never a reflection of our friendship, just her reserve.

"Hi! You too!"

I'm taken aback by the warmth of her greeting, as well as how incredible she looks. Younger, very thin, and her hair's longer, too. After plummeting to the depths, she's on the upside of the roller coaster. Looking at her, you'd never guess in a million years what she's been through.

"Listen. What I really want to say is *thank you,* Kate. From the bottom of my heart, for your friendship. Because without you . . ."

"It's fine, Jo. Really. You're more than welcome." Embarrassed, because this isn't why I came here, I steer her toward the bar, where we order lunch, which Jo insists on paying for, then take a table by the window. But Jo hasn't finished and clearly feels the need to explain herself.

"Last time you came round, Kate, the day I yelled at you, I think it all caught up with me. I'm so sorry you were on the receiving end."

"It's okay," I say to her. "I understand." Then I take a breath. "I heard about Alex causing trouble. It must have been the last thing you needed."

Her eyes widen; then she shakes her head. "I was trying not to think about it. I suppose it's round the whole village by now?"

When I don't reply, she carries on. "I know people love gossip, but it really wasn't anything. Just a crush. You know what teenagers are like—here today, gone tomorrow. Rosanna was over it and was thinking about university. . . ."

A single tear trickles down her cheek, and I reach out and touch her arm. She tries to smile, but her eyes are full of sadness.

"It's no excuse for how I behaved toward you," she says quietly. "The trouble is, I was frightened, Kate. I felt everything spiraling out of control." She pauses. "I haven't told you or anyone, but last year, I was quite ill. I suppose I'm not very good at coping with things. I started drinking too much, and then I ended up in rehab. I'm fine now. I mean, I don't drink, not like then, but after Rosanna . . . Well, Neal told you, didn't he? That I went away. I wasn't seeing straight at all. I was on these pills just to get me through. Anyway, I'm off them—at least for now."

I'd suspected as much, and in fact, it explains the flatness of her mood, the lack of emotion whenever she spoke about Delphine.

"It can't be easy, Jo. But you must feel better, now that you're off them, I mean."

She sighs. "I do . . . kind of. Only they muffle everything, Kate. They take the edge off pain, make the unbearable more bearable, but when you stop them, that's the really hard part. The pain's still there. You have to confront it. It doesn't go away."

"You don't have to hide it," I tell her, wondering what triggered her breakdown the first time. "Or apologize, either. You're allowed to feel angry or hurt or whatever else you feel. You can yell, too. Okay?"

She looks down at her smooth hands, shaking just slightly. "Being home is much harder. It was easier there, because everyone understands. They've all been through something traumatic. And now I have to stay off the pills on my own. . . ."

"You're not on your own, Jo. You have me. And Neal."

She nods. "I do know that."

We eat—or rather I eat, while Jo professes that hers is not that good, but not to worry, as she wasn't really hungry. Then I change the subject, because as well as Jo, someone else is on my mind.

"How's Delphine? She must have missed you terribly."

Jo's expression changes. "She stayed with a school friend most of the time. But you know I told you before that she was strong? I'm not so sure. I need to talk to her, don't I? I've been no help to her."

I'm relieved to hear her say that, because if it had been Grace switching off her feelings and retreating into herself, even now it would worry me, let alone Delphine, at the age of twelve, bearing the full, unsupported burden of her grief.

"You shouldn't beat yourself up about it, Jo, but you must be worried. It's a lot for a young girl."

"I know. And it is. But we're all different, Kate. And Delphine does the same as I do. When it gets to be too much, she turns inward. You've probably noticed,"

It's true. I've seen Jo many times locked away somewhere inside her head where no one can reach her.

"And Neal?"

Her face lights up. "He's good. We're really good. I didn't tell you that his charity has been nominated for an award, and there's a dinner on Friday! You won't believe who's going to be there, Kate. . . . So many stars—even royalty, if you believe the rumors. Anyway, we're going to London for the weekend. Five-star luxury all the way. I can't wait!"

"Wow! That's exciting, Jo! I love London before Christmas! Think of the shopping! The lights will be on, too! What will you wear?"

She glances behind before leaning toward me conspiratorially. "I had this dress made," she says in hushed tones. "Spent a fortune. But it's worth it. It's green, fitted, but not tight. And flowing." Her eyes are dancing. This clearly is terribly important to her. "But it's worth it. It has to be right. Rosie would be so proud of him," she adds, suddenly slightly choked. "She'd want us to celebrate."

Then I have an idea. "Why doesn't Delphine come and stay with us?"

A strange look flickers over Jo's face, as though she's not really listening, before she says, "Thank you, but she's staying with her friend."

I've always believed friendship to be measured as much by shared confidences as by what stays unsaid, while reading between the lines or second-guessing, the way close friends do. It's a belief that leaves me questioning the measure of my friendship with Jo—not my outward, vocal support of her, but those burning issues I keep quiet about, like Grace's fleeting visit home, my encounters with Alex, the fact that Laura and I talk about Rosie over cups of tea. Things I can't tell her. But then I remember, I haven't even told Angus some of these.

After coffee, we wander outside.

"Have a wonderful weekend, Jo. Both of you. You really deserve it." I kiss her cheek.

"Thank you. We will! And come over soon, Kate—so I can tell you about it!"

I nod, already seeing myself on Jo's brand-new sofa, listening, a little enviously, to her blow-by-blow account of her glamorous night and the celebrities she was rubbing shoulders with. In her beautiful dress, fighting to keep smiling while her daughter's never far from her mind. To stay off the pills. And though I don't want it to, an image of a shining star comes into my head, dazzling everyone with its brightness, flaring up one last time before imploding.

It's Jo I'm thinking of yet again as on Friday evening, around seven, I'm driving past the village shop and see a small figure weaving along the pavement. As I pass, it lurches into the road just in front of me. I slam my foot on the brake, only just managing to stop in time.

I leap out to give whoever it is a piece of my mind, then stop, completely horrified, as I realize who it is.

Rosie

It's an autumn day, with mist and curls of smoke from burning leaves. I'm excited because Mummy's taking me and Della shopping, then out for lunch.

We drive to a huge shopping center. Inside smells of popcorn and Starbucks, and there's music playing and pretty lights, like a whole make-believe world inside the real world. As we walk past the shops, I imagine living here, dressing in a set of new clothes every day, trying on all these shoes, sleeping in those big, soft beds in shop windows, eating pizza and marshmallows.

I watch as she takes us to the Disney store. She buys Della a Minnie Mouse to make up for the one my father took away when he was mad at her. Then she takes us to a movie, where we eat ice cream and sit on cinema seats the color of blood.

Then after, she says, we have to buy Daddy a birthday present, a really special present that we'll choose together, because it would make him so happy. "It would be wonderful, wouldn't it," she says, "to give him a

really special birthday?" Choosing all these presents,
then, once we're home, wrapping them, tying them with
long, pretty ribbons.

The day of his birthday, she cooks a special dinner
she's been planning for ages, just as she's told me and
Della which dresses we must wear and not to upset him.
Only, I come home with a letter about the school ski trip.
I remember how desperate I am to go. How I can't wait to
tell Mummy about it. But as soon as we get home, before
I can show it to her, she hurries us upstairs into our bed-
rooms.

"Get changed," she whispers. "Then come downstairs, and we'll give Daddy his presents. Dinner's going
to be a treat! And please, girls, be on your very best behavior."

I see it on my face—how "best behavior" always
means the same thing. No joking, no talking unless we're
spoken to. And I get a sinking feeling, because if I don't
tell her about the ski trip, if I don't sign up tomorrow, the
places will all be gone. But I do as Mummy says, putting
on the navy-blue pinafore dress with the lace blouse she's
chosen, even though she knows I don't like it. But I'll do
everything she says; then, later, if I get the chance, I'll
ask her.

Della pushes my door open and comes in.

"You look so pretty," I tell her. Her dress is like mine,
only pink, dotted with little butterflies. "Shall I do your
hair?"

Della nods. She sits on my bed as I brush the tangles
out, then tie it into a swingy ponytail with a silver hair
band. Then we go downstairs and quietly take our places
on the sofa.

Opposite, my father doesn't look up, just drinks whiskey and reads a newspaper.

"Girls?" Mummy prompts. "Isn't there something you want to say?"

I look at Della. What does Mummy mean?

"Go on . . . ," she mouths, looking worried. "Hap-py birth-day . . ."

"Happy birthday, Daddy," Della says, while I say, "Happy birthday."

He actually looks at us properly.

"Thank you," he says quietly.

"Would you like your presents, darling?" Mummy says. *I notice how dressed up she is—in one of her party dresses, with her gold chain and sparkling earrings, smelling of perfume.*

"Oh, yes, please," he says in the same fake jolly voice he uses every year. "Oh! I love presents!"

I sit there as Della gives him the fur-lined gloves she chose. I wait for him to poke fun at them, but miraculously, he doesn't. Then he opens the card she's spent ages carefully drawing for him and says, "Thank you, Delphine. It's quite nice."

Next, I give him my present, a world atlas, because he travels so much. Maybe, too, he'll discover a load more places to go to a long way from here. He looks bemused. "Funny present," *he remarks.* "What do I need that for? Is that my card?"

As he tears open the envelope, it takes the corner off the card that's inside. He barely glances at it. "Ruined," *he says.* "Oh well, never mind . . ." *Then crumples it up and drops it on the floor.*

I swallow my hurt, hating his birthday, being in this

stupid dress, acting out this whole stupid pretense—just to keep him happy, as Mummy puts it.

He opens Mummy's presents next, huge, shiny parcels tied with ribbons, while she sits nervously.

At the end, surrounded by piles of new clothes, he says, "Very good, Joanna. You've done well. I think now I'd like dinner."

Mummy rushes to the kitchen and fetches the bottle of wine she's warmed. He pours some into a glass, swills it round, then sniffs it, while she watches.

"Mmm, not bad," he says.

After we've eaten, Della and I silently, Mummy over-attentively, my father reasonably happily, I get up and start clearing the table.

"Bit quick off the mark, aren't you?" he says sharply, even though I always clear up. "Anyone would think you wanted something." Then he pours another glass of wine.

My cheeks go hot all of a sudden; then I feel them burning red. I shake my head. "No," I tell him. "I don't."

He raises his eyebrows, gives me a knowing look. And I see open in the kitchen, on the side, ready to show Mummy, the letter.

"Don't lie." He bangs his fist on the table.

"She didn't." Mummy rushes to his side. "Did you, Rosanna?"

"I didn't want to spoil your birthday," I say.

"Well, you have." He thumps the other fist on the table.

But instead of yelling, his eyes squint at me and his voice is ice-cold quiet. "It's my birthday, and my daughter's lying to me. Wonderful, isn't it?"

I don't speak, because if I ask about the ski trip, that

will be wrong, and if I say sorry, that will be wrong, too. Next to me, there's blood on Della's lip.

That's how birthdays were in our house. All the same. All hateful charades of pretty clothes, expensive presents, and ugly words.

14

I leap out of my car, over to her side.

"Christ, Jo! I nearly hit you. . . ."

Even with me holding her arm, she wobbles as she gets up. Then one of her ankles gives way, and as she flashes a lopsided grin at me, I realize she's blind drunk.

"I thought you were going to London! Come on. I'll drive you home."

I take her arm and help her into my car, where the extent of her inebriation becomes apparent as she fills it with what smells like pure alcohol fumes.

"I'm fine, Kate. Really! Look how happy I am! I'm just fine. . . ." But her words are slurred; her intonation is too exaggerated.

"You're not." I wind down the window, the blast of cold, damp air in my face welcome. "Do you have your keys?"

She opens her bag and rummages messily and unsuccessfully, by which time I've pulled up in her drive. Hoping to God she finds them, because it doesn't look like anyone else is home, I take her bag.

"Here." I dangle them in front of her. "Come on. I'll walk in with you."

I unlock the door, fumbling around in the darkness for a light switch. Jo totters down the steps and almost falls over.

"I'll make us some coffee," I tell her.

"It would be much more fun if we have a drink!" She falls onto the sofa. Under the electric light, her face is blotchy and her eyes are bloodshot. Then she leans back and throws up her arms. "I know! Vodka, Katie! Loosen up a little! Let's get completely trolleyed. . . ."

"Jo, you don't need another drink. Why don't you stay there? Put your feet up, and I'll get the kettle on."

I leave her muttering about how Neal doesn't like feet on sofas. *Neal, Neal, Neal . . .* Without her watching me, I take in the empty vodka bottle, which I drop into her bin, then use the wrong tap to fill the kettle, before switching it on and hurrying back to check on her.

I sit down next to her. "What happened, Jo? Why aren't you in London?"

The drunk smile wanes as the corners of her mouth turn down. Something happens to her face, as if she's been slapped really hard. Then it crumples.

"Oh my God . . ." She gasps, raising a slow-motion hand to her mouth, uttering a moaning sound as pain hits her. Her eyes slowly turn to mine, blinking, trying to focus. "He doesn't want me." She garbles it so quietly, I miss it the first time. When I ask her to repeat what she said, it's like I'm asking her to rip out her heart.

After that, she doesn't say much, just makes small,

pitiful mewling sounds, all the time holding her head in her hands, rocking slightly. I make her coffee she doesn't drink; then, before I can help her upstairs to bed, she lies on the sofa and closes her eyes. In seconds she's asleep. I find two of her beautiful hand-stitched cushions and slip them under her head, then search for a throw of some kind to drape over her. Finding nothing, I venture upstairs.

It's the first time I've been up here, and it's like a five-star hotel, with thick, pale carpets and new, immaculate everything, interior designed to within an inch of its life, as though it's waiting for someone—a rock legend or a Hollywood star kind of someone—to move in. Eventually, I find a blanket like no blanket I've ever owned—softest cream cashmere. After creeping back downstairs and covering Jo with it, I tiptoe out.

I know the next day she won't want to see me. I wait until nine, to give her a chance to sleep it off, before I go round there, ringing her bell several times. When there's no answer, I open the letter box and call through it, "Jo? I won't stay. But I do need to know you're all right."

Only after I stand there several minutes longer, repeatedly ringing the bell, does she let me in.

I close the door behind me. "How are you, Jo? Are you okay?"

She shakes her head. "No. I don't think I am."

She looks terrible. I take her arm and lead her over to the sofa, the same place it looks like she's just got up from. It's then that I notice the strips of green silk ripped and torn on the carpet.

Her beautiful dress.

"Oh, Jo . . ."

She covers her face with her hands. "I feel a fool. Such a fool."

"You're not a fool, Jo. You've done nothing wrong."

She searches for the right words, or maybe it's the courage to speak them.

"Neal doesn't think so." She whispers it.

I can't believe he's upset her, not again. "What happened, sweetie?"

"Says . . . *ugly*," she mutters. "I'm . . . *old. Embarrassing* . . ." I strain my ears to make out her words.

Then suddenly coherent, she sits up and says, "He didn't want me to go to London, because he was meeting someone else, Kate. He's having an affair."

"He can't be." What she's saying is outrageous. She's more unstable than I'd realized. And although they have their ups and downs, he *can't* be having an affair. "Surely not." I shake my head. "Maybe you're misunderstanding things, Jo."

"Oh, Kate," she says, looking at me sadly. "I thought you'd realized. Don't tell me you're another."

"Another what?" I've no idea what she means.

"You can't bear the thought that Neal and I are anything but a devoted couple, can you? It would be too hard, too unfair, after losing Rosanna, for us to lose each other, as well. . . ."

I gasp. I've thought exactly that; of course I have, as anyone would. Told myself that at least each of them knows how the other feels, that there's the smallest comfort to be found in sharing their pain, that being alone would be too unbearable.

"You just want everything to be perfect," she says, gazing out toward the garden.

This time she's wrong. "Believe me, Jo. I don't do perfect. I do gardens, things that grow and evolve with all the imperfections that make them beautiful. Anyway, one person's paradise is another's nightmare. Each to their own. I just think, well, you and Neal, after all you've been through, surely he'd see you're better off together than apart?"

"You don't understand." She clasps her hands, then gets up, her voice ragged. "No one can, Kate. It's not the first time. He does this, and I have to live with it—because I can't leave him."

I spend a large part of that day shoring her up, not sure what to believe and what to dismiss as fabrications of her clearly troubled mind. But the more I learn, the more I realize I'll never truly understand how it is to be Jo.

Angus is wary. "Just be careful, Kate. I know you're worried about her, but Jo's world is about Jo. What about Delphine while all this is happening? Is she even thinking about her?"

"Delphine's fine. She's with a friend this weekend. Which is just as well," I tell him. "Neal's a complete bastard. If you knew the half of it . . ."

"So why does she stay with him? She doesn't have to. She's not stupid, Kate. No one sticks around if it's that bad."

"I know," I say, weary. And he has a point. "But don't you think, when you've lost a child, that maybe there are different rules? And you're not exactly sympathetic, Angus. God, if it was us . . . if we'd lost *Grace* . . ."

He's silent, then pulls me over, hugs me tight against him, his chin resting on the top of my head.

"She'll be home soon."

"Two weeks."

Two weeks . . . That's all it is until her Christmas break starts, with the decorating, the present wrapping we always do together, the cooking, with the inevitable last-minute shopping, because no matter how organized you are, there's always something you forget.

Suddenly, I miss her terribly.

I'm at Jo's early Sunday morning, tidying the kitchen while she's upstairs having a bath, when Neal arrives back home unexpectedly.

"Kate?" He seems surprised to see me. "What are you doing here? Is Jo all right?"

"Not really," I say quite coolly. "But then, it's hardly surprising, is it? She was really looking forward to this weekend."

Neal puts down his bag and stands there, looking puzzled. "Wait a moment. . . . What exactly are you saying?"

I stare back at him, speechless. Astounded at his nerve.

Then he nods. "I see," he says softly. "She told you it was my fault."

I frown. Confrontation's not my style, but after the weekend Jo's just had, I can't stand here and say nothing."All she told me was what you said to her, Neal."

He walks over to the window and stands there, looking out, so I can't see his face. Then he turns, and I see how weary of this he is, too.

"Did she tell you all of it? That on Friday, before we left, she was drunk? So completely off her face, she couldn't walk, least of all make it to a hotel and the awards dinner? Honestly, Kate, she was in no fit state to go any-where."

"She told me you called her ugly. And embarrassing. God, Neal. She's so fragile. . . ."

He turns and walks slowly to the door through to the hallway, then quietly closes it before turning to face me. "I did call her embarrassing. And she was. It was sup-posed to be my big night. *Our big night.* Recognition for all the work we've done. I wanted my beautiful wife to share it with me. And what does she do? Gets smashed and bloody ruins it." He clenches his fists. "Too right she's bloody fragile. But believe me, Kate . . ." I see him take a breath. When he looks at me again, the anger has gone. "I love her. There's nothing in the world I wouldn't do to help her."

He's so sincere. So utterly convincing. I apologize profusely, muttering about there being two sides to every story, and about how worried about Jo I am, before crawling away, mortified. But the conversation niggles at me until days later, I put it separately to both Angus and Laura.

"If you have two equally convincing opposing stories from two people who love each other, how do you work out what's true?"

"Gut instinct," says Angus, turning the pages of his newspaper.

"The truth is often somewhere in the middle," says Laura.

"It's probably quite simple," Angus says.

"The thing is, one person's truth is very often another person's lie. There are small giveaway signs, too, which sway most of us without us really noticing," she goes on. "Body language, for one. And eye contact. It takes a sea-soned con artist to look you in the eye and lie outright."

"We all do it," says Angus. "Say things that aren't exactly the whole truth. It's human nature."

"Of course, the other thing," says Laura, "is the reason for the lie. Unless someone's a pathological liar in the first place, they'll have reasons of their own for twisting the truth."

Rosie

There are always two camps. Good and evil. Beautiful and ugly. Winners and losers. Andersons are never losers, just as they're never anything less than perfect.

It's why I'm drawn to Kate, in her old jeans or patched jodhpurs, dusty boots, and shapeless T-shirts. Ask her horses, because they know, too. What matters is the part of you inside.

Did you know that a horse reads your tension, your unease, your every mood? That it doesn't care how old your clothes are, but hears that thing in your head that's really irritating you? That if you empty your mind and fill it with love, the horse will feel its undulating wave ripple the air between you?

When I'm twelve, I'm shopping with Mummy for new clothes for the body I don't want, with the breasts and curves that weren't there before, feeling the self-consciousness that comes with them. I want to hide in jeans, rock-star T-shirts, and tiny shorts, the same as other girls wear, to blend in and be just another teenager, but Mummy won't let me.

"*Appearance is everything, Rosanna,*" she tells me. "*In the first few seconds when someone meets you, they decide what kind of person you are just by looking at you. That sort of person*"—she glances across the mall at some girls, brash, quite loud, a little overweight in their too-tight stretchy dresses, with long hair extensions and layers of makeup—"*or like us.*"

I look at the girls, then at Mummy, beautifully dressed in pale, pressed linen, her hair soft and styled, and my own baby-pink jeans. Look at the girls again—chattering and laughing loudly, arm in arm, sharing a joke. Secrets, even. At Mummy again, who looks perfect and does not smile. And I know which I want.

Over time I gather a few items no one knows about, hiding them. A black high-rise T-shirt. Denim shorts. Fun clothes that make me feel good, sneaking them on when my parents are out, wishing I could keep the feeling even when I take them off. And I'm smart about it. Every so often I change the hiding place, but even so, she finds them. Takes them away, telling me they're vile and cheap. "*Slutty,*" she says, spitting out the word.

It doesn't end there. Not with my clothes.

When I'm fourteen, Della and I are sitting at the dining table. We have a roast Sunday lunch every week like clockwork. Only this time, when Mummy puts my plate in front of me, I stare at it, thinking there's been a mistake, because apart from a sliver of meat and some vegetables, it's almost empty.

I say nothing, just eat it, waiting for the dessert that follows, ravenously hungry. But when it arrives, I don't get offered any, just feel my father's sideways look at me as I open my mouth.

Della stares, too. "*Why isn't Rosie eating?*"

"*Don't call her that,*" snaps my father.

"Sometimes it's good to eat less," says Mummy. "Rosanna needs to lose weight."

Her words shock me. I've never thought of myself as fat. I glance at my hands, still a child's hands and wrists, the same as they've always looked. Then my mother reaches for the water jug. As her hand closes round the handle, I see skin stretched over sinew, bone, hard lines. No softness.

It's the day I first notice she doesn't eat.

I can't help think the question, Am I ugly?

The less food I'm given and the tighter my body becomes, the tauter inside I get, a stretched wire that I know with certainty will one day snap. And as my body shrinks, the question grows in obesity, taking over my head as I try to answer it. Am I fat? In the full-length mirror, is the softness not in fact softness, but grotesque bulges that shouldn't be there? Needing to be starved out of existence?

Looking now, I see only the flawless, slender body of an adolescent, one who still has a child's innocence, who under my mother's endless quest for perfection is malleable. It's when I see, too, that all those weeks she'd go away, "visiting friends," it was always the same friend. The surgeon's knife, carving, whittling her away, to expose the perfect woman buried beneath.

Far from being naturally beautiful, my surgically enhanced mother has created a vocation out of perfecting herself. One of such importance to her, she just has to pass it on to her daughters.

But even now, as I watch, I don't see why, because the more perfect she becomes, the more her soul and mind go unnourished, shriveling and dying like the fallen leaves in the woods, withering, decaying to nothing.

15

December

I tread carefully with Jo in the days leading up to Christmas, seeming to come so soon after Rosie's death. It's a time of year I've always loved, appealing to my home-making side, as I make our house pretty, invite friends, gather treats and presents for my family. This year in particular, Grace's first since starting university, and because Rosie's death still hangs over us, is far more precious.

"Oh, we have an artificial one, thank God," Jo says when I offer to get her a tree. "They make such a mess. It looks quite real. You'd never know."

If I didn't know Jo was a clean freak, I'd have wondered if it was a put-down. I think of the hint of plastic-paint smell, instead of the resinous wafts of pine that I love, or the absence of needles, which are still appearing six months later, but if they weren't, in a bizarre way, I'd miss them.

"You must all come over. For a drink," I say on impulse. Only after the words are out questioning whether it's wise, in the light of what happened a couple of weeks back. "Bring Delphine, too, if she'd like to come."

* * *

Just days later, in the midst of flickering Christmas lights, the warm glow of candles lighting the windows, I find myself somewhere much darker.

Laura's phone call one evening comes as I wrap presents and write a few last-minute cards. "I won't keep you, Kate. I know you're busy, but I thought you'd want to know. The police have taken Alex in for questioning."

"God." Feeling my legs suddenly weak, I sit down. "Are you sure?"

"Completely. It seems the friend who gave him an alibi has since retracted it. Seems it was a lie and they've fallen out. Kate? Are you there?"

But I'm not listening, images drifting through my mind of Alex, at the garden center, silently working; in the clearing in the woods where Rosie died; zooming in as angrily, bitterly, he tells me about Neal, words weighted with menace, implied threats, and veiled warnings. Even so. I'm shocked.

"Kate?"

"Sorry. I was just thinking. I can't believe it—that Rosie would be with someone who could do that. . . ."

"Well, at least they've got him. You know what this means? Obviously, there'll be a trial, but at last you can all get on with your lives."

Slowly, it starts to sink in, that it's not so much a weight lifting as a relief, just to *know.* For all of us—except Jo and Neal. Delphine.

"There was something else, too." Laura's voice is serious. "Only, Alex was done for assault—a couple of years ago. He beat up this guy who was stalking his then girlfriend."

"But surely that's just teenage emotional stuff?" I say to her. "It must happen all the time. Boys punching boys . . ."

"Not on this occasion," she says quietly. "This guy ended up on a life-support machine. Alex very nearly killed him."

Jo and Neal come over that evening to a house that's cinnamon scented from the mulled wine Angus has made, the kitchen warm from the Aga's cozy heat, the needles already dropping from the tree, which I've brought in early just for this evening. I've decorated the fireplace with ivy and larch from the garden and lit candles. It's as it always looks in here just before Christmas. Untidy. Homey. Welcoming.

For drinks, which is just that, drinks plus a few mince pies, I'd usually pull on clean jeans and my velvet and chiffon top. A little more makeup than for every day, maybe even nail polish. Festive, but not over the top, but knowing Jo will be glammed up to the nines, I've made an effort.

"A dress?" Angus looks shocked, then disconcerted, because he knows the code, too, and I'm breaking it. "I thought this was just drinks?"

"It is," I reassure him. "But there's nothing wrong with dressing up a bit, is there?"

My bemused husband shakes his head, then glances down at his chinos, as if wondering if he ought to wear a suit.

I catch his eye. "You look great."

I wish Grace was here with us, but she's not due home

until tomorrow, and, anyway, being Grace, she'd have her own plans. We've invited Rachael and Alan, and our neighbors, too. Ella and David, both arty types and gentle people, sensitive to what's happened to Jo and Neal—and being childless, a little removed from what's happened. David's an architect, and Ella paints, mostly fine art, and though we're not of their world, we get on well enough. They arrive early, Ella picking my brains on her garden, while David brainstorms the conservatory Angus yearns for and can't afford.

"But as long as Kate has her horses, we can't stretch to it," my poor, deprived husband says mournfully to David. "Do you know how much they eat? What their vets' bills cost?"

Before David can sympathize, the Andersons arrive.

I've primed Ella, because she doesn't really know her, that Jo will look like a movie star and will probably flirt her arse off with her husband, if she's on form. Ella doesn't care, and, anyway, arty types have their own obscure dress code. But as Jo and Neal walk in, I'm knocked sideways.

She's wearing the skinniest skinny jeans and a loose top from which her legs and arms stick out like little pins, her hair messily swept up so she looks girlish. I realize that, quite simply, I've overdressed for my own party.

Neal shakes Angus's hand and kisses me, my accusations of the other weekend clearly forgiven, his warm bonhomie drawing our neighbors over, so that while Angus fetches drinks, they're soon chatting like old friends. Jo hovers in the background.

"Hi!" I hug her. "No Delphine?"

"She's at home, not feeling great," says Jo. "Poor little thing. I just want her better by Christmas."

It's the most motherly thing I've heard her say about Delphine. "I know what you mean. Come and meet our neighbors."

Shortly after that, Rachael and Alan join us.

The Andersons are on a charm offensive. Appearing to exist only in the moment. Looking at them, you'd never guess that we were bystanders on the edge of their tragedy. Neal takes David's card and says he'll pass it on to a colleague of his who badly needs a good architect, while Jo declares she simply has to see Ella's work, because for ages she's been looking for something *different*. Then the conversation inevitably turns to the prestigious award Neal was nominated for, but he won't be drawn.

"I feel tremendously humbled," is all he'll say on the subject. "Do you know how many unsung heroes there are out there? They're the ones who deserve it, far more than we do."

I glance at Jo, her expression unreadable, as she watches him.

I'm expecting a somber evening. It's still so soon after Rosie's death, after the news about Alex, which is why I've kept this gathering so small. But it's a good evening. We drink a little too much, say one or two things we'll probably regret, and Rachael's laugh fills the house. We part late, as old friends sharing heartfelt, even happy, Christmas wishes. Angus and I watch them walk down the drive, breath freezing in clouds, feet crunching on the gravel.

"That wasn't a bit as I expected." He shakes his head. His arm goes round me. "I thought we'd have fireworks or a drama of some sort, after everything you've been saying. Really nice people, aren't they?"

I thread my arm under his sweater. "They are. But I

feel so sorry for them, don't you? It's their first Christmas without Rosie. . . . It'll be so hard—for all of them." Then I reach up and kiss him. "Thank you."

He looks surprised. "What for?"

"For understanding. For stopping me from getting too sucked in. For always being here."

Rosie

It's only now, when I see what was concealed, read the spaces and the darkness and the hidden things, that the pattern emerges. The zigzag of lost jobs and broken hearts, embellished here and there by my mother's attempts to create perfection. The barbed wire hung with diamonds, or rusting iron sprinkled with stardust, because under the glitz, that's what the Andersons really are.

It's another town, another house, another school. But this time it's different. It's a home somehow, not because of the big, pretentious house. Nor is it the school, which is okay, but I've seen too many schools.

It's subtler, suspended in the air, carried in the stream that's hidden by the rushes. The Canada geese that gather their numbers here know about it. And the swallows that come every summer. The wind bursts with it. Have I stumbled on a portal to something bigger, or is it a premonition of what is coming?

It's when the fear starts, too, in flashes at first, then like in those dreams where you're running from someone so close that no matter how fast you run, you hear their breath coming in harsh gasps and their feet closing on you, knowing they'll stop at nothing until they hurt you, so that when you wake up, you taste fear, even though you know it was just a dream.

Only now when I awake, when my eyes open and familiar sounds reach my ears, it stays with me. Even with Alex, I know I'm not safe, that danger has somehow woven itself into my life like a time bomb. And that I'm waiting for the ticking to stop before it explodes.

It's not a life I wish for. Instead, I crave a small piece of Grace's life, the way you want tickets to the Arctic Monkeys or the new Abercrombie & Fitch hoodie or the hot boy in school to ask you out. To wear it, be Grace for a day, to know how it feels to be Kate's daughter. Grace is cool. Funny. Pretty. A butterfly flitting between her friends and her pretty life.

While I'm the moth who sees the flame too late, leaving my wings charred and my body lifeless. Like everything that went before, it was written into the small print of my life, meaning whatever happened, wherever I was, there never was any other way.

16

With Grace's arrival imminent, I rush around, adding last-minute touches of eucalyptus from the tall tree in the garden, cutting pine and more ivy, their lingering scents combining with that of wood smoke. Wanting everything to look perfect. Grace loves Christmas as much as I do. She bursts in, long hair flying, eyes sparkling with excitement.

"Mum!" She hurls herself into my arms, little girl Grace of years back. I hug her.

"I've missed you. . . ." Breathing in the fresh citrus scent of her hair.

"Me too." She pulls back. "I can't believe that guy we saw is Rosie's murderer."

I nod. "I know. Nor could I."

"It's so sad, isn't it?" Peeling back the past months to reveal old wounds still healing, her eyes now glistening with tears.

I nod, realizing the weight I've been carrying. That all of us have. Of worry and responsibility, for Grace and her friends, that though it receded slightly had never left us—until a murderer was behind bars.

"We're going to have a good Christmas," I tell her softly, because the past is what it is, watching her eyes light up.

"I've got presents for under the tree. And we need to decorate it. Can we do it today?"

"I've done the tree, Grace. . . ." Her face falls momentarily. "But I've left the cards. Only I thought you'd want to look at them first."

My heart warmed by her familiar smile.

We go outside to help Angus carry her stuff in; then, while he stacks the firewood that's just arrived on either side of the fireplace, Grace and I ice the Christmas cake. We've a month stretching ahead before she goes again, a month in which our family will be complete. A rare peacefulness washes over me and, with it, a kind of thanks. That it's Christmas, that my husband is here and my daughter is safely home. At this moment, there is nothing more I could wish for.

Can we at last move on? With Alex held in custody, I start to imagine we can, until my world is rocked yet again and the closure, the sense of security that briefly crept in, goes up in smoke. Laura calls with the news that Alex has been released, pending further investigation. It seems there's simply not enough evidence against him.

Rosie

Trust is fragile. Hope means nothing. And like I said before, disappointment eats you away, so you stop believing in people. Since losing me, Della, too, is learning this.

Between the pictures, I find myself back at home. It's the same house, yet it's changed. There's a darkness that wasn't here before, a menacing presence within its walls. And there's the apple tree in the wrong place. Even I know that. Alex told me how trees need light and space to grow and spread their roots. They shouldn't be crammed in with other plants, like this one is.

In the time that's passed since I was last here, Della, too, has been removed from her old life and dropped headlong into this one. As I slip through the window, she's in her room, writing stuff, so engrossed she doesn't notice the bed sink slightly as I join her, or that the feather touch on her hair is my hand.

It should be a lovely room. Big, bright, with the hand-carved bed and the girly-pink covers she's yet to grow out of. The heavy rug and bespoke curtains, neat, de-

signed, perfect—but not quite. On her mirror a picture is stuck—crooked—of me, taken earlier this summer. I watch her look at her reflection, see both of us.

It's still and lifeless. Lightless. A room of sadness and shadows. Then I see that it's not so tidy, either, and that the floor is littered with torn-up paper, joined by more as Della rips another sheet several times, scattering the pieces like snowflakes.

"Kate." I whisper the name, a sound wave rippling into Della's head. "Kate can help you, Della. Kate's good. You can trust her. You need Kate. . . ."

If she hears it silently, I can't tell. Della writes. Slowly, deciphering her thoughts in neat, precise letters. Then more rapidly as I read over her shoulder. Realize she's writing to me.

> *Dear Rosie,*
>   *Are you there? I wish you could hear me. I'm really frightened. Is it going to happen to me, too? Is that what you meant when you knew what was going to happen? Because I feel it, as well. Unless someone does something, I'm going to die, as well, and I . . .*

A tear falls, smudging the letter, so it isn't perfect anymore, making Della scribble, then gouge angrily into the paper with her pen, before she picks it up and shreds it, flinging more pieces in the air. As they flutter down, I blow, wave my arms, hoping she'll notice the ones that change direction, swirling upward in little currents.

For a moment, I'm back in that room with the baby who's crying. Standing there, saying, "It's okay, Della. You're not alone."

I stand in front of my sister now. Reach for her hands, stroke her face, wipe her tears away, wanting her to feel my arms around her. To know that I love her, that I'm okay, that she'll be okay, too.

Then the miracle happens. She looks up, straight at me, our faces just inches apart.

From her intake of breath, for a moment, I almost believe she sees me.

17

It's a Christmas that's subtly different. Maybe in the reference to loved ones at the midnight service at our village church, in the way people suddenly have more time for each other. In many ways like any other, with an excess of food, mulled wine, and family gatherings, but with a jollity that's muted. A New Year's Eve party at Rachael and Alan's follows, where our mood is defiantly riotous, after which Angus returns to work and I drive Grace back to Bristol. Then, for the first time in a month, I'm alone.

Part of me welcomes the silence, the days I have to worry only about my own life, stopping only to cook a meal for two when Angus comes home, sleeps, gets up early, and is gone again. But it's quiet. Too quiet.

And before I have time to adjust, it changes again.

"They want me up in York for a while," Angus tells me, late back from work yet again. Dark gray circles under his eyes give his face a haunted, skeletal look. "The senior chap up and left, just like that. They're really stuck, Kate."

"For how long?" I knew he had extra work, but not this.

Angus shrugs, then yawns, one continuous motion of tiredness. "They don't know. A few weeks, most likely. Maybe longer. But I'll be home on weekends."

"Can't someone else go?" Not liking the thought of having two separate lives. I know people do this, but with the exception of a few days here and there, Angus and I have never been apart.

He hesitates. "It might be a smart career move, Kate, running that office. And the trouble is, there isn't anyone else."

After he tells me, it seems no time passes before Angus leaves. Bereft, missing him more than I ever imagined, I call over to see Rachael.

"You have no idea how lucky you are." Her blast of no nonsense is exactly what I need. "Look at this place. It's a pigsty, Kate. No, wipe that. Even the pigs live better than this."

We both know she's lying. So her kitchen is a mess, piles of washing, letters from school, the detritus from breakfast covering the worktops, but it's the kind of untidiness that shouts of family and children and purpose, all so lacking in my own home.

"Laura still thinks Alex is guilty," she says, glancing behind her, as if any moment he might walk in. "A crime of passion. Alex wants Rosie back, she agrees to meet him, and when she doesn't give him what he wants, he loses it." She shrugs. "Sounds plausible to me. They just lack evidence."

"How will they prove it?"

"Forensics, I suppose. Eventually. We're back to waiting, aren't we? Just promise me, Kate, because I know you go to that nursery where he worked. This time, stay away from him, okay? Coffee?"

She turns to rummage in her dishwasher. "If I can find some mugs . . ."

Against the clatter of china, my eyes are drawn to a familiar face on her small TV.

"Rachael! Quick! Look at this. . . ."

She stops what she's doing, and I turn up the volume just in time to hear Neal's voice. But unlike last time, this isn't about Rosie, as instead he gives a dispassionate yet penetrating account of surviving in a war zone.

I don't speak, just watch him disbelievingly. From his expression, his tone of voice, he gives away nothing about his own tragic loss.

"God," says Rachael when he's finished. "From watching that, no one would have a clue."

Slowly, I rediscover the solace in ordinary things, finding I like it. A good book or a TV program Angus wouldn't want to watch. Clearing out my desk. And *time* to do these things, where I'm not clock-watching, not cooking the next meal, so busy that time itself becomes a gift. While it rains, I spring clean. Then, when the clouds clear and the sun comes out, I pull on my boots and start on the vegetable garden, clearing the weeds, digging in compost, in readiness for planting the first seeds. And with clients' gardens to design and my horses to look after, life goes on. It's just a different life.

I bump into Laura at the farmers' market one Saturday. After spending Christmas at home in New York, she's back for a few days, catching up on Rosie's case, where nearly five months on, evidence is still sketchy and, on the surface at least, progress minimal.

"Do you think Rachael would mind if I planted some bulbs?" she says, looking at the stall laden with pots and bowls of budding narcissi and hyacinths.

"You have bulbs," I tell her, picturing pinprick shoots just breaking the surface in her garden on either side of the front door. "It's only the end of January. Wait a month and you'll have flowers."

If the murderer still hasn't been found, if she's still here.

As we walk together to the car park, she sighs. "I keep thinking someone, somewhere, must have proof. They *must*. They're just not telling."

"You really think it was Alex, don't you?"

Laura nods. "You've got to admit everything points to it being him."

I frown. "But if it was him, someone must know. Surely they'd tell the police—especially with an innocent teenager murdered."

"Believe me, Kate, there are plenty of people who wouldn't. Put it this way. Imagine, just for a minute, if Angus had done something terrible and you were the only one who knew about it."

I look at her as though she's mad, then think of Angus, back at home for the weekend, enjoying a rare late morning in bed. It's impossible to imagine him hurting anyone. "Sorry. It doesn't work. Not Angus."

"Okay, maybe he's not a good example." She hesitates. "But when people are continually exposed to violence for a long time, the shocking becomes less shocking. And, of course, if you want to badly enough, you can make excuses for anyone, like 'It's not his fault. His uncle abused him as a child.' Or 'Her mother used to beat her and lock her up.'"

And while I know it happens, it's so far off my radar, I shudder.

Laura frowns. "You'd be amazed what people will put up with, Kate. The trouble is, for so many of them, especially when they're vulnerable, it's easier to stick with what they know, however brutal or awful that is, than to change it or walk away, like you or I would. The devil you know wins every time."

"But surely the most likely explanation is that Rosie got abducted by a total stranger who murdered her."

"It's possible." Laura's thoughtful. "Only, you have to ask how she ended up so far off the beaten track before she was killed. With no obvious signs of a struggle, until that point."

Which means only one thing.

It's not something I've even considered, and I think it rather than say it, but the thought sends shivers down my spine. If Laura's right, Rosie must have known her murderer. Bringing me full circle.

Back to Alex.

"Laura said something that made me think," I tell Angus later that evening, after supper by the fire and a bottle of wine. "Because Rosie was found quite a way into the woods, she thinks she must have known her killer."

"The police will be working on it." Angus slumps down into the sofa and kicks his shoes off and rests his feet on the coffee table. "I have missed this fire."

"Mmm." But it's back in my mind, that only someone

she knew, and must have trusted, could have done that. Pointing more and more to Alex.

"I forgot to tell you. We're moving into an apartment," Angus carries on. "Now that Ally and Nick are up there, too."

"What was that?" Suddenly, he has my full attention.

"I'm going to be sharing this palatial, luxurious apartment with Ally and Nick."

"Sharing?" I repeat it as I work out how this makes me feel.

He nods. "It's a huge place. You'd love it. Great views of the city."

"Sounds good." Swallowing what I want to say, because this arrangement sounds anything but. Ally's young and very glamorous and ambitious, which is one thing. But I've seen her eyes on Angus, watched her body language around him give her away. And while I doubt he's even noticed, I don't trust her.

"I can't wait for you to come up," he says happily.

Laura asks me to keep my ear to the ground. But when I do catch sight of Alex, it's in the distance at the nursery while I'm buying plants. Unnerved by his presence, not expecting him to be out and about, because he's still a suspect, I don't speak to him, and he goes out of his way to avoid me.

Then I go to see Jo.

Whether it's the start of a new year that's done it, the fact that she's survived Christmas, or whether it's superhuman reserves she's found inside, she seems calmer and more peaceful, as though she's turned a page and begun a new chapter.

"I need to do something more with my life," she says. "I mean, I'm still here. I shouldn't waste it, should I? I've decided to go on a course."

Yes, she's right, and wasting a life won't bring back Rosie. Life *is* far too short, and too unpredictable. But it's still early days, with Rosie's killer yet to be found. I hope Jo's not pushing herself too hard too soon.

"That's great, Jo. It really is. Have you something in mind?"

She looks worried. "Actually, I've signed up for an IT course. Don't look surprised! It's not something I talk about, because I'm really quite ashamed, but I've never got to grips with computers. I've never had to use them much, apart from basic word processing for Neal. It's residential—for a week, with another week later on. Then I can do the rest distance learning. What do you think?"

But I'm thinking of Delphine, without her mother yet again.

She picks up on my hesitation. "I know. I could have found a course closer to home. It's just . . . I need to do this, Kate. To get away. Think about something different." Her eyes pleading with me to understand.

"Sounds perfect," I tell her, silencing my misgivings. It's clear enough she needs to do this. "And when you're an expert, you can teach me!"

"I start next week." She smiles, too brightly, but then it falters. When she looks at me, the same devastating, blinding sadness is back in her eyes.

"You can be honest, Kate. Do you think it's bad I'm doing this? Now? So soon after . . ." Her voice breaks.

"Jo, of course I don't. . . ." I reach out and touch her arm. "Anyway, it's not for me or anyone else to say what's right. And even if it only distracts you, there's nothing wrong with that, either."

"It's hard to know what I should do," she says quietly. "Everyone likes to tell you to do this and that, and *not* to do this and that, until you want to scream. And if I stay in this house, I'll go crazy, I know that much." There's an edge of panic in her voice. "I'm firefighting, Kate. This course will get me through another hideous week and give me something else to think about. It may be too soon, but I have to try."

She takes a deep breath, battling with herself, and I feel my own heart twist inside me.

"You'll have to tell me if I can help. With Delphine? Or anything . . . You will say, won't you?"

She nods. "Thank you, Kate. But we should be all right. Neal's taking some leave." For a moment, she looks anxious. "It's about time. He needs a break . . . after, you know, *everything*. . . ."

"I'm glad, Jo. Maybe it will be good for all of you. And do tell him, won't you? About next week? That he only has to ask . . ."

A weekend follows when Angus doesn't come home. That work gets in the way of a precious weekend infuriates me; that he appears unbothered makes it worse. And then, swept along with work, I forget about Jo being away and my offer, until one morning halfway through the following week, Neal arrives at my back door. I'm mid-call to my newest client, trying to gently talk her round to what I know is best for her garden, when he waves through the kitchen window at me. I beckon him in.

"Two minutes," I mouth at him, scribbling notes as I watch him stand looking out the window, with his arms folded.

"Sorry," I say when eventually I put down the phone.

"That was one rather elusive client I've been trying to talk to for days. How are you?"

"Yeah. Fine. I'd no idea you were so busy. It wasn't urgent. I can always go. . . ."

"No! Have a cup of coffee with me, if you like. Is everything okay?" I turn away, aware of his presence dominating my kitchen, as I fill the kettle and rummage for mugs.

Behind me, I hear him pull out a chair. "Thanks. I'm adjusting, I think you could say."

"Milk and sugar?"

"Just milk. I'm not so sure my charity work's a good idea." Not sounding at all happy about it.

"What? You mean the orphanage?" I ask him.

"I've stepped back a bit—for now." There's a pause. "I don't know what she's told you, Kate, but the truth is, these days it's much harder to leave Joanna."

I feel my breath catch. "I thought she was doing so well, especially now that she's started this course."

"You think?" He's silent. "I don't know. Maybe you're right. It's hardly the best timing, though. There's Delphine to think of, for one thing."

"She'll be fine, won't she? You're home at the moment."

Neal's eyes narrow, creasing at the corners, as he looks at me. It's a very direct look, and for some reason it unnerves me. "You probably think I'm old-fashioned, but I've seen hundreds of orphaned kids, Kate. In Afghanistan. They've witnessed the most horrific violence. Their hearts and homes are broken, and their families destroyed. They might be three, nine, fifteen years old. It doesn't matter—they all have *nothing*. You should hear them, Kate. Crying for their mothers. Always the mothers." He lowers his eyes. "You are right, though, about Delphine. It isn't the same at all."

"It's amazing what you do out there, Neal." Rarely venturing out of my own very small world, I find it truly humbling to think of how selflessly he confronts war and poverty, putting his own life at risk, and all in the interest of humankind.

"I ought to do more," he says. "Honestly? If I didn't have Joanna or Delphine, I'd go. Never come back. Make it my life."

He speaks as though he means every word. Putting the mugs on the table, I sit opposite.

"Thanks," he says. "The other thing is, I'm crap at cooking."

"Why not bring Delphine over for supper?" I say brightly. "I'm cooking for only one these days . . . well, during the week."

"Oh?"

"Angus is working in York," I tell him. "Monday to Friday. So honestly, you'd both be more than welcome."

He gives me an appraising look. "He wouldn't mind?"

"Angus?" I say incredulously as the implication of his question sinks in, that I'm inviting Neal for dinner while my husband's away. "Of course he wouldn't."

I get the full, uncensored warmth of a Neal Anderson smile. "Then thanks. We'd both like that."

I slow roast a chicken with baked potatoes and herbs I've picked from the garden, because it's easy, adding vegetables for the last hour, pouring myself a glass of wine as I tidy up and set the table for three. I haven't dressed up, just changed into clean jeans, adding a touch of makeup and a splash of perfume, because it's just a kitchen supper with friends.

But when I open the door, I'm taken aback to see Neal's alone.

"Delphine's busy tonight," he explains. "I'd completely forgotten when you invited us. Look, we could always make it another day. I'd quite understand—if you'd rather?"

"Of course not. You might as well come in. I've already cooked. . . ." I'm too bright, overdoing it. Trying to hide what he's picked up on—the truth, that I'm a little thrown. I'm not sure why, but it feels a bit too cozy. His physical presence is powerful, unnerving. And now it is only the two of us, I'm not sure what Angus would say. Or, for that matter, Jo. Then sheer bloody-mindedness kicks in. It's just dinner, for God's sake. And Angus went to York, didn't he? I know he doesn't always eat alone.

"Cool. I'll open this." He produces a bottle. "Assuming you like red?"

"Red is good. Thank you."

I find him a corkscrew, filling an awkward silence that doesn't thaw, in spite of Neal's best efforts. Was it naive of me to invite him here? Only I didn't, I remind myself. I invited Delphine, too.

"So where's Delphine?" I ask.

"With a school friend," he says briefly. "I'm not much good at remembering the family stuff. What with being away so much, I've always left that side of things to Jo."

"God, you're as bad as Angus," I tell him, taking the glass he holds out.

His eyes twinkle at me. "Us men, hey? I know, we're all the same. . . . Cheers." He clinks his glass against mine.

"Cheers . . . You're not so bad," I say lightly, meaning

men collectively, rather than just Neal, and downing some of my wine quite quickly. "Shall we eat?"

"Good plan. Smells fantastic, by the way. You wouldn't want to see what I can manage in the kitchen. And you must tell me, how's your daughter getting on?"

"Grace? Really good. She's loving her course. I miss her, obviously. . . ." My voice trails off as I serve the food onto plates.

"It's okay," he says quietly, topping up our glasses while I put the plates on the table. "I asked. And it's not wrong to talk about her. She's your daughter. You should."

"You know why I don't?" I tell him, wondering how I can tell *him* this, but not Jo. "Because when I mention her name to Jo, I feel so guilty."

He shakes his head. "You really shouldn't," he says gently. "It's not your fault Rosanna died. Or any of ours. And life goes on. It has to, Kate. I have to believe that. It's the only thing that gets me through this."

"It must drive you insane. Not knowing," I say softly, my awkwardness gone, finding I'm suddenly flattered by his shared confidences, the way he talks so openly to me.

There's a pause before he says, "Yes."

We eat in silence, finish the wine; then as I look across the table at him, I feel a connection between us that's tangible, born out of empathy, because he's so brave, so strong. And he has no one who's strong for him.

It's as if he reads my mind, putting down his knife and fork as my heart flips over, and somehow, across the table, our hands link.

"How do you do it?"

"What? Touch your hand? Easy, Kate. My fingers close round yours, like this, and . . ."

His tone is light; his voice hypnotic. His fingers are

strong and warm wrapped round mine. How can just touching hands feel like this?

What am I doing? What is he doing?

"I don't mean that." I want to pull my hand away, but there's a force keeping it there, the same force that's making my fingertips tingle, my pulse race, and my insides flutter. I try to ignore all of them, to focus. "I mean survive, keep strong after what's happened?"

He sighs. "Oh. That. Sometimes, Kate," he says, "you really don't have a choice."

When I don't rally with some flirty aside, the shutters go down. Slowly, he disentangles his hand, then gets up, offering to help clear up before glancing at his watch.

"Thanks, but it's no problem," I tell him. "Look, there's hardly any washing-up."

His eyes flicker around the kitchen. I see it through his eyes for a minute. Small and untidy instead of pristine, stripped wood instead of gleaming steel. The washing-up's stacked in the sink; ingredients are spread over the worktops. Then I stop myself, because this is my home and I love every untidy inch of it.

"It was a lovely meal," he says finally.

"Sorry. I should have made a dessert. I could make coffee, if you like?" But my offer is halfhearted.

A silence falls between us, filled with unsaid words. Then he says, "I think it's best if I go. Thank you for tonight, Kate."

He takes a step closer, and like my fingers were sparking earlier, I feel my traitorous heart skip a beat.

"It was nothing, really. You're welcome."

I don't say, "We must do it again." I'm too aware of the physical effect he's having on me to say anything else. And then, before I can stop him, he leans toward me, his lips closer, then touching mine.

Rosie

I see the blue-eyed boy in worn jeans working in our garden, the one who knows the seasons and how to sell them to people like my parents, who, above all, want to look good. To bask in admiring glances because they have the biggest house and the most impressive garden.

Am I drawn to him that first time because my parents would hate even the idea of their daughter touching him, kissing him, joining her body to his? Or do his kind gentleness, his sensitivity, the way he reads me mean it's as inevitable as night falling or storm waves crashing on the shore? How can I tell?

Alex shows me the first shoots poking up through the earth. "It encapsulates nature," he tells me. You have these small, brown, knotty things buried in the earth that, with the right conditions, grow and produce something beautiful. First leaves, which are each their own shade of green, followed by a tiny snowdrop or a sweet-scented narcissus or bold tulips, which keep growing, changing color, even when you cut them. "But," he adds, "the potential was always there, even if you couldn't see it."

The way he speaks makes it simple, that what needs nurturing isn't the blowsy, transient flower, but what's underneath. Like with people, what's inside is far more beautiful than anything produced by the surgeon's knife.

He shows me there's beauty in imperfection. In petals that drop, then wither and brown, leaving the seed pods, which birds feed on. In lichen-covered bark; rich, crumbling soil; and the rose with different colored blooms. Their own kinds of beauty beyond the obvious.

It starts with our eyes. Our shoulders brushing. Fingers making contact as I hand him a mug of tea, until one day, he puts down the mug. Strokes a strand of hair off my face, then leans down and kisses me.

His touch is as seductive as the first breath of honeysuckle or the sun's warmth after a long winter. I don't know how I've lived so long without him, how empty I've been, until the moment his hands first hold mine, when I breathe in the earthy, fresh-air scent of him, which makes me long for him. It's when I realize for the first time, I feel truly alive.

It's a moment I can't take back. There's nowhere else to go after falling in love, with its dancing air and light feet. It's life changing, reaching into my psyche, lifting it. I can breathe. I can talk. I can be. Is it love that does this to people, or being surrounded by the silent strength of trees, the unstoppable force of the wind, while at your feet the most delicate flowers grow?

Alex shows me another world: the tallest hilltops, with the world spread at our feet; the highest clouds that herald a storm. The movement of the tides while we light a driftwood fire and sit, his arm around me, my head against his, watching the sky, shades of blue fading to peach purple before stars pierce the darkness.

And in between, it's enough to snatch moments, no less precious because they're fleeting.

I'm so careful. Cover every trace of us with finely drawn lies so no one knows. Until the day I don't see my mother come back after her hair appointment's canceled and they forgot to tell her. I don't hear her car, because she parks it on the road. Nor do I see her silently open the door and go inside, then tiptoe through the sitting room to the kitchen, where she stands and looks outside.

Is the shock on her face because his arms are around me, or because she sees on our faces something she knows she's never felt and never will?

It no longer matters what my parents think. This kind of love can't be wrong. But I know, too, it isn't always like this. That there are some people, like my parents, who would be better as passing strangers. Or best, never meeting at all.

18

What happened with Neal that night haunts me, even though it was just a kiss, and I pushed him away, and even though I picture Angus drunk in a bar, his eyes blurry as he gazes adoringly at a nameless someone, always a *pretty* nameless someone, as he flirts, almost definitely in a harmless, tipsy kind of way—but always harmless. The results of the "How much do you trust your husband?" test are in. He passes with flying colors. I trust him implicitly. With our marriage. With my life. Like he trusts me.

Several times I pick up my phone to call Rachael, but something stops me. Is it fair to put her in the middle of this? Or is the truth that I'm too ashamed?

Just a kiss. That was what Neal said before he left last night.

All his fault. How sorry he was. He said that, too, before he left.

I could have stopped him sooner. I'd sensed what was coming. Let it happen. That's no one's fault but my own.

* * *

I escape on Zappa, who's still with me because although his owner doesn't want him back, she cannot bring herself to sell him.

This morning, he's restless, jumpy, feeling the cold through his clipped coat and not liking what's in my head any more than I do. Only when I turn him into an unplowed field and let him fly do we leave my thoughts far behind, fixing instead on the pounding of his hooves, the mud spattering in all directions, and the wind.

This majestic horse senses my every mood, even when we get back and I turn him out with Reba and Oz, when he spurns their company and instead comes and stands, his head close to mine, his breath warm against my hands, as if he knows. And for a short time, I forget. But when I get back to the house, shower the mud off, and am making lunch, with damp hair, Neal turns up.

"You should go," I tell him, my cheeks flushed, not meeting his eyes. "Please. I love Angus. I don't want this."

But he doesn't. He just stands there, saying nothing. I risk a sideways glance at his face, edging toward his eyes, feeling them riveted to me.

"Kate?" How can one word, just four letters, hold so much?

Is this how affairs start? Is this all it takes? One person overstepping the line, persuading, sweet-talking the other to take a chance, to give in to that rush you've all but forgotten about, because it stops when you've been married as long as we have?

There's a silence. Drawn-out minutes that feel much longer, after which, with an iron will, I turn my back on him. Wait for the latch to click as he closes the door behind him, listen for the crunch of male footsteps on gravel, count the number of seconds I know it takes to walk the length of our drive, before I turn, only to catch the back of him as he disappears out of sight.

I slump to the floor. However he makes me feel, I'm relieved he's gone.

After he goes, and though I don't want it to be, shame is like a black armband or a battle scar, drawing sympathy I don't deserve.

"I'm missing Angus," I say if anyone comments on how pale I look, hearing, "Liar, liar, pants on fire," in taunting tones behind my back. As well as almost cheating, I'm a fraud, too.

As if he knows, the cloud of my guilt stretching all the way to York, he doesn't come home that weekend.

"I'm sorry, Kate. I completely forgot, but there's this dinner on Saturday. If I'd remembered, you could have come, too. . . ."

"You will be back the next weekend, though, won't you?" Disappointment spiked with relief.

That weekend, her course over, Jo comes home. And as my guilt intensifies, her words come back to me. *He's having an affair. . . . It's not the first time. He does this, and I have to live with it. . . .*

Suddenly, I feel so stupid. I was such easy prey. So easily flattered that he just reeled me in—and I let him. It's when I decide I can't tell her that her husband came on to me, that I didn't encourage him, but he did what he's done many times before, playing it over and over in my head.

Sitting across the table, our hands clasped.

Or did I?

His lips on mine.

Does he see it like that?

But I stopped him—nothing really happened. It meant nothing. My guilt peaking when I see her outside the village shop.

"How was the course?" I ask her.

"Really good," she says. She looks tired. "I met some interesting people. And, God, so many nerds, you wouldn't believe."

"Yes, well, that's computers," I say lightheartedly, as if I know.

"They've given us the next part of the course to do from home," she says. "But it was good to get away from here, even just for a few days." She looks wistful for a moment, and I wonder what she's going to say. "Kate? Don't you ever need to escape?"

"Me? Not really, but I am going to stay with Angus. In March. Swap my wellies for heels," I joke.

She looks quizzical, as if trying to imagine it and finding it faintly ridiculous.

"There's more to me than jodhpurs and riding boots," I quip, but she doesn't smile, just looks at me sympathetically.

"Are you missing him?"

"Actually . . . I am." Surprised to hear my voice wobble.

She smiles a little sadly. "Don't be lonely, Kate. I'm always here if you need me."

Suddenly, I can't speak, touched beyond words that in

the midst of her problems, she can still find room for mine.

But after that brief meeting, in the way she often does, Jo goes to ground. Normally, it would be my cue to go and check on her, but with Neal at home and always there in the shadows, this time I keep away.

Rosie

In front of me is a day that, though I want to, I can never forget. My twelfth birthday was my puppy birthday. The day I lost Hope. And now it's Della's.

The week before, my mother takes me shopping to choose clothes for Della. Expensive ones. Expensive skin-care products. Underwear. Holds things up against me, too, then shakes her head, says only a certain figure can wear this dress or those jeans, even though now I'm thinner, and if I eat a full meal, I've become practiced at sticking my fingers down my throat afterward. But this isn't about me; it's about Della.

And just as much as I wanted a puppy, she wants a camera. I remind my mother.

"She doesn't really," my mother says. "She only thinks she does. What does your sister want with a camera?"

"But she does, Mummy." Della's shown me a digital SLR with a zoom lens. She wants to catch portraits, street scenes, people, reportage style, without their seeing.

"I'll talk to your father," is all she says, gathering up another armful of shiny, shop-scented clothes.

The morning of Della's twelfth birthday isn't like mine was, even though the sun shines and it stays dry. It's worse.

When she opens her presents and sees her camera, her face shines with so much happiness, the air sparkles around her. I sit there, pleased, but I'm mad, too. If she gets what she really wanted, why couldn't I have had Hope?

Then she opens the clothes presents, and I see what I didn't see before. They're the wrong size. Tiny doll sizes, far too small for Della's frame. Her face is puzzled.

"Thank you," she says politely, then picks up her camera.

"Try them on," orders my father, seizing the camera from her. "Come on. Your mother's spent all this money. I want to see how they look."

She catches my eye. She's seen how small they are, knows that voice of his, and she's afraid.

"I'll come with you." I jump up, help her scoop up all the stupid, too-small clothes.

"Sit down, Rosanna," roars my father. "You'll stay here."

My mother looks worried. And then I'm mad at her. For her part in this cruelty. For letting my father bully us. I almost get up, but I know if I do, he'll lose his temper. I want to shout at him, tell him how fathers should love their daughters; or to walk out of here and never come back. But I can't, because Della will be alone.

She comes downstairs, head down, shoulders slumped, in one of the dresses she's pulled on, the sleeves cutting into her arms, the hem riding up her legs.

"There." My father stands up. "Head up, Delphine. What's the matter with you?"

She whispers, "I can't do it up."

He marches over and roughly spins her round, yanks at the zip, pulling it hard. I count two seconds as my father walks back and reaches for the camera.

"Smile," he booms. "Pose, Delphine. Come on. You're not a little girl now. This is a woman's dress. Be a woman."

I feel sick just watching him, seeing our fear, wondering where he's going to draw the line, a line that seems to move almost daily.

Della moves minutely, and as my father aims the camera and snaps, there's a ripping sound. And that's the memory. Della frozen, her face washed red with shame, the gaping seam exposing soft white flesh, to a soundtrack of my father's cruel laughter.

Later, he says he'll take us out for dinner. At six o'clock. I help Della put away the hateful clothes. Wipe the images from her camera, wishing it was as easy to wipe them from her head. We get ready. Find one of the new tops that nearly fits her. Six o'clock comes, and we go downstairs. My father sits, watching TV. I can't see my mother. At seven o'clock, he pours himself a whiskey.

"Are we going out?" I ask.

"Out?" he says, with fake surprise.

"For Delphine's birthday? You said you were taking us out."

"I've changed my mind," he says calmly. "Your mother agrees. You saw what happened with that dress."

Della sobs, runs back upstairs. I watch myself face him. Is he enjoying this? What does he get out of belittling his own daughter?

"That's not fair," I say quietly. My voice shakes.

"Fair?" he says, with that ice-calm way of his. "I'll tell you what's not fair, Rosanna. It's fat, ugly children

who don't do as they're told. Who don't appreciate what they have. Who don't make any effort and will never do anything with their lives, because they're too lazy and too stupid."

I gasp as crucifying pain hits me. Then, just as quickly, it vanishes, and I feel myself rise above it, completely numb.

"You can't say those things," I cry, not caring what he says. Can he be worse than he is? "Not to Delphine. She doesn't deserve it."

He gets up. I wait for another onslaught of words, but I wasn't watching when the line moved. He raises his hand and hits me.

Delphine

"Give it time," everyone says.

"It gets easier."

"You'll miss her less."

"Feel less sad."

"Start to enjoy life again. There's nothing wrong with that. Enjoying life."

That's when I know they've never lost someone. If they had, they'd understand.

That you always miss them.

That the pain doesn't go.

That life stops.

19

February

As the first daffodils push their heads aboveground, as I ask Rachael over for a gossipy catch-up, several things happen at once.

Jo calls me, a call that leaves me mystified. It's cryptic, to say the least.

"I have that software you asked for. I can bring it over this morning, if it's convenient?"

"What are you talking about, Jo?" She sounds like she's talking to a stranger. And it's the first I've heard about any software.

"Perfect," she says brightly. "Would twelve work for you? I know you wanted it installed as soon as possible. . . ."

"Are you okay, Jo?"

She ignores me. "Don't worry. It shouldn't take long. I'll see you later."

"That was peculiar," I tell Rachael. "It was Jo—only she sounded very odd."

"Hardly surprising. If it were one of my own kids and the murderer was still on the loose . . ." She shakes her head. "It would do my head in. On the subject of murderers . . ." She looks at me expectantly.

"You mean Alex? Unless they find more evidence, I guess he's in the clear. And walking around like anyone else. It all takes so long, doesn't it?"

Rachael slurps her coffee thoughtfully. "I know. Sometimes I wonder whether life will ever get back to normal. Talking of normal, how's Angus?"

"He's quite happy, I think. Too happy." Happier than I am. Making me wonder if he's putting down roots.

"Oh well," says Rachael. "I bet you don't miss the extra washing and cooking. And if you do, I'll give you some of mine." She glances at the clock, then frowns. "Oh, fuck. I forgot." Looking horrified, she leaps up. "I was supposed to be at school ten minutes ago. Milo's teacher wants to see me. I am already *so* in the shit with that woman, you wouldn't believe. . . ."

She dashes for the door, blowing me a kiss. "So sorry to run like this. Give Jo my love."

But she's barely gone when Jo arrives, early, in a fluster of cold air and confusion.

"I'm sorry about earlier, Kate. . . . Neal was listening. He does that now—he listens. To everything." She's nervous, on edge, can't keep still.

"I'm not with you, Jo. Why shouldn't he know you're coming here?"

"He knows I talk to you. And he's been hiding something, Kate. Something he doesn't want anyone, even me, to know about."

Oh God. My mouth is dry. Has she found out about what nearly happened between us?

She runs her fingers through her hair, her face fraught,

speaking in fragments, as she pulls out a chair. "Can I just have a minute? I will tell you. . . . God, Kate. It's too much to take in. I can't think straight. . . ."

"I'll make some coffee. Are you all right, Jo?"

But she doesn't answer, just sits, staring ahead. I fill the kettle, worried about her, but before long, she's talking again.

"You know I said how useless I was on computers? I hardly ever touched the things. But obviously now, since the course . . . Anyway, yesterday I was trying to find a document I'd saved, but . . ." She breaks off.

I place the mugs on the table and sit down.

"Go on."

She picks up a mug, and her hands are shaking, slopping the coffee over the sides. She puts it down again, then fixes her eyes on mine.

"I've been using this laptop of Neal's. An old one I didn't even know he had. I found it buried in the bottom of his wardrobe, of all places. . . ." She pauses. "I was looking for something I saved on it. I found these files, Kate." Her voice is deathly quiet.

"Oh God!" She runs her hands through her hair. "I'm not sure I can do this."

"Jo . . . what is it? Tell me."

She stares past me, then takes a deep breath. "They're awful, Kate. I've never seen anything like it."

A sick feeling fills my stomach as I start to wonder where she's going with this.

"He's into porn. The worst kind. Horrible, violent sex, rape . . . killing people."

The "killing people" comes in a whisper, a wild, terrified look in her eyes, like those of a rabbit frozen in headlights, before she continues.

"There's more. Links to all these Web sites. I can't begin to tell you. . . ." She breaks off, and her hand goes to her mouth. "I couldn't look at them. . . ."

Jesus. My mind goes crazy with possibilities. Then I shake my head. For all his faults, I can't imagine in a million years that Neal would be doing this.

Then her eyes are dead as she says, as if in a trance, "You see, Neal's always taken care of things."

My blood turns to ice. What does she mean?

Jo's face is white. "It's all there, Kate. There are dates. Even an idiot like me can tell when it was last opened or looked at, or whatever. All the dates, Kate, they're all *before.*"

Her eyes are huge.

"What if he killed her?"

There's silence as the words hang between us. As I stare at her, appalled, trying to work out what she's telling me.

Fleetingly, I think of the night he was here. Did I share supper with a murderer? Did the hand that touched mine kill Rosie? Then common sense kicks in.

"That's ridiculous," I tell her. "No way could Neal have committed a murder. Certainly not his own daughter's."

But Jo stares, a ghostly stare that makes my skin prickle.

"You don't know him," she says. "You don't want to, either. You probably won't believe me when I tell you. Nobody does. . . . But there's another side to him." All the time her eyes glued on mine, imploring, begging me to believe her. "He's damaged, Kate. He has a twisted, brutal, cruel side. Whatever he may have said to you, he enjoys hurting me, enjoys telling me how ugly I am. Oh,

not just that once that you saw—so, so many times. How
it would be better for all of them if I was dead . . . He's
said that, too."

A sob erupts from her.

"I've tried so hard, Kate, to be the woman he wants me
to be. To be his wife, a mother. To be beautiful, to make
him proud. But nothing I do is ever enough."

Her eyes are spilling over with tears, with hurt and de-
feat, and she slumps, the fight visibly draining out of her.

When she starts talking again, her voice is full of sadness.

"He's always been like this, all the time we've been
together. In the beginning, he was just rough. Sexually. I
thought it was normal, Kate. That he felt so passionately
about me, he just got carried away . . . And then, other
times, he could be so gentle and thoughtful, treating me,
always buying me such beautiful things. . . ." She hesitates, and I see her looking back, dredging up more
painful memories.

"Over the years he's got worse. I've always known he
can be violent. He hits me, Kate. . . . After, he hates himself, but he can't help it."

I watch, sickened but unable to look away, as Jo
slowly unwinds one of her huge, soft scarves to reveal
fresh red bruising on her neck. My hand goes to my
mouth.

"He strangles me, Kate. Even when I beg him not to.
During sex. Until I pass out. It excites him. That's the
kind of man he really is."

She speaks slowly, detached, as though she's talking
about someone else. I'm utterly shocked. I've heard about
this going on between consenting partners, but against
her will, that's assault. It's why she wears those scarves,

no matter how warm it is. Because her husband gets his kicks by throttling her. How can the revered, exalted, saintly Neal Anderson be such a monster?

"The last time he did it, when I came round, he said he'd been planning where to bury me," she gabbles. "He laughed, but he wasn't joking, Kate. It's a big enough garden, isn't it? He'd just tell people his crazy wife had left him, and they'd sympathize, wouldn't they? Everyone always believes him. No one would ever know. . . ."

She's shaking, her hands clasped so tight that her knuckles are white, her eyes begging me to believe her.

Then she continues in a low voice, "I saw him hit Rosanna. I don't know what else he did to her. I know it's wrong, and I'm weak and pathetic, but I couldn't ask. He bullied her, Kate. Didn't let her do anything, have friends, have a social life. And when he got angry . . . I know you don't believe me, but truly, he's evil."

As she speaks, though, there are other words echoing in my head. Words I've heard so many times. *Amazing man . . . He's an amazing man. . . .*

"And this has been going on how long, Jo?" I know she's just told me, but it's too much to take in, that she needed him so much, she'd forgive him anything, even this.

She stares back. "Years."

I stare at her, horrified. "How could you put up with it? That long? What about the girls?" Doesn't a mother's every instinct scream at her to protect her precious children?

She hesitates. "I don't expect you to understand, but when you've seen that darkness, that vulnerable side of him, you want to help him. It's not right, but I've made excuses for him. He can do such good things, too. You

know that. Look at the orphanage. . . . And I always believed he needed me. I know he did. Only . . . I never
dreamed he was capable of this."

By "this" she means killing Rosie. I try my hardest to
understand how the amazing man is so suddenly an evil
monster. How the truth can be so twisted. So invisible.
How all this time Jo has deceived herself and everyone
else, and only now, presented with unmistakable evidence,
has forced herself to face up to what he is.

Then she leaps up, agitated. "Oh God. What if he
knows I've got it? If he comes here?"

My heart misses a beat; then I remember. "He won't,
Jo. He doesn't know where you are."

I notice her hands shaking.

"Where is it? The laptop?"

"I brought it with me in my bag."

She lifts it onto the table and opens it.

Then what she shows me, I'll never forget.

"What do I do? *What do I do?*" Her voice drops to a
whisper again as I look at the screen, appalled.

"Jo, I really don't know."

I say it because the cogs of my brain have seized up as
I try to imagine the truth as anything, anything at all,
other than the awful, shocking reality she's painting. But
however I turn it round, whichever angle I look at it from,
double-checking, just in case, the answer's the same.

Rosie

My father is an actor with many faces. Otherwise known as a liar. Everyone who meets him sees the charm, the looks. The handsome, famous news reporter looking back at them out of their TV as he risks his own safety in war zones; the same face now ashen, after being shot at while trying to get at the truth; grim as he talks about what happens out there; earnest as he describes the orphanage; angry as he details how little help there is for too many children; softening when he's asked about his wife and family.

He's his own one-man show, my father. Imagine Neal Anderson: The Life Story, *always with the right face, no matter what's underneath, however many flirtations or tawdry affairs happen invisibly behind doors that always stay closed. Whatever violence he inflicts on his wife or anyone else for his own kicks. Whatever abuse his children suffer as he controls and manipulates and destroys.*

It isn't love that turns him on. It's the chase. The catching of eyes, manufacturing excuses to be together. The risk. The realization that this woman, too, like all the others, finds him irresistible.

And then he'll walk back into our house, unreadable. See a dirty coffee cup and hurl it across the room. Speak quietly, then, seconds later, be consumed with rage and fury because his shirts haven't been ironed or the lawn hasn't been mowed. And the picture doesn't fall off the wall and smash on its own. He wrenches it off, hurls it onto the floor. Makes spiteful comments about the family next door because he's so much better than they are; then, when he sees them next, he's their friend.

After a lifetime of acting, the real Neal Anderson is unknown. Is there a person behind the faces? Or underneath, is he so less than perfect, so despicable, so damaged, been hidden so long that he's vanished?

But it doesn't matter, does it, as long as the women keep chasing him? As long as the face is there? The one people expect to see. Which never slips.

Like my mother always says, he's an amazing man.

20

After Jo's call to the police, I hear, don't see, how it happens from different sources, but the village comes to life, whispering with rumors that Neal Anderson has been arrested and questioned, then held for further questioning. That the Andersons' house has been searched again, and the laptop taken and fingers are pointed.

"There was always something about him. . . ."

"Poor Jo . . . To think all this time, she didn't know. . . ."

"How could she not know . . . ?"

"She must have guessed, surely. . . ."

Idle talk that only makes it worse, while understandably, Jo goes away for a few days, and yet again, Rosie's murder is everyone's business. In the middle of it all, my thoughts turn to Delphine. I assume Jo takes her with her, but she doesn't answer my calls, and I worry about both of them. How much more can they go through?

Angus is speechless when I tell him, relieved that this isn't a weekend I spend alone, that he's here. *"Jesus."*

He shakes his head. "The guy was in our house. I liked him."

Both of us questioning our judgment.

"I know. It doesn't seem possible that someone could do that. And poor Jo . . ."

Angus sighs. "How do you ever come to terms with that? I mean, her *husband* . . ."

I curl my arms round his neck, leaning close against him, feel the thump of his heart against mine.

"It makes everything else seem so small."

He nods into my hair. Not knowing what I'm not saying. How I'm trying to cast out the memory of cooking for this man, of his company, his touch, his lips. I pull away; I can't help it.

"I'll open some wine."

Laura can't take it in, either.

"Bloody unbelievable, isn't it?" She puts down two mugs of tea in front of us. She is in boyfriend jeans and a huge sweatshirt, her hair twisted up under a cerise hair slide, and looks more like a student than the glamorous reporter from New York.

She hunts around for a pen, then comes and sits back down. "Some of it I already know, but I'd really like to hear your version of what happened."

"I had this cryptic call from Jo about some mythical software I hadn't ordered. It was a smoke screen, because she didn't want Neal following her. Anyway, she came round and said she was using an old laptop of his when she found these files. Horrible, violent sexual images, links to Web sites . . . She didn't say much more. She was too upset."

Laura stops scribbling for a moment. "I can't imagine how she must feel. And she thinks he killed Rosie."

I nod. "If she hadn't been in that IT course, she'd never have found any of it. She was useless with computers. And he'd still be walking around, and none of us would be any the wiser."

It really did come down to that. To Jo's course and some lost files she stumbled upon on a computer she shouldn't have been using. Coincidences, flimsily strung together by twists of fate, a conclusion that's somehow startling.

"Well, for five whole months, no one has known," Laura says. "But we do now. Did she say anything else?"

Just for a moment, it crosses my mind to mention Neal's advances, but I decide not to. I shrug. "I don't think so. Do you know he abused her?"

Laura nods. Not for the first time, I wonder where her information comes from. "I had heard. You'd never have guessed, would you? I mean, he really has something, doesn't he? Like George Clooney. Women the world over are besotted with him. If only they knew."

"And then there's the orphanage," I remind her. "It doesn't make sense."

"I know, but look at it this way. It was the perfect cover," she says. "Everything about him, the public face of Neal Anderson he's so painstakingly constructed, completely hides what he really is." She frowns slightly. "My contact happened to get talking to his lawyer—a bloody expensive one, I might add. And not discreet at all. Kate, do you know where the Andersons' money comes from?"

I frown. "No idea. They obviously have plenty, though, if you look at the cars, the house. . . . And Jo doesn't

work. Yet the girls were at the same school as Grace. . . .
I just assumed it was his salary."

Laura shrugs. "Maybe."

A shiver runs down my spine. "I still can't believe it."

"I know. He's a talented liar, as we know. It's a pity
the police didn't find the murder weapon. Still, when they
examine the laptop, hopefully things will be clearer."

Since Rosie's body was found, the worst moment is
yet to come. Another shock, piled on shock, when Laura
calls to tell me that Neal has been released on bail—in
spite of Jo's testimony and the files she found on his
computer.

"I don't understand." I can't believe he can be free.

"The police have charged him with assault, but there
isn't enough evidence to charge him with murder," Laura
explains. "They can't hold him indefinitely."

"God, what about Jo?"

"There are post-bail conditions. He'll have to stay away
from her, Kate. If he has any sense, he'll keep to it. It's a
serious charge. We just have to hope the police find more
evidence."

Suddenly, no matter the conditions attached to Neal's
bail, I'm frightened for Jo.

With Jo still away, her phone apparently switched off,
I watch her house for signs of life. A week passes before
I drive past and notice lights back on and her car parked
outside. As I'm in a hurry, I don't stop, just text her quickly,
wondering how it is being in the house, knowing Neal has
been released, before hurrying home to feed the horses before it's dark.

Then, that evening, as I'm washing up in the kitchen, something flutters through my letter box. Seeing an envelope lying on the floor, I guess a neighbor's put it through, but when I open the door, no one's there.

And it gets more curious still when I open the note.

Rosie

The final scene of the movie brings fear, an ocean of it, coursing through me, its sulfurous presence pervading the air.

It's the night I'm leaving Alex's house, where there are no mirrors, no disapproving eyes, where his arms hold me close and the air shimmers with love. Poppy's covered for me. Her heavy makeup and harsh tongue, the too-tight clothes my mother detests, the brassy hair hide a kindness not many people know about.

There's a reason I'm walking away from him, alone. As I quickly move through that night, I feel the weight of knowledge of something, and of where I'm going. A feeling of dread.

It's a warm night, starlit above the soft cloak of darkness wrapped around me. I'm thinking of Alex, filling my head with thoughts of him, twisting my fingers through the necklace he gave me, feeling his love, because even when he's not here, even when we argue, I can do that. Feel his love.

I'm not expecting the car to pull over, then stop beside me. I'm surprised, not expecting this. Not wanting to get in, but swayed with clever, persuasive words. We need to talk. To start again. We should walk. It's a beautiful night under the trees, the moon so bright, it casts shadows.

Feel uncertainty ripple like the surface of a pond. Then we walk, and as words unspool, mostly about the past, I realize that all I'm to do is listen.

Such a beautiful night to walk in the woods . . .

As we turn up the path beneath the trees, I hear of desperation, longing, a willingness to do anything to make amends for something bad that's happened. How some mistakes are too big, and sometimes you have to do what's hardest, because however much it hurts, it's for the best.

We're deep in the woods, where the ground is soft from fallen leaves, a circle of trees around us like an ancient chapel, dappling the moonlight, looking up at that deep, tranquil sky.

Until an unseen force hurls me backward. Cracking my head, the air knocked out of me, the roughness of bark under my skin.

I struggle. Blink to clear the mist around me. Feel myself pulled, thrown backward again, hear a voice scream. Pull away, but the sky is spinning.

A million thoughts fill my head at lightning speed. Then more, as I realize that it's this person whom I trusted, with whom I've walked willingly to this place, who is doing this.

No! This can't be happening. It's wrong. There's been a mistake. The trees recoil as my silent cry hits them. I can't let this happen. I have to stop it.

But I can't.

In shock, in slow motion, I feel my legs crumple. Work out I'm hurt, that I'm falling. Hear my voice scream out, a sound I've never heard.

Feel a splintering, agonizing pain as my head explodes into a million pieces of light. As time stretches out to infinity. And then snaps backs. As my own warm, sticky blood coats my hands, an invisible stain in the darkness.

Then the pain is gone and I'm floating.

And that's how it ends. Watching the last vicious, brutal, stabbing, slicing motions that twist and rip my insides, as the last gossamer threads holding me to my body are broken, setting me free to move toward the light I hadn't seen, which is coming nearer. I feel its warmth soaking into me, its brightness comforting me, so there can be no shadows ever again.

But before it reaches me, it pauses, hovering just out of reach. Then it moves again, cruelly, away from me, even though I reach out my hands, call out, begging it to come back. "Please, come back. . . .

"Don't leave me here. . . ."

21

In my hand, there's a small white piece of paper with frayed edges where it's been ripped from a larger sheet, the words on it printed clearly.

If you only knew the truth.

Even though it's late, I call Angus, but it goes to voice mail. On impulse, I call Laura.

"You need to show the police, Kate. It might be linked."

"Why send it to me, though?"

"It might just be rubbish. Some local nut who knows you're friends with Jo, stirring up trouble."

"Do people do that? Really?"

"Yes. They really do. You shouldn't worry about it."

The next day, I call Sergeant Beauman, who sends someone round to pick up the note, then go to see Jo, expecting her still to be reeling from hearing about Neal. Instead, I find her having a massive clear-out. What's more, she's taking delivery of a new carved oak bed.

"I'm redecorating," she tells me after welcoming me with open arms. With her hair tied messily back, and wearing a checked shirt that swamps her, she looks about Grace's age. And scared, but energized. "You understand, don't you, Kate? About the bed?"

"God, yes, of course I do. Can I do anything to help?"

"You could take one of those downstairs." She points to a row of smart matching suitcases. "They're Neal's clothes. I can't bear to have them in here. They can go in the garage—at least for now." Barely pausing for breath before she starts again. "I've been thinking about moving, and I still might, only we've moved so many times, Kate. I'm sick of it. Every time Neal fell out of favor with people. It was his answer to everything. New house, new people . . . Anyway, I can have the house how I want it now. How *I* want it!"

She's elated, unable to stand still, her thoughts running too fast for me to keep up.

"Are you all right with him being released?"

"Not really." Jo's too quick, her eyes darting frantically, and I see then, she's on a knife-edge. "But I have to believe he won't come here. If he does, the police told me they'll arrest him. He would hate that."

"I wish I'd known how bad it was," I tell her. "You should have said, Jo."

She shrugs, pulling up her sleeves. "What I should have done was leave him. Years ago. I've wasted so much time. And once he's in court, everyone will know what he's really like. That he killed his own daughter." Her voice wobbles as she deposits an armful of bed linens into a garbage bag. "I want nothing on my skin that's touched *him.*"

"Over here, please," she says as the men carrying her

new bed survey the scene with an amusement that's out of place, because nothing about this is remotely funny. It's horribly, desperately sad. "By the window. Thank you. That's perfect. *Oh God*. The curtains."

She rips them down and stuffs them in the bag with the bed linens.

Holding the bag open, I try to help her. "I tried to call you . . . several times. Where were you?"

"I'm sorry, Kate. I was in such a state, I forgot my phone charger. I just drove until we found a B&B. I had to get away."

As I carry the suitcases downstairs, I notice here, too, evidence of her catharsis. Already, there are new cushions, coordinated perfectly with the sofas. Therapeutic brochures on the coffee table, next to liberating pages of paint charts and fabric swatches.

"You wouldn't believe how this helps," she says, coming down the stairs behind me, empowered by what she's doing, clearly relishing cutting Neal out of her life, as well as putting her own stamp on the house, not for one moment seeming to miss him. Too much so for me not to worry.

"Come on. I'll put the kettle on. Actually, it's nearly six. I'll open a bottle."

It's five thirty, but if a glass of wine is what it takes to wind her down, I decide I'll share one with her, because the manic way she's behaving, I'm convinced she's heading for a breakdown.

"It's like she feels nothing for him," I tell Angus when he calls me later that evening. I'd left Jo making inroads into the rest of the wine, getting her to promise also to eat supper. "Even though they've been together all this time, she's simply cut him out of her life, just like that. I don't believe anyone can do that—not without it catching up with them at some point."

"She's probably relieved," he says. "You can understand why. Once the court hearing's out of the way, it'll be easier for her." He pauses. "Just please don't do anything to our house while I'm away. Are you still coming up here in a couple of weeks?"

"I hope so," I tell him. "I miss you."

"I miss you, too. I'd suggest you come earlier," Angus says, sounding regretful, "only I really have to work this weekend."

"It's fine. I should probably work, too." And I would if I wasn't so preoccupied with Jo.

"How's Rachael?" he asks, picking up on my restlessness. "Why don't you plan a girls' night?"

"I haven't seen her. She's tied up with work and the boys."

"Well, why don't you go and see Grace?" he suggests. "Get away from there for a bit. A change of scene would do you good."

I know what he's really saying. It's his unvoiced reminder to me not to get too drawn into Jo's problems. He may be right. And the thought of seeing Grace is irresistible.

Rosie

You can't know that air shimmers. Or that a north wind is violet streaked with indigo, and a southerly wind is the color of a sunflower. That it carries the sound of bees swarming and angels crying, even though you can't see them.

You can't know any of this. How it feels to have none of the residual sensation an amputee might have. No wraithlike limbs or ghostly body, like in movies. But that doesn't mean I'm not here. That I'm not something. Just because there are no words to describe it.

Colors have become ever changing; faraway sounds, knife sharp. Time elastic, catapulting me from a night that's lasted forever into the middle of the building storm.

The randomness of the universe isn't random at all. I see that now. Take the molten metal streams of silver raindrops, snaking downward, streaking the forest floor. Or the storm, a product of heat and moisture in the air, swirling like an ocean current or riptide, charging the clouds until they explode into their own light show.

Across the woods, I glimpse a streak of white. As it comes nearer, I realize the storm has brought me a horse.

I know Zappa instantly, as light and fluid as the rain. Kate says I have an affinity with horses. That horses read your soul. Is that what I am now? I call out to him.

"Hey! Hey, boy! Zappa . . ."

He throws up his head, startled, and I realize he's heard me. Then I see Kate riding him. Urgently, desperately, I need her to hear me, too, to know the truth, to send someone out here to help me.

"Kate . . ."

As the thunder crashes, I scream her name. Hear it echo, see the air ripple, taking it to her. I try again, and this time her face is stricken with terror.

"Kate, it's me. It's Rosie. . . . Help me. . . . Please. Help me. . . ."

For a moment, I think she's heard. Then I realize, even if she hasn't, Zappa has. He bolts, galloping too fast. Kate can't stop him.

I have to do something, help them both, but all I can think of is to bring them here, where the ground is flat and the trees will protect them. To show Zappa where the path is. To take away Kate's fear. To bring them to me.

In my mind, I see a glow around me, under the trees, casting shadows that move with the wind, and then it's there. Dim at first, slowly growing brighter.

As if he reads my mind, Zappa turns, takes the slope in two long strides, then, seeing me, stops dead, his huge, astonished eyes trying to figure out what he's looking at, as Kate pitches onto the ground.

Zappa stands there, spooked, snorting at me.

"Good horse. Good boy. It's okay, Zappa. . . ."

He doesn't get it. How can he see me? I don't get it, either. But he's okay. I turn to Kate. She isn't moving.

Somehow, I'm beside her, at her head, hearing her whisper a breath, and I reach out, a butterfly touch to her cheek.

"It's okay, Kate. You're okay. I'll look after you. . . ."

But I don't see what happens to her. I'm floating away, even though I'm grasping at branches, which my hands just slip through. Calling out. I don't want to go. I can't leave her.

Then it's dark again, the sky a mass of twinkling stars calling me in a million voices to be one of them. But I can't. Not yet. Even though my body's lifeless, my last breath squeezed from my lungs. I've seen my life flash by. Seen the truth about those I thought were close to me. I'm supposed to move on. But there's a reason I'm still here. It's because I've lost someone. Someone I know I have to find.

Then I'm overcome with a strange, sinister feeling. And in front of me more pictures start, only these are darker, faster, more menacing. The story behind my own story. The part of the story no one knows.

22

Only when she's caught unawares do the cracks show.
Jo's expression when Delphine asks about the school
trip to Paris. The pile of bills mounting up, on the side,
unopened. A call from a police counselor that leaves her
unduly flustered.

"I'm fine. I just need some space," she says snippily.
"I wish they'd get off my back."

All pointing to how vulnerable she feels.

She makes no mention of money, and I don't ask.
Then, with her work on the house finished, the last wall
painted, the last piece of new furniture in its place, her
mood of euphoria collapses.

"It's beautiful, Jo. You've done a great job with it."

"Thank you. Better, isn't it?"

I look around at the walls, painted a different neutral
shade from before, with new curtains hanging, furniture
shifted slightly. All that aside, it's disturbingly reminis-
cent of how it used to look. Immaculate. Too tidy. It's the

same upstairs, a glamorous interiors photo shoot rather than a family home.

"I love it," I tell her. "So now that it's done, what next?"

She looks puzzled.

"I was thinking about the course you started. It was going well, wasn't it?"

"I don't know." She sounds unsure. "After all this business with Neal, I—I can't think that far ahead."

And though she hides it well, I see a change. After that, every time I see her, her world closes in a little more, until it's shrink-wrapped around her. She shows me new china or the latest high-tech gadget. And then she has absolutely nothing else to say.

"Jo?" I have to ask her one day, as we sit there, barely speaking. "You're not yourself. What is it?"

"I don't know," she says, looking at me blankly. "I thought with Neal gone from here, the house decorated, I'd feel good. But I don't, Kate. I feel terrible. Every day it gets worse. And I don't know what to do. . . ."

"You've been through so much," I say, worried she's on the verge of another breakdown. Under her makeup, her skin is gray, and there are dark circles under her eyes, as though even when she sleeps, she doesn't rest. "Seriously. Maybe you should talk to someone. A professional, Jo. Don't you think it might help?"

For a moment she looks as though she's tempted, but then she rallies. Laughs a brittle laugh. "There are people far worse off than I am, Kate. Honestly. I'll be fine."

But I know she isn't, and as I drive home, I'm preoccupied. I know enough to realize that stress can creep up on you and hit you when you least expect it. I'm guessing that's what's happening to her again. In which case, she really does need some help. I decide to call her and try to convince her, but when I get home, I'm distracted by another of those envelopes and, when I open it, another note.

In a world of people, I'm alone.

Rosie

As the next picture unfolds in front of me, it's mono-chromic and dark, like through a tinted lens. I see a girl I've never seen before. She's small, her hair a mass of pale curls, her old-fashioned dress tied behind her in a bow. She's in a garden behind a large house, a dull sun high above the tall trees surrounding it. As she walks across the grass, she stops suddenly, her hair caught white in the sunbeams through the branches as some-thing lands on her hand. A large, patterned butterfly flex-ing lace wings as the girl holds her breath and doesn't move.

Then it flies, fluttering upward out of her reach, and she watches, then flings skinny arms out and runs, leap-ing across the garden, featherlight, following the path of the butterfly through air that glimmers, with a happiness that soars, too. Until the voice comes out of the sky.

"Joanna? Joanna? Come inside, child."

She's done nothing, but her world darkens with a fear she can't explain. Her feet take her inside. They always

do. Because if she doesn't do as they say, bad things happen.

The door closes behind her; then the sun starts to sink
slowly, then faster, gaining speed in this black-and-white
world, until the last rays spike below the horizon and turn
it to darkness.

23

I leave the note at the police station for Sergeant Beauman, then turn up my music and set off for Bristol, with each passing mile feeling my heart lift as I think about the weekend with Grace.

As if she knows, when I get there, she's sitting outside, waiting for me.

"I can't tell you how glad I am to be here!" It's true. As well as giving us time together, being miles from home gives me a changed perspective on Jo and her problems.

Grace's eyes sparkle at me. "I know, Mum. I'm glad, too. I thought we could go to this Italian tonight, if you like? It isn't expensive."

I notice the nod to her impoverished student status.

"Don't worry about that, Grace. My treat! This is great, though," I add as we walk into her dormitory. "I love what you've done with your room."

The empty space we abandoned her to all those months back is no more. What's here reminds me of her room at home, only with unfamiliar pictures on the walls, photos of friends I've yet to meet. And flowers. Grace's cheeks flush pink as she catches me looking at them.

I raise a questioning eyebrow.

"Mu-um! Okay." She rolls her eyes. "They're from a boy. He's called Ned, and he's cool. You'll really like him."

Ned. I haven't met a Ned before. I wonder if he's good to her, what he looks like.

"Here." She thrusts her phone under my nose. "This is him."

A kind, boyish face looks back at me. A little older than Grace, maybe? If he's important to her, I'm sure I'll get to meet him.

"Is he coming out with us?"

"God, no. I might see him after, though. It depends."

Her social life yielding to allow us a few precious hours together before snapping her back into its midst.

"Party?"

She nods. "But it doesn't matter. I don't have to, Mum."

"You go. I'll be happy with an early night."

Grace shows me round the campus, chattering about the clubs she's joined and the movies she's seen. Then we drive into town and find the B & B I've booked, which is clean and homey, with a soft bed and a rooftop view punctuated by chimney stacks. Then we walk through the streets to the restaurant she's chosen, with its stripped wood and bare bricks. We eat pasta and drink red wine, and after filling her in about Jo and Neal, suddenly weary, I change the subject. I want to forget about them, everything I've left behind, just for a while.

I've booked my room for the weekend, fully aware that Grace will have her own life to lead, but needing the change of scene, glad that there are no visitors, no intrusions. That I can spend time with Grace, or just explore the shops, be lazy, please myself.

The following morning, on a whim, I book myself in for a manicure with a pretty, very made-up girl called Mollie, who tuts about my hands and says she's never seen anything like them.

"Let me guess." She stares at them. "Horses?"

I nod, slightly taken aback.

"And gardening. I know. I'll put this lovely cream on them. You won't recognize them when I've finished, and it's got all these cool ingredients, like calendula to soothe the skin and almond oil. . . ."

I tell her I've never had a manicure before, then let her get on, sitting back, half listening to the idle chitchat around me, about holidays and reality TV shows, until one sentence jerks me back to the moment.

"You know that TV reporter bloke that killed his daughter?" says a gossipy voice. "Well, seems like his wife's done herself in. . . ."

"Excuse me?" I spin round, yanking my hand from Mollie's. "Could you repeat what you just said?"

"Joanna what's-her-name. It was on the news, love."

I turn back to Mollie, numb. "Sorry. I need to make a call." Pulling out my phone, searching for Laura's number, noticing Mollie's puzzled face. "She's my friend."

The timing is ironic—or is it? Guiltily, I wonder, if I'd been there, if Jo had known I was just a couple of miles down the road, instead of a couple of hours away, would it have happened? And with Neal no longer around, who's taking care of Delphine?

I make my excuses to Grace, feeling horribly guilty about that, too, that I'm letting her down. In spite of her assurances that it's fine, that she understands, that we'd had a lovely evening and now she was free to go to yet another party she'd been invited to without worrying about leaving me alone, the guilt lingers.

"I could have gone with you," I tease her, seeing the flicker of alarm in her face before she giggles.

"You'd hate it, Mum. All that spilt beer and smoking. You hate cigarettes. And drunk teenagers . . ."

"Yes, but I might have met Ned," I point out.

"If you really want to meet him, I'll bring him home. For Easter. If we're still together, that is."

I think of Easter. Spring. Grace. Maybe now, Ned . . . Vibrant, beautiful things, full of life and hope. Then Jo, tortured and fragile, unconscious but stable, according to the nurse I spoke to. And, of course, in all this, there's Delphine.

It's late afternoon when I reach the hospital, where it seems the entire world has turned out to visit their loved ones. The extortionately priced car park has no spaces, and after being sent on a wild-goose chase through corridors heavy with the cloying scent of disinfectant, I at last find the right floor and the right set of swinging doors, only to be confronted by the ward sister.

"I'm sorry, but Mrs. Anderson's not allowed visitors." She says it most imperiously.

"I don't think you understand," I try to explain. "I'm her closest friend—especially since she's been on her own. I don't think she'd be pleased if she knew about this."

Trying to ignore the fact that I've cut short my week-end with my daughter, that I'm hungry, worried. How Jo has no one else who cares enough to be here.

The sister ignores me, writing something on one of the charts spread in front of her before turning her back on me. I wait, studying the board that tells me exactly where she is, and when the sister strides away out of sight, I slip into Jo's room.

Rosie

I see the child again, the one with pale hair and my mother's name. Joanna. With the story that's stitched into the background of mine. She's in a house of silence, seated between upright, unsmiling parents lost in the pages of their books.

A tasseled lampshade hangs center ceiling, throwing a dim light on furniture that's as dark and heavy as the air they breathe, air that fills her lungs and sticks in her throat, slowly suffocating her. Now and then, glancing from one parent to the other, she shifts in her chair.

While they carry on reading, ignoring her.

She crosses her legs, with the same anxious, pleading look I've seen so many times.

"Keep still, child," says the woman.

"But please, Mama, I need to be excused," she says.

"You must wait," the woman says abruptly.

Joanna waits until she can't wait any longer, then gets up and tiptoes toward the door, hoping she can slip out before someone stops her. As her hand reaches for the door handle, the man slams down his book.

"Where do you think you're going?" He's on his feet, marching toward her, a dark-clothed monster towering over her.

"To the toilet," she whispers, looking at him, panic-stricken.

"You were told to wait.*"* His voice is hard, hateful, makes her cower. *"Go and sit down."*

The child quivers, then flinches, not taking her eyes off him, eyes that fill with terror as a pool of warm urine trickles down her leg. She's waited all this time, and it's too long.

She freezes while his eyes wander down, as he sees what she's done. Waits for the angry cuff across her face, before he grabs her wrist too tightly and drags her through the door and up the stairs, into the special room that has no window and no light.

I know before she gets there, from the fetid blanket of fear that stops her breathing, from her eyes. This is what happens. He pushes her in and locks the door. Inside, in the darkness, I hear her whimper, watch her fall on the floor in her sodden clothes, clasp her arms, rocking back and forth, before the screams start.

They go on for hours, long after darkness falls, while I slip through to be with her, to fold my arms around my mother, try to comfort her, tell her that this isn't her fault, that her mother's cruel and her father's evil. That she's a child. She deserves soft words, strong arms to hold her, and love, so much love. The love that I have inside me, if she'd ever looked.

But I haven't been born, and she can't hear me.

24

I slip into the little room that Jo has to herself, then crouch beside the bed, trying to stay out of sight.

"Jo? Jo? Can you hear me?"

I look at her, a small gray doll on the starched sheets, threaded with plastic tubes that link her to drips and screens. The air rings with electronic noise that no one should be able to sleep through, but she doesn't stir.

Glancing through the door, checking that no one's in earshot, I whisper her name again.

"Jo?"

Then I watch as she stirs, the slight movement of her head turning, then her lashes, a flutter, as if she's dreaming.

"Jo? It's okay. You're not well. You're in hospital."

Briefly her eyelids flicker open, then close again as I hear footsteps behind me.

Then my heart sinks, because it's the same ward sister, just as uncompromising as before. "Kindly leave. I made it very clear you weren't to come in here."

"And as I said to you earlier, I'm her closest friend.

And quite possibly the only visitor she'll get. She opened her eyes just now. While I was talking to her."

Reaching for the buzzer, she's still glaring. Then the room fills with nurses, and a female doctor jostling round Jo, trying to elicit another response from her. But failing.

I stand out of the way, praying for Jo to open her eyes again as I listen to medical terminology I don't understand, only at the end catching up to the doctor as she leaves.

"Excuse me, but can you tell me what's happening?"

The doctor hesitates. "You are?"

"Kate McKay. Her closest friend. I've been with her through the most awful time. Yesterday . . . she seemed all right. Otherwise I wouldn't have left her."

I can't believe it was just yesterday that I left for Bristol.

"Your friend took an overdose. She should be all right, but we're concerned about what else is going on. After everything that's happened, it's possible she's suffering from some form of post-traumatic stress disorder. As you know, she's lost her daughter. We won't know how she's dealing with that until we can talk to her."

"She has been quite surprising," I say. "She's been up and down—obviously—but has somehow found a way to carry on. She took a course not so long ago. And she was working for her husband before—" I stop, wondering how much this doctor knows.

She nods. "Her sister-in-law gave me some of the background. But where in all this has she taken any time to grieve? It's a massive loss she's suffered. And now, whatever the circumstances are, her husband is another huge loss she has to face. . . ."

Hearing it put like that, I realize how accustomed I've become to Jo's incredibly difficult life. And how foolish

I've been, too, even imagining she could get through this without some kind of meltdown. Something of the magnitude of losing a child can hardly be assimilated, accepted, moved on from in just a few months—if at all.

I've done it again. Been too close, seeing only her lion's courage and brave face, not what's underneath. Jo hasn't been coping; she's been burying her head in grief's insidious quicksand. And it occurs to me that in her shoes, it would be so much easier to let it suck you down and slowly close over your head, rather than face what lies ahead. Alone.

I call Laura when I get home, just to fill her in.

"I went round to see Joanna. Yesterday. I was going to talk to her about the notes." Laura sounds shocked. "It was just to ask if she had any idea where they might have come from. I asked Delphine, too."

"What did they say?"

"Joanna looked quite shaken when I told her. Do you think there's any possibility that she sent them? She's under such strain. A kind of cry for help, perhaps?" It's not something I'd considered, but maybe she's right. "I don't know. Possibly. She hates admitting she needs help. . . ."

"Delphine just looked blank," Laura says. "That child worries me. She gives nothing away."

"So what now?"

Laura sighs. "See if you get another. A similar thing happened during another case I was following. It turned out that some batty old dear thought the victim had deserved what she got. Kind of posthumous hate mail, you could call it."

I'm astonished. "People do that?"

Laura laughs. "Kate! People aren't all nice! They can be devious and evil, you know. Look at Neal."

"That's the thing," I tell her. "If Jo hadn't found the laptop, he's the last person in the world I would have suspected."

Laura sigh is audible. "Welcome to my highly confusing world."

Rosie

Love is devious, deceptive, misleading. In Joanna's black-and-white world, love is that new dress or those pretty shoes, if you half close your eyes and don't look closely. It's about control.

Thirteen-year-old Joanna stares at herself in the mirror. At the awkward girl with the chubby face and the velvet child's dress, a bow stitched at the collar. The child's shoes, black patent, which she's wanted ever since she was ten.

Just behind, her mother looks, too, pleased, not seeing that the dress is for a child's body, that her daughter is no longer a child. That the shoes no longer thrill.

"You're such a big girl," she says. "You'll be bigger than me soon." Straightens the lace collar. Adjusts the matching Alice band round her daughter's head. "There. How nice you look."

She looks at the faces in the mirror. The two strangers. The child who wants to be small and the round-eyed mother controller with toxic thoughts, who offers sweets dusted with cyanide and nitric acid lemonade.

It's a drinks party rather than a tea party, full of her parents' friends and neighbors, in twinsets and lounge suits, drinking sherry. With laughs that tinkle and roaming, lecherous eyes. Joanna slips among them as it starts again.

"Haven't you grown?"

"What a big girl you are!"

How big, big, big . . . inflating, until it explodes in her ears and deafens her, when all she wants to do is disappear.

Once she starts, it's easy. "I'm not that hungry." "I had a big"—that word again—"lunch at school." "I have a tummy ache." While her poor hollow stomach rumbles and her sandwiches get thrown in the bin. But none of that matters when she sees how flat her stomach is, how her clothes hang. How without its baby fat, her face has a haunted kind of beauty.

Then, when she's forced to eat what's on her plate, even though she doesn't want it, because it's too much and will sit heavily in her stomach, she's learned, too, how to quickly stimulate her gag reflex. Only she can control this, no one else. And as well as the jutting bones and the childish shape, which she's so proud of, the benefits come flooding in.

"She's so slim!"

"You look lovely, dear."

"She has a lovely figure. . . ."

"That dress looks so pretty on you."

To be admired, to hear good things said about her for looking pretty, for exhibiting such admirable self-control, for making herself the best she can be, for all but starving herself, gives her a warm feeling inside. It's closest to love.

25

As there's little I can do for Jo, and Delphine is with a good friend, I go as planned to visit Angus. During the long drive up, with what feels like the wings of a dozen butterflies fluttering inside me, I'm not sure how this will go. But rather than taking me into the apartment he shares with Nick and Ally, after meeting me at the door, Angus surprises me with a luxury hotel suite.

"You didn't have to do this," I tell him, looking around at the lavishly furnished living space and the king-size bed and the en suite. The orchids on the elegant furniture and the champagne in a silver ice bucket. I walk over to the window. The views are spectacular—and I realize this must come at quite a price. "The apartment would have been fine, Angus."

Feeling his presence behind me, I turn round. He pulls me close and looks into my eyes.

"You're worth it," he says softly. "Anyway, I wanted you to myself. I don't like being away from you."

His brown eyes are serious, and suddenly his words

are all I can think of, because somewhere along the way, over twenty or so years of being married, of being easy in each other's company and taking each other for granted, we've lost sight of how much we mean to each other. How much our marriage means. And it's taken being apart for me to realize this. As I look at him just for a moment, at the face I know like my own, at the tears in my husband's eyes, I wonder, *Like I did with Neal, has he, too, come close?*

He opens his mouth to speak, looking at once worried, loving, apologetic. "Kate, there's something I have to tell you."

"Shh." I place a finger on his lips. "Enough talk. I've a better idea."

And then I take my husband's hand and lead him to the bedroom.

It's an episode of our marriage that threatens everything we've built together, but for those few days we forget, pushing it into the background, instead filling lazy days wandering the city and long nights where we forget about being husband and wife, parents, with jobs and responsibilities, and instead strip back time and are just lovers.

I've always believed in honesty, even if it hurts. But I learn there is strength in silence—wisdom, too. We talk, but the unspoken part stays just that. Unspoken, so that I leave there with my suspicions unvoiced, still not sure what, if anything, he didn't tell me.

But as I drive, my doubts linger, unresolved. And I'm uneasy, because it's the first time Angus and I have kept secrets from each other. Are some things really better left unsaid, or have we slipped over one of those invisible lines that crisscross life, waiting to trip us up?

And can we ever go back to how we were?

When I get home, I find Jo's been transferred to a small, exclusive private hospital tucked away in the Surrey countryside, a tranquil location enclosed by beech hedges and ancient cedars, a sweeping gravel drive leading to the entrance. I can't help but wonder how she can afford this.

The front door opens into a grand hallway, which at first glance could be mistaken for the reception area in a country-house hotel—until you see the blankness in the faces, the suffering not quite hidden behind their eyes.

I wait until one of the nurses takes me to the lounge, where Jo's sitting by the window with her back to us, facing out across the garden. As I walk over, she turns round.

I hardly recognize her. "Jo?"

I lean down and hug her. Not once in all the time I've known her have I seen Jo without makeup, and only here, within the safety of these walls, is the extent of her sorrow bared for the world to see.

"Thanks for coming, Kate." So humbly grateful to see me.

I pull a chair up close to hers. "So how are you doing?"

She sighs. "I've got myself in a bit of a mess, haven't I?"

"I don't know about that. It all got too much, didn't it?"

"I suppose it did." She sounds perplexed, as though she can't understand how it's come to this. "Stupid, though, letting it get this bad . . ."

It's a bleak attempt at humor. Her lips stretching into a smile and stopping short.

Even now, she's in denial. Or is she doing what she always does? Playing down her pain for my benefit? It's impossible to tell.

"How long will you be here, Jo?"

"A few days," she says. "Something like that. They don't tell me." A tear trickles down her cheek.

"Oh, *Jo* . . ." I fish in my pocket for a tissue and gently wipe her face.

"I keep crying," she says, her voice wobbling. "I can't stop it. . . ."

I don't know what to say, just lean toward her and hold her hand.

"It's okay," she says slowly, her eyes drifting toward the window again. "They do understand here. They say they can help me. I've been hiding, Kate, haven't I? I can't do that—hide. Not anymore."

From the way she speaks, it's clear she's on medication, and I can see, too, that without it the pain would destroy her just as surely as a heart attack or an aneurysm would.

"Is Delphine with someone?"

"Carol collected her. She's Neal's sister." The "sister" is slurred. "They live in Devon. Carol's like you, Kate. She'll be fine."

"Can I call her? Just to say if she needs me to, I can help?"

Jo nods weakly.

"Do you have her number?"

A vacant look crosses her face. "I'm so tired . . . ," she mutters.

Then her eyelids start to close, and her head droops.

Rosie

A hospital where uniforms, beds, floors, walls, everything's white. Joanna in a white dressing gown, across the desk from a doctor.

Silence while he reads her notes, then takes her blood pressure, then asks her to undress and get on the scales.

It's the worst part—the scales. They fill her with dread, as with each day in this hateful place, she watches the fat creep on, loathing that the numbers are going up, picturing the hideous ounces like lumps of lard when there should be just white skin and jutting bones, so small she can slip past people and through doorways, unseen. Hating that she's so big and solid. Has form and shape, bones and muscles. All she can see is the fat.

But she has to play his stupid game and bear this. Tolerate just enough pounds of the extra fat, solid, hateful weight to reach a tacit agreement where he'll sign her off, ask her to come back in a month just for a checkup.

Even though they both know she won't, just as they both know the pounds will be starved and purged and ex-

ercised until they're gone again, just as fast as she can make them.

Joanna's flat is small—tidy, clean, unadorned—a place of impermanence, the fridge all but empty. Half a dozen books on the single shelf. The TV and a handful of videos. The bathroom, however, is a place that holds endless possibilities. It's luxurious, her private sanctuary.

Each day starts here. Each day, which might offer endless possibilities for changing her life, and so she sets her alarm, leaving time for it to go wrong, to start again, until it's perfect.

There's a ritual. Shower, scrubbing until she's raw. Hair washed, then washed again. Every day. Legs de-fuzzed, nails scrubbed, too.

Then, when she's dry, hair scraped back under hair band, to start on the face. And this is where her skill shows, because Joanna can paint herself anything. Beautiful, brazen, brave, reckless. Mostly, she settles for simple, understated beautiful. She's done her homework. Sees how women who have it all—who have the lifestyle, the looks, the man—present themselves. The base coat is smooth; the foundation flawless, the perfect shade mixed herself; eye shadow the latest color; mascara the newest waterproof, glossy tube. Life proof, *she always thinks.*

Each day is the same. After the ritual, that flutter of anticipation as she gathers her bag and puts on her coat. Or is it nerves? Down the flight of stairs, wondering what the day will bring. Always what the day will bring, not what Joanna will make of the day, how she'll embrace it, filling each precious minute. She doesn't know about such things, just believes if she waits long enough, things will happen to her.

She takes the first step outside, gasps as she breathes in the cool early morning air and enters the world, which must be how babies feel, she's thought more than once. Only a baby has a mother's arms, her warmth, her breasts, her love. Is safe.

While Joanna is alone.

26

Thinking of Delphine, I try to get Carol's number from the receptionist, but understandably, Jo's records are confidential, and as she's now asleep, I have to resign myself to putting it off until I'm next here.

Instead, I drive home and walk down across the field, feeling the cold air on my skin, in my lungs, sharpening my thoughts. Oz and Reba are pleased to see me, nosing gently in my pockets for tidbits, jostling each other, but Zappa hangs back, taking no notice of us.

It's not like him. Usually, Zappa's at the center of everything, and as I look more closely, I notice his eyes are dull and listless. Then, as I watch, he stamps a hind foot underneath him. It's at this point that alarm bells start going off, because I know this horse. I know his body language, and something's wrong.

When I coax him into his stall, and I have to coax him every step of the way, he's no more comfortable, just stands with his head lowered, every so often turning to stare at his flank. Across the yard, Oz and Reba shove impatiently at the gate, demanding the same level of attention that he's getting, but unusually, he completely ignores them.

At one point, he raises his head and looks at me. For a moment, I can almost see his life visibly draining out of him, while at the back of my mind, a chilling thought occurs to me. *Has Zappa been poisoned? Is someone trying to get at me, too?*

The sender of the notes?

Quietly, I tidy the yard, imagining footsteps that aren't there, constantly glancing over my shoulder, while keeping a careful eye on him. But an hour later, he's no better, and I call my vet, Helen.

By the time she gets here, it's dark. Zappa's in a sweat, his condition deteriorating rapidly, and I'm wishing I'd called her sooner.

I have known Helen for years and trust her implicitly, standing at Zappa's head while she checks him over.

"He's quite poorly, isn't he?" she says, gently stroking him. "Poor old boy. I'm fairly sure it's colic."

"Do you think there's any chance he's been poisoned?"

Helen looks at me sharply. "It's impossible to tell without a blood test, but if you think he may have been, we'll do that. Let's try and get him comfortable for now. I'll give him a jab for the pain and another to relax him. Hopefully, it will pass, Kate. Can you keep an eye on him tonight? I'm on call, so let me know if he gets worse."

I nod, anxiety gnawing at me, at how wretched this vibrant, lovely horse has rapidly become. "I'd better tell his owner."

"He's one of your liveries?"

I nod again.

"You probably should."

After she's gone, I call his owner, but she doesn't pick

up, so I leave a message, then let myself back into Zappa's stall, where I stroke the soft coat and rub him gently behind the ears.

"It's okay, boy. You'll feel better soon."

I leave him only briefly, but when I come back, he's down on the straw bed, and the next minute, despite my efforts to calm him, he starts thrashing around.

I call Helen. She comes straight over and gives him another sedative, then, when he's quiet, examines him again thoroughly.

"It's not good, Kate. There are no gut sounds. Given the pain he's in, he's almost certainly twisted something. His best hope is surgery—this evening, as soon as possible. Can you get him over to the practice?"

"I have a trailer, but I've never loaded him."

"You better hitch it up, and I'll help you."

Thank God Helen's here to make me do this, because not only do I have massive doubts, but a sixth sense tells me he isn't going to make it. Even though he's been here only a few months, I've bonded with this horse. I know he's really sick.

I reverse the trailer as close to the stable as I can, while Helen coaxes Zappa to his feet. While I hold the end of his lead rope, he takes a reluctant step toward the ramp, and then all hell breaks loose as he leaps forward and crashes into the wall.

"It's the pain." Helen grits her teeth. "I'll have to give him another shot."

She goes to her car while I stay with him. He's shuddering, coated in sweat, and though I try to stop him, he goes down again.

"Helen . . . hurry. . . ."

She reappears instantly, holding a syringe. "I'll get this into him first. Then we'll get him on his feet."

Poor, poor Zappa. Brave horse that he is, he tries so hard to do as we ask. Once, he almost makes it, but his legs give way and he collapses back onto the straw.

"God . . . I hope it's not too late. We have to get him in that trailer, Kate. It's his only hope."

And though we pull, push, try to rock him gently to his feet, we fail. And as the implications of this sink in, I feel the sickening wrench inside as my heart twists and breaks.

Whispering quietly to him, I crouch down on the floor beside his head.

"Zappa . . . beautiful horse . . ."

But even as I gently stroke him, he doesn't move. Behind me, I hear Helen come back in. "Kate? I'm sorry, but you know we can't leave him like this."

Still stroking Zappa's noble head, I nod as a tear rolls down my face onto his.

While she goes out to her car, I lean forward and kiss his silver nose. Apart from the rise and fall of his rib cage, he doesn't move.

"It's okay," Helen says as she comes back in. "He's out of it. He won't know a thing."

Loss is one thing, but standing between life and death, making the right decision for the right reasons, is almost worse. It's Zappa's body being winched away, which I don't watch, because I want to remember his beauty, his intelligence, his talent, not this last, most undignified part at the end.

It leaves me raw, bleeding, and devastated, then angry, needing someone to stick needles in, to inflame, to hurt as much as I'm hurting. I pour a large medicinal whiskey, which I hate the taste of, feeling it burn my throat and numb my pain, after which I phone Angus and tell him.

"God, Kate. How awful. Are you all right?"

"Yes. *No.* I feel horrible, Angus. That poor horse . . ."

"You did what you had to," he says quietly. "I wish I was with you, Kate."

Suddenly, I miss him. Hate that he's not here when I most need him; that I can't crush my body against his so that I can feel his heartbeat, his energy, reminding me that there is life and it does go on, regardless, as it always will.

Seized with recklessness, I let whiskey-tainted words rip out of me. Words I've kept inside for far too long. "This sucks. . . . I hate you not being here. Everything's different, Angus. You're different. I'm different. . . ."

"Hey, Kate. We're the same. I'll be home in a couple of months. All this will be behind us."

But I deserve to hurt, to be hurt. So does he. Pretending we're fine is too easy.

"Neal came on to me." I blurt it out, air from a balloon escaping, squealing in my ear. And almost immediately regret it.

He's silent. *Is he going to tell me, too?*

"And?" His tone is steely.

"And nothing. He kissed me. I pushed him away."

Do I stop here? Do I tell him how Neal made me feel? How revolted I am that I touched a man who murdered his own child?

"Stay away from those fucking people, Kate. They're bad news, both of them. You've changed. Look at you. The old Kate wouldn't have dreamed of this."

"How dare you?" Shouting, stung. "You're hardly ever here, Angus. And I didn't do anything. You're the one who went away. *How dare you!*"

"We're married, Kate. Remember that? Because from

where I am, you seem to have forgotten." His voice is cold, distant.

"Yeah, well, it didn't stop you from leaving me, did it? Or whatever else you've been up to while you're there."

Another bitter, anger-filled silence resounds in my ears.

"Just . . . leave it, okay? I can't talk to you in this mood. I'll call you."

Then he hangs up.

I slump onto the floor, tears pouring down my cheeks. Is this it? The end? Only later do I realize he's explained nothing. Denied nothing. Maybe he's done nothing, too.

For the first time ever, did I read him wrong?

Rosie

There's a reason Joanna doesn't go to parties or out drinking with friends or to see a show, getting dressed up, sharing a meal afterward. There's something of such importance that it's spreading into all the corners of her mind, taking over her every waking hour. Something that the most careful makeup in the world can't paint over or conceal.

I follow, a shadow in her shadow, even on this gloomy day, as she takes the Tube to Regent's Park, then walks the short distance to Harley Street and up the steps to a glossy front door. Hesitates, but only minutely.

Inside is bright white. Makes her think of sunshine, warmth, a perfectly ordered world where everything is as it should be. More so when she meets Jean Pinard. Their first meeting. First of many.

"Are you certain?" He traces the outline of her nose, presses it gently this way and that, wonders why such a lovely young girl needs to endure the anesthetic, the slicing of skin and cartilage, the pain, all for a few millimeters less.

"*We can make a small difference.*" She likes the word small. *The way he says it, in that accented voice of his. Maybe he can remove inches of her height, her arms, her fat at the same time.*

She insists, and he does it. He's right, too. The difference is small. So small that when she returns to work, her colleagues don't notice the nose, just how pale she is. How can someone go to Turkey for three weeks and be so pale?

But Joanna knows that this is the first step. Her new nose for the new life that one day she's certain will be hers. She isn't sure what it is yet, just that she'll recognize it when she sees it. And piece by piece, if she perfects herself, the rest will follow. How can it not?

27

Is there a rebalancing going on in my universe? A price to be paid for a mistake or a bad judgment call? The cost of almost cheating on Angus? Zappa's life for my marriage?

Stupid, I tell myself. *It doesn't work like that. You didn't cheat, anyway. You feel guilty because just for a moment, you wanted to.*

As I contemplate the future of my marriage, Zappa's loss leaves a bigger space in my life than I'd have thought possible. His owner is sad, of course, but she didn't really want him, and her insurance paid out, effortlessly resolving her dilemma.

For all the animals she's surrounded by, Rachael remains a farmer's wife—almost.

"Thank God it wasn't one of yours," she says, unemotional, completely unable to comprehend that ownership doesn't come into it. That Zappa had crept deep into my heart.

I remain unsettled. Missing something. My husband and my daughter. And now this beautiful horse. What happened to all that spirit, that energy? Did it dissipate into the straw in his stall when Helen pulled the trigger, or did it cross over to somewhere I can't see? An image of Zappa comes to me, out there, a streak of silver galloping through the darkness. A ghost horse ridden by the ghost girl with pale hair.

And while I flounder, Jo's progress is also slow, the trauma of past months seeming to have her in its stranglehold.

"Your visits are good for her," one of the nurses tells me. Carla stays close to Jo, shares my concern for her with more than simply professional interest. "She needs to remember there's a world out there. She seems to have completely detached herself from Delphine, but that's because at the moment, just being Jo is too painful for her."

"It's what I've seen her do before," I say. "Just switch herself off."

"It's a defense," Carla says, looking troubled. "A wall between her and her pain. And when she does it, we can't reach her."

"Has she talked about her marriage? I know it's not my business to tell you, but there are so many things. . . ." My voice trails off. The hospital should know, but I'm not Jo's family. Unfamiliar with the protocol, I'm not sure it's my place to say this.

"Listen, Kate. We need to know anything that will help her. I know her husband is suspected of murdering their daughter."

I take a deep breath. "Do you know he abused her? Physically?"

Carla's eyes tell me she doesn't know. We sit down together in a quiet room away from everyone else, and slowly, over the next hour, I tell her what I know.

* * *

It's when I realize how straightforward, how uncomplicated my own life used to be, but also how now it's anything but. When Laura comes over, primarily to ask about Jo, I try to explain.

"It's since Angus went, really. We've been together for so long, I've forgotten what I was like without him."

"But he'll be back soon, won't he?"

"Another couple of months." I hand her a cup of tea. "He comes home most weekends, but it's not the same. Anyway, we argued."

Regretting the words as soon as they're out of my mouth. Wishing, like with Angus, I could take them back.

"It can't be easy. It's a long time to be apart. It's bound to put a strain on things."

"You think? Wouldn't most women love that there's less washing and cooking, that they're free to please themselves, you know . . . ?"

"To start with, maybe. But it's a long time. It's nothing serious, though, is it?"

"I'm not actually sure." I put down my tea. "Okay. I wasn't going to tell you, or anyone else. And I'm not proud. At all. But Neal Anderson came on to me."

Laura whistles. "You've kept that one quiet. What happened, Kate?"

"To be honest, I wanted to forget about it. I invited him for supper while Jo was at her course. I was just trying to be neighborly. I invited him and Delphine, but he turned up without her. She was at a friend's. He'd forgotten all about it."

"Or so he said."

I stare at her. It hadn't occurred to me that he'd done it on purpose. "I'd already cooked, so he stayed. Then, when he left, he tried to kiss me."

She looks at me sharply. "What? You mean he forced you?"

"No. Not like that at all. He was very charming. And so bloody seductive, Laura." And though I hunt for another, they're the only words that accurately describe him. "Anyway, I pushed him away. He left. Then, the next morning, he came back for another try. I told him to go." I shrug. "That was it."

"God. What a bastard." Laura's thoughtful. "Does Jo know?"

"I haven't told her. How can I? I'm supposed to be her friend. . . . I've no idea if he did. Knowing what sort of man he is, he might well have."

"What about Angus?"

"I told him. The other night, after Zappa, when it all got too much, Laura. I was a mess. I probably shouldn't have. But it's too late now."

"Oh, Kate." She contemplates her tea. "You didn't actually do anything wrong, did you? It was all Neal."

"Oh . . ." I shake my head, thinking of my body responding to him, the mixed messages I must have given him. "I think there must have been some body language going on there. I must have encouraged him, or he wouldn't have tried it, would he?" A horrifying thought occurs to me. "Oh God . . . Do you think the police should know?"

"I wouldn't say it's exactly relevant, is it?" she says gently.

"Isn't it? Doesn't it show how disreputable he is? How traitorous? That stupid women like me fall under his spell?" To my embarrassment, I'm nearly crying.

"Kate. Enough. You stopped him," says Laura.

My eyes meet hers. "You want the truth? Honestly? I stopped him, yes. But I didn't want to."

Laura shakes her head disbelievingly. "Kate! You've been married far too long! I don't mean that in a bad way! But all women are allowed fantasies, aren't they? Well, the living and breathing ones, at least. You shouldn't feel guilty. You didn't act on it. You turned down the revered Neal Anderson when millions wouldn't. It makes you practically a saint!"

"You think?"

Is she right? Did Neal set the whole thing up?

"God, *definitely.*"

The weight starts to lift.

Then I think of Angus's cold, reproachful voice, and it crashes back down, leaves me gasping for air.

Rosie

Some people have thirsty ghosts not just behind them but still with them, somehow intertwined in their lives, even though they can't see them. People like Kate, Grace, Auntie Carol.

But not Joanna, who has lost her ghosts, has no love behind her, no one beside her in her expanse of empty life, until that sunburst day at a mutual friend's wedding, when she and Neal meet. A cherry-blossom day full of promises, scattered like the confetti outside the church. The moment he sees her, light, beautiful, pliable, slipping off the silk coat she's saved for such a moment, her hair catching the sunlight, as she looks around for a familiar face, then turns and sees his, such is their attraction of extremes, a collective sigh goes through the cosmos, followed by a whisper of hope—tinged with relief. And danger.

Something strange happens to Joanna. Not the vodka she had earlier to bolster herself—she's used to how that feels. It's this sense of déjà vu. She has no idea about what but absolutely knows, feels it in her parched, shrunken heart, when she sees him. This is he. And from that first moment, they're white powder and rusty metal that's slowly corroding, the heat building until it ignites.

The fireball catches everything in its path, drawing it into the inferno. Only it isn't about love; it's about large and small. And with his handsome, head-turning, commanding ways, no one's ever made her feel smaller. He's powerful, too, and she instinctively feels herself respond, bending and flexing to his every whim. She can't help herself.

She's found it. The beginning of the rest of her life. She can't let him go. She's seen, too, the Joanna-sized space in him that she has to fill.

28

It takes time, but while Jo crawls from the depths toward daylight, Neal's trial draws closer. The assault charge is conclusive enough, according to Laura, though whether he'll be charged with murder is still questionable. The police have various accounts of what happened that night, along with the files Jo found, but the murder weapon has yet to be discovered.

"He may be the prime suspect," she tells me. "And you wouldn't believe the number of people coming forward with axes to grind. From work colleagues to ex-lovers. But the police need more concrete evidence."

She glances at my face. "So many of them, Kate. Seems Neal's upset a lot of people. It does happen, you know—particularly in the case of successful, powerful men, like he is. They think they're invincible, until one day, they take a step too far. And then it all catches up with them."

What she says is completely plausible, yet one thing puzzles me. "It's hard to picture the same person involved with the orphanage."

"Yes, well, seems they'd had enough of him there, too. He left a few months ago—under a cloud. Something clearly happened, though as yet no one's saying what."

"But the charity awards." I'm puzzled. "He was nominated for one at the end of last year. He and Jo were going together, making a weekend of it. Only in the end, he went without her. She got drunk before they'd even left."

"What? I hadn't heard about this."

"That afternoon, apparently, Jo was drinking. Heavily. I'm not sure why. By the time I found her, he'd gone."

Laura's shaking her head. "But if he'd severed his connection to the orphanage, he wouldn't have been nominated—or would he? Maybe it was for past work. Did he win?"

I try to remember the Sunday morning at Jo's, when he came back early. "He didn't actually say." But my brain is whirring. "What if," I say slowly, still thinking, "it was all a facade? He got her drunk rather than tell her the truth—that they'd fired him—then pretended to go alone, only instead spent the weekend with another woman."

Laura frowns. "It would be easy enough to check if he was there or not. Not that it's really relevant to Rosie's murder."

"It's very relevant to Jo, though. He had a way of bulldozing over her. She felt terrible that she ruined that night for him. It might be empowering, especially now, to know that he set it all up."

"Who'd have thought it?" Laura shakes her head again. "You know, you think you can figure people out. Work out what it is that makes them tick. But honestly, Kate, sometimes you can't tell the half of it."

*   *   *

With the trial pending, speculation resurfaces as the press digs up all the dirt it can get on him. The messy trail of affairs and his systematic abuse of women, who until now had chosen silence for their own reasons. Even Jo's history of illness. It leaves the image he's built up over the years in tatters.

"God. What an utter bastard." Rachael's disbelieving. "More fool Joanna for staying with him. She didn't have to, did she?"

"She loved him," I say quietly.

The last straw for me are the unsubstantiated reports that Rosie was pregnant. And suddenly, I'm completely sick of the gossip, the speculation, the lies, every last bit of it.

Still fragile, Jo holds up bravely. "It's lies, all of it. Don't you think I'd have known? Everyone knows what the press is like. I'm not going to let them get to me, Kate."

Head held up, internalizing it the way she does everything.

Maybe the cosmos decides I deserve a break, because two things happen that revive my flagging spirits. First, I'm asked if I'll take on a horse. An ex-racehorse that through no fault of his own has become homeless. And so Shilo arrives, wary and apologetic, wondering how long he'll be staying before he's uprooted to yet another yard, but with honest eyes and a calm way about him, which I instantly warm to.

The second is Grace suddenly comes home.

"I wasn't expecting you for another week!" I hug her,

noticing the unfamiliar car parked outside. "Who drove you?"

As she pulls back, I see her cheeks flush pink. She fixes twinkling eyes on me.

"Now, Mother, you did say you wanted to meet Ned, remember? Well, now you can."

He comes in, tall, tousle-haired, in slouchy jeans and an oversize hoodie, holding out his hand.

"Hi, Mrs. McKay. I hope this is okay. . . . I told Grace she should have called, but I guess you know what she's like. . . ."

His manner is both bumbling and familiar; then he grins as Grace pretends to punch him. I shake his hand, liking him immediately.

"Yes, I do! Hi, Ned. And it's Kate! I'm really pleased to meet you. This is *such* a lovely surprise!" I turn to Grace. "How long are you home?"

"The weekend? If that's okay? Then we were going to Ned's parents for a few days. But I'll definitely be home for Easter, Mum. . . ."

The ground rocks under my feet just for a moment, as I figure both of them are staying, but in separate rooms? Grace's room? It's the first time I've been faced with this, and so out of the blue I don't know what to say. Then quickly decide it doesn't matter—they can work that one out themselves.

The combined presence of Grace and Ned, with Shilo out grazing with my own horses, restores much-needed equilibrium in my soul. I can feel my way in what is once again a hospitable world, with familiar routines of meals that need cooking and rooms tidying. With people.

After a thrown-together lunch of homemade soup and

hastily unfrozen bread, Grace and I walk across the fields to see the horses. Ned stays behind to watch football, so he says. I halfheartedly twist his arm, then silently thank him for this time he gives us alone.

As we approach the horses, they lift their heads and study us. Grace stops.

"It's so weird without him," she says quietly, thinking of Zappa.

We stand, watching them, remembering his majestic presence, each lost in our own thoughts about him. I know Grace felt it, too. Only every so often do you meet a horse that touches your life as he did.

"Come on." I reach for her arm. "Come and meet Shilo."

She wipes away a tear and grins bravely, a grin that wobbles. And as we get nearer, Oz nickers at her and jogs over.

"I've really missed them." She's emotional, far more than she usually is, and I wonder. Is there another first going on here? Is she in love?

"His owner is ill, and no one wanted him." Shilo wanders over, and I stroke his nose. "She has cancer. I've no idea how bad it is. He's here indefinitely, until we know."

"He's sweet." She hesitates. "Mum? Can I ask you something? Is Dad okay? I thought he'd be home this weekend, but when I spoke to him the other day, he said he was staying in York. And he sounded weird." She pauses, and it's as though ten-year-old Grace is beside me, looking up at me with tangled hair and pink cheeks as she reaches for my hand, seeking reassurance.

Fleetingly, I glimpse how it would be to tell my child that everything she'd grown up with, taken for granted, had been swept away by the two people she believed she could always count on. *This,* after Rosie.

"It's just the job. It's taking more of his time than he thought it would." Wondering if she'll notice my voice, overly bright. "Why? What did he say?"

"Not much." She screws up her face. "That's the thing. Usually, he makes bad jokes and asks me loads of questions—you know what he's like—but he hardly said a word."

It's as though the sun's dipped out of this wonderful day, and I shiver. "I expect he was tired, Grace. He's working too hard."

She shrugs. "Maybe."

"Don't worry yourself about the adults! They can take care of themselves. Now, tell me all about Ned." I link my arm through hers, and she smiles, a proper, warm, sunny Grace smile.

"What do you want to know?" She's suddenly cagey.

"Well . . . is he good to you? Are you happy?" Are there any other questions worth asking?

She nods. "I really like him. I think you will, too, when you get to know him. You don't mind, Mum, do you? About him staying?"

"Of course I don't! I'm really pleased."

She's silent, framing the question I already know is coming. "Is it okay . . . if he sleeps in my room?"

"It's fine, Gracie. I did think he might."

"What about Dad?"

"He's not here, is he? And even if he was, don't worry! I'd talk him round."

Though I can imagine how Angus would be about the other man in his daughter's life, checking him out and inevitably finding him lacking, because no boy would ever be good enough for his little girl. *Nice boy, but don't you think . . . ?*

"Cool." Her cheeks flush as she glances behind her. "I better go back and see if Ned's okay." She plants a kiss on Oz's nose and, her child self again, whirls back up toward the house.

Rosie

Joanna looks in the mirror at the face. It's a too-perfect one, nipped and tucked by renowned plastic surgeons, every line, every wrinkle smoothed out, the skin of a twenty-year-old. The worst pain she's known, but worth it.

The face is framed by lustrous, pale, long hair—not her own, but Neal hates short hair, so in the end, she got extensions. It was worth the day it took to have it done—just for Neal's reaction. It was there, on his face. Desire, in big letters. He still wants her.

It's the face of a girl who has everything to live for. One who has the world at her feet, especially when you read about how she lives. It registers only dimly as phony and unimportant before she pushes it from her mind, thrilled she can look like this.

Round her neck is the heavy gold chain. A gift from Neal. He gave it to her just after they were married, as she stood in front of another mirror in another house, feeling his breath against her cheek as he came up behind her and placed it round her neck.

"You're mine, Joanna," he whispered. Words she'd waited so long for, to be wanted, sending adrenaline through her veins like an intravenous shot, that meant she could go through any number of days of self-denial, not eating, enduring increasingly strenuous workouts, all because of him.

"Every time you look at this, think of me," he said softly.

She gazes at it, admiring how slender her neck looks against its weight, how it's the perfect length to wear with anything.

Remembers hearing the tiny metallic click as the catch snapped shut.

Only later glimpsing the back and seeing the padlock.

29

Over the rest of the weekend, missing my husband, I get to know my daughter's lover, liking how he smiles at her, how his eyes follow her, how quickly he learns to navigate his way around the kitchen and make tea for us all. On Saturday night, I book the table by the open fire at the local pub, and over plates of hot food, any awkwardness that remains between us melts away.

As I watch them together, I realize that however much I tell myself otherwise, I wish Angus was here to share this.

When we get home, instead of collapsing in front of a movie with Grace and Ned, I head for my office and, closing the door, call him, hoping with all my heart that he'll pick up. That he'll listen and hear what I want him to hear, that I'm sorry, that I love him and I don't ever want to be without him.

But he doesn't pick up.

As I go back to join them, Grace eyes me anxiously. "You okay, Mum?"

"Fine. I just remembered something I had to do, that was all. Who'd like tea?"

"I'll make it if you like." Ned stretches his arms up and starts unwinding himself from Grace.

"It's okay. You two stay there. I'll do it. You can light the fire." I scurry out before Grace's X-ray eyes see right through me.

I'm bereft when they go. Disproportionately so, considering Grace will be back in only a few days. But I'm in a melancholy mood, and it's a taste of the future I'm seeing. I tell myself I'm doubly blessed to welcome Ned into our circle, but also realize I have to share Grace.

I spend an hour with the horses, who, sensing my mood, are watchful. It's Oz who comes over and thrusts his muzzle into my side as he tries to get to the root of what's bothering me. Feeling no better, I walk back up the field toward the house, self-pitying tears blurring my vision.

I'm at the back door, pulling off my boots, when I hear a car pull up. Quickly, I go inside, wiping my eyes, not wanting to be caught like this, at the same time wondering who on earth could be here. Then my heart quickens as I hear footsteps outside coming toward me and a man's voice that I'd know anywhere.

"Kate?"

"Angus?"

He comes into the kitchen, and I go to him, and then my arms are tightly round him, my face buried against his neck, as slowly I feel his arms go round me. And all the tears I've been bottling up come pouring out of me.

At first, he doesn't notice, then gently pushes me away so he can see my face.

"You're crying," he says. "Please don't cry. I've missed you so much."

"I've missed you, too," I wail. "I'm so sorry, Angus. . . . I didn't do anything, but I'm so sorry I hurt you."

"Shh." He pulls me against him so I feel his chin resting in my hair. "I'm the one who should be sorry, leaving you to cope with everything. . . ."

"But I don't have anything to cope with, do I? Just a friend whose messy life I can't stay out of and Zappa . . ."

But the thought of Zappa finishes me. I can barely say his name before emotion completely overwhelms me.

I discover how big my husband's heart is. How lucky we are, too, that we're better together than apart.

"How long are you home for?" I don't ask him until much later, not wanting to spoil the pleasure of his body against mine in our bed, where we've never needed many words.

"However long you want me here," he says softly, stroking a wisp of my hair off my face.

"What d'you mean?" I prop myself up on my elbows and look at him properly. "Of course I want you here."

He's grave, his face questioning. "For a moment there, I wasn't sure."

I lean forward and kiss him. "I've hated you being away."

"That's good," he says, his eyes a mixture of anxiety and relief. "Because I've finished there. I may have to go back for the odd few days, but that's all. Next time round, I'm going to tell them they'll have to send someone else."

I look at him, feeling his words sinking in and a sense of peace descending on my world.

Rosie

Another snapshot of my parents flashes before me. They really are a perfect match. Complementing each other. As Neal grows stronger and more successful, so Joanna fades and shrinks, the equal and opposite reaction to his every action.

But after a while, it isn't enough. Not for Neal. He wants more power, over her emotions, her life, her happiness, such as it is. Needs to push limits and to control how she feels. See her need for him in her eyes, watch her stabbed with hurt as he rebuffs her. Or use all the tricks in the book to seduce, turn her on, making her body want his, before closing his hands round her neck until her eyes close and the fight goes out of her, so that she has all the desire but none of the release. It's the ultimate control, over whether she breathes or not. Brings a surge of heat like he's never known.

Joanna's kept his sordid, sad little secret. Only this time, I'm witness. To him locking the bedroom door behind them. Dragging Joanna across the room, shoving her against a wall, pinning her there, one hand round her neck while he rips at her clothes, tearing them off her.

While she begs him not to.

"Please, Neal."

Because she's terrified, and she knows what's coming, because he's done it many times before. Knows each time could be her last sound, her last breath.

But she can't stop him.

"Please, Neal, not like this."

He doesn't listen. He can't hear her: he's lost in her pain, her fear, just holds her neck with both hands and pushes into her.

This is where I want to shut my eyes, long for the picture to be sliced in two, my father in one half, taken away, those hands torn off first, then his tongue. I try to pull him off her. I scream at him to leave her, that he's a vile monster everyone hates. How is it they can't hear their own daughter?

But they don't, and I'm forced to watch as it just goes on for what seems like forever, in hideous slow motion, as he squeezes tighter round her neck, pushes harder, until her eyes bulge and her head lolls over. Until the noise stops.

A silence that holds its breath is broken by a whimpering sound, coming from the small figure slumped on the floor against the wall. It gives way to a hoarse crying, because her throat is so sore, her neck red and throbbing. She's alone. He's downstairs with his whiskey bottle, and I sit beside her, stroke her hair, tell her she has to leave him. "This isn't love. There isn't a name for what he does to you."

But she can't hear, just reminds herself how lucky she is, even though she fears him, fears the pain he causes her, the marks he leaves both on her skin and so much deeper, underneath.

He loves her, doesn't he? How long she's waited to feel like this. So desired. So perfect. So minutely small. She winds one of those scarves round her neck, thinking how much she has to lose. How many scarves she has. How she's married an amazing man.

The baby isn't planned, not this first one. She knows they'll have a family, just not yet. She isn't ready, anxious at how her skin is already stretching and her belly is swollen, at how her shape is out of her control, and how the small foot that protrudes ripples not just her skin but her heart.

There's conflict, between the baby and her looks, because looks are not about the brightness of her eyes or the glow her skin has or the new life she's carrying; they're about the size she has become.

And she's frightened.

Doesn't know if she can do this.

Each day her fear grows, but in the end, she doesn't have to. The pain comes too early, when the baby's too small, with lungs that can't breathe. I watch as the light in her eyes that shone briefly fades with the baby's heartbeat. With the heartbreak of touching him, holding him, then losing him. Seeing him for the first time, so strong and handsome. So pure.

The baby she wanted only when she'd lost him.

But he's more.

He's the brother I didn't know I had.

30

Angus has two weeks' leave before he goes back to work—this time in London. Grace comes home for Easter and brings Ned with her. I start to ride Shilo. And as my happiness blooms with the earliest bluebells, for the first time I realize how fragile it is.

Just before the trial is due to begin, one of the papers runs a full-page story leaving no one in any doubt as to Neal's guilt. According to their source, before Rosie died, she had a row with Neal, just as Alex said. Neal left the house in a drunken rage, blundered back in, still blind drunk, just before dawn, after luring his daughter into the woods, where he stabbed her.

Horrific though the truth is, it seems to give Jo the impetus to face her demons, and just a week later, she comes home.

"I'm taking her some food," I tell Angus. "Because otherwise she won't eat. And I promise I won't be long."

"Look, it's okay, Kate. Take as long as you like. She really needs you at the moment. I understand."

I walk over to where he's sitting and lean down, brushing my lips against his. "And so do you. We have months to catch up on, remember?"

He grasps my arm and pulls me onto his lap, a gleam in his eye. "If we did the catching-up bit now, you could always see her later. . . ."

"Sorry." I kiss him, then twist away. "She's expecting me, I'm afraid. But definitely later . . ." I blow him another kiss.

Jo's front door is open, which is unlike her, but as she tells me, she has nothing to hide. All she wants now is a fresh start.

"I've thought long and hard about this," she says, "but I think it's best if I sell the house, Kate. I've talked to Delphine about it. We agree. . . . Too much has happened here."

"But can you do that? Before the trial's over?"

"I'm seeing a lawyer. If I can't sell, I'll rent it out. Anyway, I need to think about money." Taking a breath, a flicker of panic in her eyes.

"But where will you go?" Even though I understand that she can't afford to stay here, my emotions are mixed.

She looks sad. "I don't know. In a way, I don't want to leave. Mostly because of you. It may sound strange, but you're the only real friend I have. I'm thinking about Devon . . . nearer to Carol, because Delphine's really fond of her. Or somewhere completely new. I haven't decided."

"Are you sure, Jo? Wouldn't it be better to give it some time, feel stronger, before you make any important decisions?"

"That's the problem," she says softly. "I think that as long as I'm here, what's happened will always be holding me back." Then she smiles bravely. "Come and have some tea."

As we sit in her kitchen, she tells me about the therapy she's been having.

"I started to face up to a lot of things while I was in there, Kate. About my childhood. How it affected my marriage. My health, too. God, look at the state of me!" She says it self-deprecatingly, picking up the loose fabric of her clothes, under which she's skin and bones. "Neal and I brought out the worst in each other. I do see that. I know how it must have looked from the outside, too, but if I'm honest, in a strange way we complemented each other. I wanted what he had to give. I wanted him, and there was a price. But there always is, isn't there?"

Is she right? Is it impossible to have it all? Did Jo crave Neal's love so much, she'd do anything, even suffer his abuse?

I'm reminded of how I felt when Zappa died. *Zappa's life for my marriage* was what I'd thought. Jo's doing what I did, mistakenly balancing emotional books. And she's wrong.

"She's planning to sell the house," I tell Angus, watching the flames from the fire casting shadows on the walls.

"Really?" He sounds surprised. "I thought from everything you'd said, it was Neal who was always on the move, not Jo."

"I thought so, too. But you can understand it, can't you? There are too many bad memories in that place. And round here, too." I hesitate. "You know . . ." I reach a hand out, gently touching his arm. "We still haven't really talked, have we? About while you were away. Do you think we should?"

And there it is again, between us. Suddenly, I'm nervous.

He sighs. "I was bloody jealous, Kate. But when I got over it, I trusted you. I've never had any reason not to— only, I suppose trust just got lost along the way."

I pause. Do I ask? If I don't, it will always be there, rearing its ugly head whenever we argue. "Angus? Was there something? With Ally?"

Again he sighs. Hesitates, which tells me all I need to know. Feeling physically sick, I lean forward to get up and walk away from him, but he grabs my arm tightly. "There wasn't. But she wanted there to be. We got a bit drunk one night. She tried to kiss me, then realized her mistake. . . . That's all. That's why I booked the hotel. . . . I hoped you'd never know."

I'm quiet, thinking that if Neal hadn't kissed me, I *so* wouldn't get this. For the first time, I tell him the full story of what happened.

"It doesn't make it right, but it was a weird time. You weren't here. Or Grace, of course. And then Jo went on her IT course. I thought it was neighborly to invite Neal and Delphine over."

Angus's jaw clenches. "Well, I'm sure it was. Only, Neal has his own definition of *neighborly.*"

"To be honest, I'm not sure he didn't set it up," I say slowly. "I talked to Laura. She couldn't believe I didn't see it coming."

He raises his eyebrows. "You told her?"

I nod. "I had to talk to someone. I felt so guilty, Angus."

He's silent. "You know what? You did nothing wrong, Kate. It *was* a weird time, but it's behind us. We're together. We've survived it, and that's what matters. Now, come here."

I wonder at what cost those words come. On the sofa, I snuggle closer to him, but in the silence, my ears prick up at the faint sound of footsteps on the gravel.

"Someone's outside."

Then there's the distinctive click of the letter box snapping shut.

"Just a moment . . ." I unfold myself from his arms and walk out to the kitchen, a hollow feeling in the pit of my stomach, throw open the door, stare outside into the darkness. But like before, there's only silence. I close it again.

Then I see it on the floor. Another envelope.

I take it through to Angus.

"If this is what I think it is, it's the third," I tell him.

He takes it from me, opens it, and frowns.

Not everything is what it seems.

"What's that supposed to mean?"

"There were two others," I tell him. "I've given them to the police. The first was, 'If you only knew the truth.' Then, a few days later, a second arrived. 'In a world of people, I'm alone.'" Words ingrained on my mind. "It must be to do with Rosie, don't you think?"

"It's hardly likely to be anything else, is it?"

"Laura thinks there's a slim chance it's someone local just stirring up trouble because I'm friends with Jo. She says there are people who do that kind of thing."

"Maybe." Angus is thoughtful. "She might be right. . . . But what if she's not? What if someone out there knows something?"

And though I know the likelihood is he's wrong, just hearing him say that sends a shiver down my spine.

I take the note back from him. "I'll call Sergeant Beauman tomorrow."

Angus nods silently, then takes my hand, pulls me toward him. "So, Mrs. McKay, you know what you said earlier on? About this lost time we have to make up for? How about now?"

Rosie

When they're first together, they go to parties, Joanna and Neal. Flirting, dancing, and laughing together, Neal whirling her round the floor while everyone watches, wanting a piece of them, wanting to know them, wanting the sparkle to rub off on their own gray-brown lives.

I watch my family take shape, piece by perfect, carefully chosen piece, each placed next to the last. The handcrafted chair that's the latest thing. The state-of-the-art kitchen, a modern wonder of polished steel and granite. The designer lamp. The contemporary art on the walls. One perfect daughter, then another. The best schools. The perfect friends.

And from the outside, you see the big house on the quiet, private lane, windows newly painted, lawns mown, flower beds in bloom. The gravel drive, so everyone hears the flash cars coming and going. You might catch a glimpse, too, of a girl's face framed by pale hair. If you get close enough, you'll see the look in her eyes is indecipherable. That whatever's going on is on the inside.

Neal and Joanna are not like everyone else. They have

such wonderful lives. How pretty they are, how charming, how much energy they radiate. He has a car men envy; their house is like a show home. But a family needs the invisible bits that hold it all together. The nuts and bolts and glue that come from strains of laughter, like music in your ears, or from the sharing of secrets and dreams, more precious than jewels.

And if you don't have these, if you don't have love, then over time it all drifts apart—the fancy house with all the stuff in it, flimsy as snowflakes. I watch a beautiful painting as its colors run, then fade to a blur of gray; a sofa go up in flames; a budding flower bloom, then shrivel and die, while the exotic holidays pop like bubbles, leaving soap-scum memories, and the family that has no gravity just floats.

Delphine

I don't know when it arrives. Whether it's blown in on the breeze or in a dream. But her name is in my head, with the screaming inside that's always there, that no one hears. With all the hate, the lies, and the truth.

I need her to help me.

Kate.

Rosie

I watch Joanna's world shift imperceptibly to one of scalding heat and hypothermic cold. Needle sharpness and invisible softness. Blinding days, and nights so dark, they suffocate her. Cruelty she doesn't notice until yet again it escalates. He shocks her, hurts her more than last time. For Joanna, and for Neal, too, there are only extremes.

But she stays. Her own personal triumph of hope over reality. That's what she tells herself proudly, not seeing that really it's a triumph of denial.

"Poor Neal, he doesn't mean it. He had such a difficult childhood, you know. He can't help himself. He's been through so much. Yes, he drinks too much sometimes, but we all do, don't we? And it's my fault, too. If I hadn't upset him, he wouldn't have got so angry.

"He's no worse than a lot of men.

"I know, in his own way, he loves me."

* * *

The heavy gold chain he gave her, the one she loves because it makes her look slender, the one that's pad-locked round her neck, they've lost the key. So she's found her dark glasses and shut out the world. Even if she wanted to, there's nothing she can do. She can't leave him.

And why would she? Where would she go, and to whom? There's no one, not since Amy. Only, Amy didn't understand, not really. She's not like Joanna. She's strong and clever. Has a job and her own house, while Joanna doesn't even have her own bank account. But why would she need one?

And there are the girls to think of. They need their fa-ther, don't they? Especially when their mother's so frag-ile. Joanna knows that she's weak, that she relies on Neal to keep their house, all their things, their world safe. That, as he constantly reminds her, she could never man-age without him. He takes care of everything. Including her. She needs to get herself together—he's always telling her that, too. To stop ruining all their lives. She's so lucky she has him, isn't she? Not many men would put up with her.

What she needs to do is think less about herself and more about him. It's not his fault she's not happy. Some people never are—and, anyway, real life isn't about hap-piness. It's about taking the rough with the smooth. The good with the bad. About making a go of her marriage, no matter what happens.

As she's said more times than she can remember, he's an amazing man. He needs her. She needs to be needed. And unlike other people, she can see beyond his brutality to the complicated, compassionate man underneath, so deserving of the unselfish, giving kind of love not many people have to offer. She's good at that. It's the same when her children are ill, when she brings them pills, mops their forehead, fusses over them. Keeps them there as long as she can, because at times like this her life is easy, her purpose valid. They're small and helpless and need her.

"Only we're not small. We're growing up!" I want to shout at her. "I'll leave, then, Della. You can't keep us here."

But she doesn't think about that. Nothing must change— because if it does, if no one needs her, what else is there?

31

True to her word, Jo's lawyer gets Neal to consent, and the house goes on the market. The fact that it happens so quickly makes me wonder how stretched they are financially. Straight away, people want to view it, throwing her into the mother of all panics.

"But I'm not ready!" she cries, running her hands through her hair, knocking her sunglasses onto the floor. She often wears them, even on the dullest day. "Half of me doesn't even want them here, prying into our lives. Everyone knows about us. They believe the gossip, don't they? I've told the agent to give me a few days."

It's exactly what she said last week. I wonder if perhaps she's having second thoughts.

"Jo, you really don't have to do this. Not yet. Put it off, even if only for a couple of months, but give yourself a break."

"But I have to, Kate." Her eyes are desperate. "Can't you see? I need the money. And as long as I stay, it's like living with a ghost."

She doesn't say whose ghost. But the more I try to reason with her, the more upset she gets, and in the end, I let it go.

"You could at least let me tidy your garden," I tell her. "Nothing major. Just cut the grass, prune the shrubs a bit. It's surprising what a difference it makes."

I can see her thinking about it. She glances outside. "Are you sure? You're so busy. I hate to ask."

"You didn't ask. I offered. It won't take me long. I'll pop in tomorrow, when I get a free couple of hours, if you don't mind me letting myself in?"

"I'll probably be here," she says, hesitating. "But if I'm not, that's so kind, Kate. Thank you."

"I can help, Mummy." It's Delphine, standing in the doorway. Neither of us had noticed her there.

"Oh!" Jo looks flustered again. "Don't worry, honey. . . . I think we're almost there."

"But there's the garage. I could tidy in there."

An odd look crosses Jo's face. "I don't think we need to worry about that. People don't care what's in your garage, do they? Before we move, I'll get someone in to clear it."

"No, Mummy. You can't do that. Remember my old books are in there?"

"They're upstairs, aren't they? I'm sure they are. . . . Why don't you go and have a look?"

"Would you like some help, Delphine?" She stands alone, this child. I've never seen Jo touch her, cuddle her, or any visible display of affection between them.

Delphine hesitates. Then it's as though something unspoken flows between her and Jo before she turns back to me. "Thank you, but I think I can manage."

*   *   *

The next day, when I go back to work on Jo's garden, the house is locked and Jo's car isn't there. I let myself in through the side gate, as we agreed, and get to work.

A couple of hours in, I realize there's far more work needed than I'd thought. The lawn's freshly mown stripes give it an instant face-lift, but everywhere I look, there's something else. After hunting around for a wheelbarrow, I start on the flower beds nearest the house, imagining most potential buyers won't venture much farther, only the trouble is, once I've done them, the rest looks even worse.

There's no sign of a compost heap. In need of something large to hold all the weeds, I go to get some gardening sacks from my car. Only, as I pass the garage, I glance in the window, to see a pile just inside, on the floor.

I try the door. It's unlocked, so I let myself in. In spite of what Jo said, it's the tidiest garage I've ever seen. A pair of shelves at one end hold one or two pots and what I imagine are the books that belong to Delphine. Other than that, there's hardly anything in here. Apart from the suitcases of Neal's clothes, there are boxes, gardening tools, and an old cupboard.

As I bend down to pick up the gardening sacks, I don't hear anyone, but I'm suddenly aware of someone close behind me. As I stand up and turn round, I'm face-to-face with Jo.

"God! You gave me the fright of my life! I was just getting these!" I wave the empty bags at her.

"How did you get in?" If I didn't know her better, I'd say the look on her face was hostile. Behind her, Delphine appears.

"Hi! The door was open. I didn't think you'd mind.

There's more to do out there than I realized. I thought I'd take the rubbish away to save you the trouble."

"I don't understand," she says, turning to her daughter. "Delphine locked it just before we went out, didn't you?"

Delphine nods.

I shrug. "Maybe the lock stuck or something. Anyway, I ought to get on."

Jo seems to snap out of whatever it is that's preoccupying her. "Yes. Of course. Sorry. You just surprised me, that's all. I'll put the kettle on and make us some tea."

"That would be great."

As I go back to my pruning, the irony strikes me that for all Neal's controlling ways, Jo, too, seems to like her life just so. The garden, however, gets the better of me. I make it halfway along the first border before deciding the rest will have to wait for another day.

As I stand up and stretch my aching back, the little apple tree catches my eye. It hasn't flowered the way it ought to, and the leaves that are unfurling are yellowed and unhealthy looking. And I wonder, *If I replaced it, would she even notice?*

Laura stops by unexpectedly with the news that the trial starts next month.

"Do you know if Jo will have to be there?" It's a question I don't dare ask Jo.

"Almost certainly. She's a key witness, isn't she?"

"I'm really worried about what it will do to her." It's too soon for her. She's too fragile.

"I know. Same."

"You'd think . . ." I hesitate. "Nothing's changed, has it? I mean, it's obvious enough Neal's guilty . . . isn't it?"

Laura raises her eyebrows. "Are you thinking about Alex again?"

Suddenly, I'm less sure. "Maybe . . . I don't know. Only, you read about innocent people being convicted. . . . What if Neal's not the murderer?"

"There's nothing innocent about Neal Anderson. Anyway, the trial will consider absolutely everything." She hesitates; then a look of surprise dawns on her face. "Oh my God. You're thinking about the notes."

Rosie

I watch Joanna stare at her reflection. Everything he said was true. The lines, the circles under her eyes, skin pulled too tight over jutting cheekbones. She sees ugliness. Ugly face, ugly hair, ugly everything, not the person inside, who's terrified of being without him, nor does she see the beauty in softness. She's become a caricature, unlike other women, for whom beauty is so natural and effortless.

She's fat, too. Look at her arms, at the loose skin under her chin. Pinching the nonexistent flesh round her middle, she feels the familiar curl of self-hatred inside her. She's hideous. No wonder he pushed her away.

She rubs her cheeks, trying to lure color into them, then stretches out imaginary wrinkles toward her hairline, picturing a surgeon's knife slicing into the pale skin, lifting it, creating perfection. How can she do that, repeatedly enduring the pain? But it's worth it, ten, twenty times over. Anything is, to be with him.

But it's too late now. He doesn't want her. But then,

she lost him a long time ago to younger, longer-limbed versions of herself, like the models on the pages of Vogue.

She's turned a blind eye to them, because that way, they go away—eventually. Only, this one's different. Serious. She's seen photos of them, online or in the press, the woman standing almost beside him or just behind him. Caught him whispering into his phone. Read the texts that leave nothing to the imagination. Private, explicit messages that he leaves for her to find, knowing they're like bullets or knives through her heart, laughing his cruel laugh, ridiculing her.

Joanna has dreaded this day. This woman's like she herself was not that long ago. Neal's type. Young, tall, beautiful, making him look good. Shouting to other men that he's better and more attractive than any of them.

Which he is. She's always known that. Whether you like him or not, he stands out from each and every one of them. Not for his cruelty or the abuse he inflicts on us. It's his looks alongside his confidence, his easy way with people. I've seen him do it too many times. Watched Joanna crippled by his betrayal as he approaches someone, engages them in conversation, maybe laughs a little, places a hand lightly on their arm, watching them, not missing an eyeblink, as they fall eternally under his spell.

Joanna's still staring in the mirror. It's exactly what he did to her. From the moment they met, he'd made her feel like the only woman in the world for him. He was the first man she'd really loved with every fiber of her being. Enough to sacrifice who she was and to endure the pain of the surgeon's knife. That's love, isn't it? But it doesn't matter how much you want someone; love isn't always enough. And now, if he leaves her, as he's told her so many times, she's nothing.

Her eyes wander toward the bottle of pills prescribed by her doctor to help her sleep. This is what she's been reduced to. An ugly face and a bottle of pills. She hasn't taken a single one—until now.

Like her body, her choices have shrunk. What else can she do?

"Don't!" I want to scream. "Don't let him do this to you. What about Della? Think of Della. . . ."

I can only watch as slowly she reaches toward them and unscrews the lid.

32

"Blimey!" Angus is reading the Sunday paper. We have a ritual as old as our marriage, which involves fresh coffee, scrambled eggs, and two or three Sunday papers at the garden table in summer or in front of the fire in winter.

Today is neither, however. Warm enough for the garden, but it's raining, so it's the sofa in front of an empty fireplace.

"What?"

"I know you're not supposed to believe everything you read, but it says here that a couple of months before Rosie died, Jo took an overdose. I thought that happened more recently? Didn't she do it when you were staying with Grace?"

"She did. . . . Can I see?"

He passes over one of the supplements, folded open at an article entitled "Family Guy." I skim through it, deciding in the first few lines that it's total rubbish.

"It says Neal was thrown off the orphanage project because he seduced one of the residents. An underage teenage girl." I look at Angus. "Surely even he wouldn't do that?"

"Probably crap," he says.

"If Jo did take an overdose, maybe it's because she'd discovered what he was up to," I say loyally. "I didn't know her that well then, did I?"

"I guess not." Angus picks up another section of paper and starts reading. "Bloody hell, Kate. Did you know—"

"*Angus!* Shh, darling! I'm actually trying to read something myself."

"Just thought you might be interested," he says huffily.

"I know, darling, and it's very sweet, but—"

"Annoying," he says, then lapses into silence.

Then I read something that utterly astounds me. "Oh my God!"

Angus raises an eyebrow in my general direction, but I can't stop myself.

"It says here Jo's the daughter of acclaimed scientist Edward Pablo. I can't believe it. Everyone's heard of that man, and she's never mentioned him. In fact, she never talks about either of her parents. . . ."

"Maybe they fell out," says Angus reasonably. "Come to think of it, I haven't heard anything about him for years."

I wouldn't know. I don't read papers to the extent that Angus does. Then a curious thought strikes me, because as well as not mentioning her family, Jo hasn't a single photo on show anywhere in her house.

I take it up with her, of course. "Don't you have any photos?"

"What photos?"

"Family ones. You know, like of the girls . . ."

"We used to have a few. I took them down after Rosanna . . . It was too upsetting."

"What about your parents, Jo?"

She turns and stares at me. "What about them?"

I shake my head, feeling stupid, deciding to just come
out with it. "Sorry. It was just that I read this article about
your father being Edward Pablo. I'd no idea. He was a
great man, wasn't he?"

I'm half expecting her to deny it, explain it away as
more rubbish from the press, but to my astonishment, she
doesn't. "It's true. He was my father. He and my mother
died five years ago. I prefer not to talk about it."

"God." I'm horrified. "I'm so sorry, Jo. How awful for
you."

"It was awful at the time. But don't be too sorry, Kate.
He was a vile, cruel man."

It's an assessment of her father that leaves me wanting
to know more, but after that, her lips are sealed. She clearly
has no wish to talk about him and changes the subject, as
she does if I mention the trial.

"Well, at least now the house is straight."

"When do the viewings start?"

"Next week. But the agent's dealing with them. I don't
want to be here when they look round."

I imagine the queue of strangers pointing, whispering
behind her back. Bad enough when she goes out, but not
actually here, in her own home.

"Have you found anywhere to go and look at?"

"Not really. I spoke to Carol. We might go and stay
there—just for a while. When the house is sold."

Even now, I get a sense of Rosie's presence, usually
when I'm with the horses. It no longer shocks me. I've an

open enough mind to believe that if a sufficiently strong bond exists in this dimension, it could just as easily overlap with the next. And then, one afternoon, my heart nearly stops when I glimpse a back view of her across the field.

I rub my eyes, then see another flash as her pale hair catches the sunlight between the trees, and I realize this is no ghost. *Is it Rosie?* Has there been a mistake? Could she be alive?

Wondering if I'm hallucinating, then realizing with amazement that it's Delphine, I start running. Oz immediately throws his head in the air and follows, and soon all three horses catch up, then overtake me, closing on the still-running figure.

Then, as I get nearer, just as I call out, thinking the horses are going to gallop into her, she stops, spins round, and faces them. Just in time, they shy away, snorting, circling her, but not going any closer. At last reaching her, I grab her arm.

"What are you doing? You might have got kicked." *Or worse,* I'm thinking, but I don't tell her that.

"I didn't know. I don't know about horses." Delphine's defiant. Self-possessed and scarily calm.

"Judging from what I saw just there, I'd say you do." I speak sternly, a little guiltily, too, as I remember how I used to welcome Rosie here. But then, Rosie would never behave like that. She never took anything for granted.

"I didn't mean to upset them." She watches them, calm, as now that the excitement's over, they wander off to graze.

"I don't think they were too upset. They were just having a bit of fun with you, like they do with each other, only sometimes they get a little carried away. Take Shilo, for example, the biggest one. He has no idea how long his legs are. When he lets fly with them, it's high spirits. He's not trying to get you, but it's not his fault if you happen to be in his way."

She nods. "You have to think like them, don't you? That's what Rosie said."

"Did she? She was right. She was good with them. They liked her."

"She told me." Delphine nods again. "I wish I could learn. Only, I don't think Mummy would let me."

I forget my irritation with her then, remembering she's a young girl whose only family is a mother who's barely coping with her own problems.

"Why not? I could ask her for you. . . . I know you're moving, but that might not be for quite a while."

I see something new in Delphine's eyes. Something raw and pure. Like hope.

"Can you? She'll probably say no. . . ."

"Leave it to me. I have an idea."

The next time I see Jo, I know exactly how to play it.

"Jo? Can I ask you a favor? With Grace away and all the time I've spent on your garden, I'm really behind with my own chores. Could I borrow Delphine, d'you think? I need help with the things I always do at this time of year, and if I don't, the season gets away from me. And there are the horses to exercise, too, if we have time. . . ."

Jo frowns. "You should have said. I'm so sorry. I hadn't realized. But I don't think Delphine would be much help. She doesn't know anything about horses."

"Oh, it's mostly stuff like sweeping out the hay store and cleaning out the tack room. We probably won't ride, but if by any chance we do, I can lend her Grace's gear."

Jo hesitates. I've no idea what her objections are, but she's clearly looking for an excuse of some kind.

"It might be good for her. A change of scene. She's had a lot to cope with, hasn't she?" This time my sentiments are genuine.

"Okay. Thank you, Kate. You're right."

"Great! Well, this Saturday, then, if you've no plans. Here she is! Would you like to tell her, or shall I?"

Playing along, Delphine looks quizzically at first Jo, then me.

"Kate asked if you'd be able to help her on Saturday."

There's not a flicker on Delphine's face.

"Only if you want to," I add, puzzled. "Otherwise, I'll manage. Don't worry."

"Okay," she says, looking blank.

It remains a mystery as to why in front of her mother, Delphine is so emotionless, as well as why Jo is so reluctant. She calls me on Friday night and says that the weather forecast isn't too good, that Delphine has a bit of a cold, and that maybe it would be prudent to put it off until a better day. In the end, I persuade her to wait and see what the morning brings.

When I awake the next day, the sun is rising in a clear sky. I call Jo and tell her we're on.

Jo drops her over, looking far from happy about it, but once she's left, I discover that Delphine's not as different from her sister as I'd previously thought. More self-possessed, certainly, especially given her age, but then after what's happened in her family, it's hardly surprising.

"What are we going to do?"

"Oh, ride, I think, don't you? I've dug out Grace's old riding clothes, and we'll find you a hat. Is that okay with you?"

She nods her head, looking pleased. "It is. Thank you."

I show her where the spare room is so she can change; then we pull on boots and head down to the yard, where I tack up Reba because she's rock solid, while Delphine watches me.

"Did Rosie ride her?" she asks.

"She did. But only once. I offered to give her lessons, too, but she didn't want to. I don't know why."

The same reason Delphine thought Jo wouldn't let her come here? I glance at her, looking for clues, but under the peak of her riding hat, the expressionless look is back.

Throughout the day she spends with me, she lowers her guard just once, when she has finished riding and slides off Reba.

"You can stroke her nose," I tell her. "She likes that."

But as Delphine walks round to the front of her, Reba lowers her head, then presses it so gently against Delphine. I watch Delphine's arms go round her, and Reba's eyes close with bliss. They stay like that for minutes, neither of them moving, until Delphine looks up, a single tear rolling down her cheek.

And just like with Rosie, I don't ask and she doesn't explain.

Rosie

Even without Alex, it would have come to this. Alex. That he's here, working in her garden, earning Neal's money, casting his filthy, all-knowing eyes over her daughter, tortures her.

It obsesses her, too. What time does he arrive? If she pretends she's going out, then slips back inside and watches from behind the curtains, she sees him digging, pruning, planting what he's chosen, which isn't impressive enough. Not nearly. Not for the Andersons.

But she must focus on the man, not the plants. See his head turn, his eyes linger when I take him a cup of tea. The easy way he talks to me, which makes my face light up. His carefully measured questions, only gently pushing as he tries to get to know me, to understand. Watch his every move as I slip from my past to my future.

He's so blatant, Joanna thinks. He doesn't hide it, not even here, on her property. Why should he, when he doesn't know there's anyone to hide from? Not like her, behind the curtain, inside her spitting blood, feeling a lifetime's rigidly contained fury explode as she watches his familiarity. But she somehow holds it in, because she knows. If she sends him away, it'll happen somewhere else with someone else. Somewhere she won't be able to watch.

So Joanna composes herself. Stills her shaking, quelling the volcano inside herself, because everything has to look perfect.

And it takes everything she has. She's not like Neal. Doesn't have that iron strength, or that way he has of arranging his face, the tilt of his head, the set of his chin. Joanna needs the surgeon to adjust the mask. She finds the right person to do the right thing, and her problems are solved.

Was it last week that Neal told her that he was going to the dinner without her? That she wasn't to bother getting dressed up like some tired, try-hard, old tramp, that he had someone more worthy to take his arm? Someone who knew how to please him, who didn't complain, didn't demand, but understood how he was and truly loved him?

He told her that, didn't he? Was it last week, last month, last year? Or did she dream it? She can't remember, fact and fantasy blurred into a delicious, delirious make-believe. And Rosanna and that boy—did she dream that, too?

And now he's told her he's leaving her. That's not a dream. She remembers the ice-cold feeling when he told her. How she begged him to stay, telling him how much she loved him.

"But how can you, when you don't have a heart?" he told her. "In there," he said, prodding her chest, "you have a credit card that's up to its limit, Joanna." He watched her flinch with every word. "And all you've given

me in return is anger, pain, and ugly, stupid children who don't know how lucky they are. Now it's time to pay the bill."

 But so far, he is still here. Just. Maybe it's not too late.

 She can make the girls thinner and more beautiful. Make them study. Buy them new clothes. Get the house re-decorated. Change her hair, flatter him, remind him about the threesome he wanted to try and she refused, because now she'll do it. She'll do anything he says to make things perfect.

 It's like she always says.

 When you want something, there's always a price.

33

"You were so helpful today," I say to Delphine when I
drop her home.

Her eyes shine back at me. "I really enjoyed it. Especially the riding."

"We'll do it again, I promise," I tell her. "In fact, why
don't I come in? I could talk to your mum now."

"I think she's going out," Delphine says, the blankness
back as she gazes out the window toward the house. "But
I would like to. Thank you."

She gets out, and I watch her go inside. There's no
sign of Jo. I wonder if she's really going out or if Delphine had some other reason for me not to go in with her.
Deciding I'm reading far too much into all of this, I turn
the car around and go home.

Then, a few days later, another of those notes gets posted
through my letter box while I'm out. And this one makes
my spine tingle.

When he gets in from work, I show it to Angus.

"I'm sorry, but that's far more sinister than a nutter talking." Surely, this time he has to agree.

He frowns. "Maybe. Show it to Laura. If anyone knows about nutters, she does."

I go to get the phone.

"Why not leave it till tomorrow," suggests Angus. "It's getting late."

But I don't want to. I'm freaked out by this one. When I call her, Laura is, too.

"You need to give it to the police," she says.

"I know. I'll call them first thing tomorrow."

I don't sleep well. I've a horrible, chilling picture in my head of someone quite calculating sending these notes to me. But why to me? Why should I be able to help? Or do I know something no one else does?

At two, I am still wide awake and, in the end, get up and go downstairs. The wind has picked up, the leaves tapping against the windows.

I pick up the note and read it again.

> *Three little babies sitting on a bed.*
> *One dies, another dies.*
> *The third baby doesn't want to die.*

Is it even to do with Rosie? What other baby died? Who is the third baby?

Leaning against the Aga, I shiver.

What is it I don't know?

"It's got to be related to Rosie's murder." Sergeant Beauman frowns as she reads the note. "Obviously, we can't be certain, but when you put them all together. . . ."

"I know." That's exactly what I've been thinking.

She nods. "It looks the same, but I'll take this and check it against the other notes. Let me know if there are any more."

I leave the note with her, then go straight home, what seem like only minutes passing before Laura turns up..

"Do you have a minute, Kate? Only you won't believe what I've found out. According to my contact, when I told her about the note, she told me there was another baby. Joanna gave birth to a baby boy. Before Rosie. Three months early. He was stillborn. Whoever wrote the notes obviously knows. And the police will know about it. If a child dies—in this case Rosie—any other deaths in the family would be flagged up, too, as a matter of course."

"Which includes Jo's parents, then."

Laura frowns. "What about them?"

"Well, they died. About five years ago. She told me only recently."

"Are you sure?"

I nod. "She didn't want to talk about them. Something about her father being 'vile' and 'cruel,' I think her words were."

"Interesting," says Laura. "Only, her father's Edward Pablo, isn't he? According to the records I checked, Mr. and Mrs. Edward Pablo are very much alive and living in Switzerland."

Our eyes meet.

"So why the lies?" I ask.

"I'm guessing she meant they were dead to her. Maybe they fell out and never made it up."

I shake my head. "It didn't sound like that. I said something about it being awful. She said it was, at the time."

"She could have been talking about a row," suggests Laura.

Could she? As I replay the conversation in my head, I wonder if maybe Laura's right.

"On the downside, we're still no closer to finding out who sent the notes," says Laura. "Is there a pattern to when they arrive?"

I shake my head. "Not that I can think of."

She shrugs. "There's one other thing. I'm going to try to see Neal. Apparently, that rumor about him seducing an underage girl was just that, a rumor, spread around by a jealous colleague because his wife had a bit of a thing for him. He was genuinely nominated for that award. Did you know that? I looked into it."

An image of Jo, excited, radiant, comes into my head, followed by another, of the ripped remains of her beautiful dress.

"So many people have it in for him," Laura goes on. "But then, if you go around seducing other men's wives, I suppose it's inevitable."

"It wasn't a secret from Jo. She knew what he got up to."

Laura nods. "What some people will put up with . . . Don't you wonder why?"

Rosie

It's the look in his eyes as they flicker down my body. His daughter's body.

It's when he comes in late, whiskey on his breath, the cruelty in his eyes, Joanna enduring his fingers rammed inside her too hard, then his body crushing on top of hers as he forces his way into her. While she grits her teeth against the dry, rasping pain, because he wants this.

Why isn't it different? Why can't she see the same light in her own eyes as she sees in mine? The light she can't look away from, even though it blinds her to look at it, because it comes from love. It haunts her that it makes my face beautiful in a way hers never can be. That she is too scarred, has too much pain.

And when he's done all that, he goes again. "To another meeting," he always tells her, his phone switched off for hours, sometimes days. Comes home, another hotel bill for her to find, left deliberately in his jacket pocket, more texts for her to find on his phone. The pretense has stopped now, of caring, of belonging, of wanting her. That's when she decides.

She has to take matters into her own hands. Do whatever it takes to remind him how much he needs her. Because she needs him. She can't live without him, even though there is no love in her husband's soul, only lust, ambition, pride.

She thinks of the pills, only that's too easy. And it's too soon. Leaves too much behind that's unresolved. There are lessons to be learned, debts to be paid. And as she's learned from the master himself, there's no room for imperfection.

34

June

May turns to early June, with talk of a long, hot summer ahead of us. Work quietens a little. After a wet spring, the rush of lush growth has slowed to a more leisurely, manageable rate.

In just three weeks' time, Grace will be home for the summer, and for now, I'm content to look no further ahead and just enjoy the prospect. She's not yet said if Ned's joining her.

I'm still thinking about them, picking salad leaves in the veg patch, when the phone rings.

"Hello? I hope I have the right number. . . . Could I speak to Kate?"

"This is Kate McKay. How can I help?"

Not recognizing the voice, I instantly assume it's a potential client. Only it isn't.

"Oh, thank goodness. Kate, my name's Carol. I'm Neal Anderson's sister."

"Hi! Carol . . ." I'm not sure what to say, but she carries on.

"I'm so sorry, Kate, to call you like this. I hope you don't mind. I know you're friends with Joanna, but . . ." She hesitates. "I'm terribly worried about Delphine."

On this lovely day, a chill comes over me.

"Go on."

"She called me. Last week. She said her mother wasn't well—again. I don't know if you're aware of Joanna's . . . *problems?*"

"I think so. But since she came home, she's been quite good, I thought."

"Is she eating?" Carol sounds worried. "You do know she doesn't eat? Just drinks?"

"Oh, I don't think so. We do go out now and then. She doesn't eat much, but she always has something."

There's silence. "Does she go to the bathroom after?"

Does she? I try to think. Is Carol trying to tell me Jo's bulimic? If so, I'd put money on her being wrong. Jo's always been thin, but that's largely due to stress. And I'm not prepared to discuss her with a stranger.

"Carol, I'm not sure if I can help you. You say it's Delphine you're worried about?"

"Terribly. Joanna isn't stable. We've never really got on, but the poor woman's had a lot to cope with, and I know my brother's to blame. Right now, she's all Delphine has. And I'm not at all sure that's a good thing."

"I don't think it's as bad as you're making out," I reassure her. "And at least when they move, you'll be able to keep an eye on them."

"Move?" Carol sounds astonished. "They're moving?"

I'm getting a bad feeling about this. I'd had Carol down as an earth-mother type, as caring, gentle, not as this woman set on stirring up trouble.

"You must know." I'm starting to feel impatient. "Jo

told me they were probably going to stay with you, just for a while, when they've sold the house, of course."

"Are you quite sure she said that?"

"Definitely. She's spoken to you, surely?"

In the silence that follows, I try to work out what's going on. Who's misunderstanding whom and, more important, whose side Carol is on.

"I haven't heard from Joanna for several weeks, Kate. We had an argument when I dropped Delphine home. Delphine wanted to stay with me—not just short term, either. She wanted to come and live with us. I can't imagine how that makes Joanna feel."

I'm struggling to believe her. Surely if something of this level of importance was going on, Jo would have mentioned it?

"She hasn't said a thing about it—not to me."

"No. She probably won't, either, knowing Joanna. I'm sure you know what I mean. But, anyway, as you can appreciate, I am concerned."

I end up promising Carol that I'll keep a closer eye on both Jo and Delphine. I know Jo well enough now to be able to gauge if she's having another breakdown.

But when I next go round to see her, everything is as it always is. The house tidy, Jo her most poised, beautifully dressed self and drinking tea as she leafs through a pile of property brochures.

"You've been busy." I pull a chair up next to her. "May I?"

"Please do. It's quite fun, actually. Have a look. I'll make you some tea."

I start flicking through them, an assortment of large houses similarly located to this one, modern and expensive-looking, on exclusive wooded estates. And I wonder, even after selling the house, how she's going to afford this.

"There's one in there I love," she calls over. "It's near Tonbridge."

"But what about Devon? Isn't Carol expecting you to move there?" I hate that I'm doing this, but for Delphine's sake, I'm testing her. After what Carol said, I feel I have to.

"To tell you the truth . . ." She puts the mugs on the table and sits again. "I'm not sure that's such a good idea. Carol's a bit inclined to . . . interfere, I think you'd call it. I'm not sure it would work."

I sip my tea, working out how to play the next card. "It might be nice for Delphine, though, don't you think? Carol has children, doesn't she? A similar age?"

I watch as Jo's smile tightens. "They're quite a bit older, actually. Look, tell me what you think of this one." She pulls out one of the brochures, with a picture of a new-build New England–style weatherboarded house on the front. "What do you think?"

"Very nice." I turn the pages. It's definitely Jo's kind of house, airy, spacious, and—dare I say it?—impressive. "If you'd like me to come and look with you, I'd be more than happy to."

"Would you?" She hesitates. "I'm waiting to hear back from the agent. Can I let you know?"

"What does Delphine think . . . about this?" I nod at the brochure.

"Oh, she's fine with it. She's used to changing schools. We've always moved. In fact, this is the longest we've stayed anywhere. So it will be nice to live somewhere else."

She makes no mention of her earlier reluctance—or of our friendship. I know some people change their homes as easily as their hairstyles, unlike Angus and I, who like the thought that having found a home we love, we'll grow into it, grow old in it, stay forever.

"I know. You probably think we're mad! And boring!" I tell her.

She looks at me. "You're just lucky, aren't you? But you deserve it, Kate."

"Very, *very* weird thing," I tell Laura, when I call round to her cottage. "I had a call from Jo's sister-in-law, Carol."

"Neal's sister?" Laura says.

"That's her. She told me she was worried about Delphine. *Really* worried. And that Delphine apparently wanted to go and live with her."

"That is strange," says Laura. "Has Delphine said anything to you?"

"No. But I don't know her that well. Were you able to see Neal?"

"Yes. I finally tracked him down to a flat in London. He's there until after the trial. Basically, it sounds as though Joanna's about as fucked up as he is. He said that he'd told the truth about the award, just as he was telling the truth about not killing his daughter. That their gardener, Alex, is guilty as hell, and what would it take for everyone to believe him? That sort of stuff."

Then Laura frowns. "You know the weirdest thing? I almost believed him. Oh, I know how manipulative he is, but I'm convinced he was telling the truth."

As the implication of what she's saying sinks in, as rock-solid certainty turns to confusion, we're silent.

"Did you ask him about Jo's parents?" I say eventually.

"Yes. He's had little to do with them. Apparently, she

had quite a strict upbringing. He didn't have much else to say. Talking of Alex, have you seen him at all?"

I shake my head. "Not for a while. He's not working at the nursery."

"You've got to admit it's odd," Laura remarks. "It may just be a coincidence, but there's Neal proclaiming him guilty just as Alex disappears."

I shake my head. "But the police didn't charge him."

"The police couldn't, because even without his alibi—who was Poppy, by the way—they didn't have enough evidence," Laura reminds me. "But if Neal really isn't the killer, I wouldn't be at all surprised to see the spotlight back on Alex. Right now, there isn't anyone else. . . ."

Rosie

*On that jewel-bright day when Neal's coming back,
when the last of Joanna's bruises are fading and her hair
is like it was when they got married, when her children
wear their new clothes, when her world is finally as it
should be, even the mask face can't hide how shocked
she is.*

*It tips the fragile scales that she's spent years care-
fully weighing, so that they teeter on the edge of perfection. Ruins everything. Wrenches the rug from under her.
She's in the bathroom, looking at the pregnancy test, then
away, then back again, in case it's changed.*

*How? She's been so careful. She wants to scream. It's
so unfair that this should happen now, when everything's
in place, and the moment she's been waiting her entire
life for has finally come.*

*She drops it into the basin, slumps onto the floor.
Hears a howling sound, then realizes it's her own cry of
anguish, drawn from deep inside her. Stifles it, because
no one must hear. No one must know.*

This baby can't be born. Because she's not just a mother, but she's also a wife. Has a duty. To give them all what's best for them. To do everything in her power to make sure none of them suffer as she has. She has to put them first, doesn't she? Put him first?

35

I go round to Jo's several times, intending to challenge
her. To ask her why she lies to me. Why she can't trust
me, *her only real friend,* to use her own words, with the
truth. Only each time, she's out.

A couple of days later, though, it's Jo who comes
round to see me, looking shaky and unsure of herself.

"I'm sorry to just turn up. I know you're busy," she
says, her eyes wide and anxious as she looks at me.

"Not that busy," I tell her. "Actually, I wanted to talk
to you. Come and have a cuppa with me."

She follows me in and sits at the kitchen table, not
talking.

"Tea?"

She nods.

I put the kettle on and get out the teapot, wondering
how to tackle this, while she sits, not moving, completely
silent.

But before I can find the words, it's Jo who speaks.

"I'm not having a good day." Her voice wobbles. "I
thought I could do it, but I don't think I can leave here,

Kate. I mean, Rosanna's buried here. And it's still Neal's house, too. What was I thinking?"

She sounds like a little girl who's lost. But what's more astounding is that she even mentions Neal's name, let alone seems to feel an obligation to him.

"Hey, it's okay, you know. Moving at any time is stressful. It's a huge thing to take on, moving away from here. And I completely get about leaving Rosie's grave behind. I wouldn't want to. But don't cloud your decision with loyalty to Neal, Jo. He doesn't deserve it."

I rarely speak to her this directly, because at the back of my mind, I'm always thinking how fragile she is. *She's bloody fragile,* to use Neal's words. And yes, even though she's been going through the motions of selling the house and moving, I've doubted all along she's ready for this.

She nods. "You're right. You're always right, Kate. I wish I could be like you. It's just that sometimes nothing's clear. Or I think it is, and then it fogs over and I lose it again." She looks confused. "I'm rambling, aren't I?"

"Here's a thought." I sit down opposite her, forgetting my earlier antagonism toward her. "If you could do anything in the world you wanted, go anywhere, be anyone, what would you do?"

It's a game Angus and I used to play, just for a laugh. He'd be Tom Hanks and I'd be Rita Wilson, in a Hollywood mansion with pots of money, even though in real life we're perfectly happy being us. Then I realize with a shock how crass I've been. In Jo's shoes, all I'd want is Rosie safe and well, and a husband who loved me by my side.

I look at Jo, leaning on her elbows, her hands shaking, wild panic in her eyes.

Eventually, slowly, she gets the words out. *"I . . . don't . . . know."*

Rosie

The house is empty, but Joanna's muttering to a nameless, disembodied someone who can't hear her as she spews out the words that are so jumbled inside her head, it hurts.

Fucking bastard. She hurls a glass onto the floor. Feels fear replace fury as she glances over her shoulder and clears up the broken pieces.

Vodka. She needs another glass. Her hands shaking so much, she almost drops it. Ice. Tops it up, then drinks it down in one and waits for the numbness to drift over her. It's not fast enough. She has another, then at last feels it enter her bloodstream, sweeping through her veins until slowly it anesthetizes her brain.

Mania turns to exhaustion in two seconds flat. She counts them, then forgets what it is she has to do.

Not so clever now, is she? Not as sneaky, deceptive, secretive as she thought she was.

She doesn't know if she can do this thing she's forgotten about, only that she can't not do it. As always in her life, she has no choices. It's always about other people. Forcing her to do things.

Like now. Drinking vodka. Feeling up, then down, then blank. Like so many things, not her fault.

But the trouble is, if you knew what her dilemma was, you'd see clear as night. She's the only one who can do this, even though she doesn't want to.

She has no choice.

36

What was intended as an entertaining diversion, a foray into a fantasy world, seems to tip Jo over an invisible edge. I forget about the questions I have for her about her parents, the baby she lost. Here, before my eyes, it's as if she's falling off an emotional rock face, and I can't stop her.

"Jo?" I grab her hands in mine. They're ice-cold. "It's okay, honey. Come through and sit somewhere comfy."

I manage to get her to her feet, then support almost her full body weight, which is frighteningly light, until I get her to the sofa, where she huddles, shaking, her face ashen under her makeup, looking as though any moment she'll pass out.

"He was leaving me," she sobs, as if to herself. "My husband was going to leave me, Kate." Her hands go to her face. "He found a young, beautiful whore to fuck, one who'd do everything he asked. . . . He didn't want me anymore. . . . He doesn't care about me . . . after everything that's happened. . . . Do you know how that feels?"

I open my mouth to tell her that actually, for a few life-changing weeks, *almost,* only she has turned away and is gazing blankly ahead of her.

"I didn't mean to . . . ," she says, as if to the air around her.

I frown. "Didn't mean to what, Jo?"

"I found the piece of paper," she says in a different voice, before she looks at me, blinking as she tries to focus. "It said, 'Kate, supper, eight.' You screwed my husband, Kate. How could you? You're my fucking friend. . . . I trusted you. . . ."

And I'm finally there, in the nightmare I've always dreaded, ever since that fateful evening, as I grab her arms, desperate to reassure her. But she pulls away.

"Listen, Jo. I didn't. He came on to me, but I pushed him away. You have to believe that."

But she's staring blankly again, not listening. "It was deliberate. . . . He wanted me to see. He always does that. Wants me to see who he's fucking, to know that everyone's better than I am. Even you, Kate . . . What was I supposed to do?"

"God! Listen to me, Jo! Nothing happened. I invited him and Delphine, but he—"

"You took Rosanna, and then you took him . . . when they're mine, Kate. Mine . . . Can't you see what he's like?"

She rummages in her pocket and gets out a small bottle, her hands shaking as she tries to unscrew the lid.

"Pills," she mutters. "I need my pills. . . ."

Gently, I take them away from her, just as her body starts shaking more violently. A look of fury on her face, she tries to get to her feet, only her legs give way.

"I'm calling an ambulance, Jo," I say quietly. "I'm sorry, but this can't go on."

Rosie

Joanna's found a way to do this. She pretends that she's someone else. She decides on a name. The first that comes into her mind. That mother she knows in passing from school, that one she has coffee with, who rides horses and drifts through life without a care in the world. No one should have it that easy.

"Kate . . ." She says it gleefully, grotesquely, as she dances around the kitchen.

"Kate . . ." Pours another glass of vodka. "Cheers!" She raises her glass to my friend.

"Kate . . . you should try it sometime," she tells Kate. "If you drink enough vodka, your mind can fly like a bird."

She doesn't really know Kate. They have lunch sometimes. Kate actually eats hers! Joanna pretends, of course. Not that Kate even notices.

It amuses her to think of Kate doing this. Not the real Kate, of course, who's far too good, too naive to even imagine such a thing. Or is she? Maybe she isn't. Doesn't everyone have their little secrets?

She laughs. A manic, screechy laugh. The laugh of a mad person. Drinks down another glass in one.

When she does this, she'll be Kate, using Kate's voice, Kate's hands, Kate's body, and all the time, Joanna will be innocent. And when it's all over, and everything's back to normal, Neal will come home.

37

"Delphine?" Jo's voice barely audible from inside the ambulance.

"What's that, love?" The paramedic turns to look at me.

"Delphine's her daughter. It's okay. We're friends. I can look after her. Can I just have a minute before you go?"

He nods.

Inside the ambulance, Jo's clearly sedated, her eyes closing. "Jo? You mustn't worry about Delphine. I'll meet her when she comes back from school. And she can stay with us. It'll be fine."

Jo's eyelids flutter. "No . . . mustn't . . . take her—"

But the paramedic interrupts us. "Sorry, ma'am, but I think you'd better leave us. We really should be on our way."

"I'll call the hospital, Jo. Don't worry. You'll be okay."

It's my last glimpse of her, lying in the ambulance, her

anguished face turned toward me, a single word framed by her lips. It's a word, even in my best attempts to help her, as someone who cares what happens, I fail to understand.

"No . . ."

Delphine

Rosie is in my head and answers my questions, like she used to. Crapshooting, we used to call it.

"Tell me the worst," she'd say.

I'd rack my brains for the worst thing I could think of, like our parents dying or the house burning down.

Rosie would look past me, her face a blank. "Not so bad, then," she'd say.

I wouldn't understand.

"Think about it," she'd say. "There's far worse things than that."

"Like what?" I'd cry, suddenly fearful.

Rosie would look sad. "Like not loving or never being loved."

But there's worse. Like dying.

Or ghosts you can't touch.

She doesn't know I can see her.

Rosie

Joanna's careful. So careful. No one must know. She works out that she has about two months, slightly less maybe, depending on how soon the baby shows.

She does her research meticulously. It's not something she knows about, that she's ever thought about before, though she knows other people do it without a thought. But every so often her breath catches in her throat. As a mother, she wishes for another way. But can't think of one.

Everyone thinks she's so stupid, don't they? When she really isn't, and she can use a computer, maybe not brilliantly and speedily, not like her daughters, but she has second-to-none typing skills, and all day, when the girls are in school, when Neal's away, shagging one of his whores, she uses her time well.

Not that she needs a computer, since now she has an iPhone. And on the Internet, as she discovers, you can find out anything. Absolutely anything. About things she wishes she didn't have to. About clinics. About what to do about pregnancies that can't happen. When there are no choices.

Hiding what she's doing, so no one will know.

Her plan obsesses her. She's not sure that when the time comes, she won't bottle out. Wishes with all her heart she could. Bottle . . . She thinks of the one that's half full of vodka. Hidden from sight, just like this latest secret she has.

Planning is crucial. So is timing. She has the information now; she just has to choose the right moment.

38

I think about calling Carol, but instead call Angus. I'm torn as to what is best for Delphine.

"You should pick her up from school and go from there," he suggests. "Jo may not be kept in for long. I'm sorry, Kate, but I've got another call. Why not wait till I'm home? I'll try and get away early."

I've no idea if Delphine catches a bus or Jo collects her. In the end, I go to the school and wait outside.

I know you can't tell just by watching them. The kids for whom divorce is an everyday part of childhood. The lucky ones for whom the worst is a grounding or a bad exam grade. And I know all kinds of things happen to families, but as I watch the car park fill with teenagers, I wonder how many have backgrounds like Delphine's? A dead sister, a murderer for a father, a deeply troubled mother, a big, glossy, empty, unhappy house. Unable to imagine anyone.

Just as I'm worrying I've missed her, I catch a glimpse of her. Alone, composed, impassive as she stands and looks around. Then seeing me, she comes over. Still her face shows nothing.

"I'm not sure how long she'll be kept in," I say to Delphine as we drive back to the Andersons' house. I've suggested she packs enough clothes for a few days and any other things she wants. "I'll call the hospital later, but you can stay with us, at least until we know what's happening."

Beside me, she doesn't speak, just nods.

"Don't worry, sweetie. She'll be okay. I think she just needs proper care and time."

"I know," Delphine says. "And I'm not worried, really."

It's a strange thing to say, but then everything about her reaction is strange. I was prepared for tears, upset, anger even—anything other than her passive indifference.

"Do you have a key?"

She nods.

I park outside their house.

"Would you like me to come in with you? I can help you carry things."

She nods. "Thank you."

I follow her up the path, and she lets us in, then pauses before unlocking the door into the garage.

"I need to get something out of there," is all she says.

While she goes upstairs to pack, I wait in the sitting room, looking around and noticing piles of papers, magazines, clothes strewn everywhere, which isn't like Jo. In the kitchen, too, there are cupboards left open and a pile of washing-up. Then I see the glass and the empty vodka bottle.

"She thinks I don't know."

The voice comes from behind me. I turn round to see Delphine staring at the bottle.

"She has it when she wakes up. And in the day, when I'm at school or when she thinks I'm not looking." In the same flat, unemotional voice.

I'm flabbergasted that I haven't seen this before. How didn't I know my friend was an alcoholic? "I'm so sorry, Delphine. I didn't know."

Delphine shrugs. "No one does. It's okay."

But it's so far from okay, I don't know what to say to her.

All the way home, I think of Jo and her drinking, then make tea for Delphine, feeling a nostalgia for when Grace was younger, when she'd chatter all the way back from school, eat about three slices of cake, pull on her jodhpurs, and run outside to her beloved Oz. Carefree, happy, free-spirited, as children should be.

And I know she's not Grace, but Delphine is so silent.

"Would you like to help me feed the horses later?"

"Yes, please. Can I borrow Grace's clothes again?"

"Of course. They're still in the spare room from last time. I hoped you'd be needing them again."

She just nods, carries on eating, the rest of my sentence remaining unspoken.

Just not like this.

Such is the magic of horses that they draw out her words and bring light to her eyes. I give her a lead to catch Reba and she comes back not just with Reba but with all of them.

Seeing a fleeting happiness in her face, I pass her a grooming brush. "Start at the top of her neck and work your way back," I tell her. "Then, when you've done both sides, you do her mane and tail."

I watch Reba's expression of bliss as Delphine brushes her, then leave her to get on with it while I fill up the water trough. When I next look up, her pale head is resting against Reba's dark one, her eyes closed, both of them still.

An hour passes, mostly in silence. As we lean over the gate, the low sun filtering through the trees and into our eyes, I'm trying to work out how to reach her.

When we get back to the house, I call the hospital, then go to find Delphine.

She's in front of the television, quite motionless, the sound turned down low. As I come in, she turns it off. I sit down next to her and take her hand.

"I've just spoken to the hospital. They're keeping your mummy in. She's dehydrated and terribly confused. They've put her on a drip, and they'll do some tests. I'm sure she'll be fine."

I continually watch Delphine's face, trying to gauge her reaction, but there is none. She seems miles away.

"Perhaps tomorrow I could take you to see her? After school."

For the first time, I elicit a reaction from her. She shakes her head quite firmly. "No. It's okay. Thank you."

It's not what I'm expecting. "It might be good for her to see you."

Her eyes turn to mine, her look piercing. "But I don't want to. It's her fault she's ill, isn't it?"

"I think that's a little unfair, Delphine. Okay, so she needs to stop drinking. But losing Rosie, what your dad did . . . It's not easy for her. Can you see that?"

She folds her arms and stares at the wall. "Is she coming back?"

"What?" Is this what's worrying her? That on top of everything else, she's about to lose her mother, too? "Of course she will. You mustn't worry, Delphine. Really . . ."

"It's not that." Her voice is hard.

"Tell me," I say gently.

Her response, when it comes, shocks me.

"I don't want her to."

"Delphine, you can't mean that. . . ."

"Why not?" Her eyes flash angrily. "She spoils everything. Why can't people see that? She's not a mother. She's *pathetic*."

Words ringing with such hatred and scorn, shocking me. *How can she hate her mother?*

"I'm sure she doesn't want to be like this, but she's sick, Delphine. She needs help, just as much as someone with a broken leg needs help."

"She won't get better. She'll always be like this."

"Is that why you want to live with your auntie?"

I say it as gently and compassionately as I can, but Delphine's head turns to stare at me.

"She called me, sweetie. Last week. She's worried about you. And your mum."

I'm beginning to understand why, too.

"Mummy hates her," Delphine says tonelessly. "She says she's common and stupid and plain. But she's not. She's kind, and she loves people. She's a proper mother."

"Would you like me to call her?"

Delphine hesitates, then says, "Okay."

"Okay. I'll do it now. I'm sure she'd like to talk to you."

But as I go to get the phone, she speaks in a completely

different voice, the voice of a child in pain, which touches my soul. "Can I stay here, Kate? With you? *Please?*"

It's only now, with Delphine under our roof, that the extent of Jo's problems fully comes to light. In her daughter, I see the mirror image of Jo's obsessions, from the food she eats to the way she organizes her room here, so neat, every trace of herself so invisible that you wouldn't believe anyone inhabited it.

"I've never known another child quite like her," I tell Rachael. "Most of the time, you'd hardly know she was there."

"God. Poor little thing. Makes you wonder what's going on in her head. Here, have some cake. I hid it from the boys."

"Thanks." Frowning as I take the plate from her. "She knows far too much for a child of her age. She told me about Jo's drinking. So calmly, it spooked me. Then she made all these angry, bitter accusations, about how it was her mother's fault that she had a drink problem. She doesn't want to visit her at the hospital, either."

"She probably can't stand them. I know I can't. Ghastly places." Rachael cuts more cake.

But I'm silent for a moment, thoughtful. "You'd think, wouldn't you, that now that it's just the two of them, they'd be closer than ever? Only they're not."

It's a thought that still haunts me when, early the following afternoon, I go to the hospital. Having been told Jo has been transferred to a psychiatric wing, I'm expecting a grim ward, not a small, sunny room that overlooks the garden. I'm not convinced she'll want to see me, either, after my revelations about Neal.

Propped up against the pillows, she looks haggard, ill, exhausted.

"How are you?" I hate seeing her like this, a shadow of the brave, tortured friend who's suffered so much. She shakes her head, but it seems to loll, too heavy for her, and I realize she's drugged.

I sit down next to her and take her hand. "Don't try and talk, Jo. I just wanted to tell you Delphine's fine. She's staying with us. Don't worry about her. I'll look after her. Just concentrate on getting yourself well."

I'm not sure how much registers, but then her lips try to move, and I think I hear just faintly a whisper. "Thank you."

I stay until her eyes close and the movement of her chest slows and becomes more regular. Then I go out to the reception desk.

"Excuse me, is there someone I can talk to about Joanna Anderson?"

A nurse glances up. "Are you family?"

"The closest thing she has," I say, realizing it's true. "I'm looking after her daughter. I'd just like to know what's happening."

It takes repeated requests and an hour of waiting before a doctor tells me that until they've carried out a range of psychiatric tests, Jo won't be going anywhere. He can give me no clue as to how long this might take, nor does he tell me what the tests are.

I call Angus from my car while I'm waiting outside the school for Delphine.

"It's bloody frustrating." In the space of twenty-four hours, we've gone back a few years, to watching what we say, not in front of Grace but Delphine.

"She can stay, can't she?"

I hear his shrug over the phone, knowing before he speaks what his answer is, reminding myself that this kind of generosity is why I love him.

"I love you," I tell him. "Here she is. Better go."

I blow a silent kiss at my phone as Delphine climbs in.

"Hi! How was your day?"

"Okay." Like everything else in her life. Not amazing or really terrible. Just okay.

"Would you like to ride Reba later?"

"Can I?"

The next couple of days pass in a similar way, with Jo caught among the machinations of the practitioners whose care she's under, while I make painfully slow progress in drawing out Delphine. At a loss to know how to help her, I call Laura.

"It's like a stalemate," I tell her when she comes over. "She just doesn't respond like any child I've ever met. Everything's kept inside."

"When did this start?"

"Four, five days ago." It feels much longer, in that strange way time can when life springs unimagined change on you, so that *before* and *after* are suddenly lifetimes apart.

"It's really good of you to look after her," says Laura, meaning Delphine. "How is she?"

"Okay. That's what she says about everything—'It's okay'—apart from some scathing things she says about her mother."

"She probably feels let down," says Laura. "Not just by Jo, but by life. When I was her age, I didn't have any worries—well, maybe about homework, that kind of thing. Nothing like this."

"What I hadn't realized was Jo has a serious drinking problem. Vodka-for-breakfast kind of serious."

Laura hesitates. "Poor Jo. But it kind of goes with everything else, doesn't it? The death of her daughter. Her insecurity . . . all the problems she's been having? It's probably how she survived being married to Neal, let alone the past few months." She pauses. "The thing is, when someone's been through what she has, there's no easy fix. She's suffered the worst things that can happen to anyone. Effectively lost half her family. How do you move on from that?"

But I don't like how Delphine has so easily been forgotten, as if she doesn't count. "She has another daughter who needs her. She can't just opt out, can she?"

"Oh," says Laura, "but she can. And Alex has been found, too. It seems he hasn't been entirely truthful. He was with Rosie that evening. Earlier on, he says. Until her mother called to say that Neal was on his way round—so he says."

"But she was at Poppy's."

Laura raises her eyebrows. "Yeah, well, it seems that was another one of Poppy's lies. Her brother's been locked up for beating up someone who used to bully her, so understandably, she doesn't have much time for the police."

"So . . ." I try to work out what she's saying here.

"Alex may or may not have been with Rosie. May or may not be the murderer, quite honestly. Poppy swears he's innocent. They both loathe Neal, but that's not the issue. And there's still one thing we haven't considered."

"What?" I stare at her.

"What if the papers were right, Kate? Only it's come up time and time again. What if Rosie was pregnant?"

Delphine

When you see what it isn't, you learn what madness is. It's a world that's different every single day. Moods without rhythm, like an out-of-time metronome. Words that mean anything or nothing. A smile that starts warm and, as you smile back, turns ice-cold and evil. It's the home that's a smart address and empty rooms. It's lies and pretense. It's vodka bottles, supposedly hidden, only not well enough. It's being alive and not being allowed to live. Having only air that's toxic. A sister you can hear, even though she's dead.

Rosie

Joanna gazes out the window. She can't tell Neal what's happening. Not ever. Like she can't tell him that I've fallen in love with the gardener, for Christ's sake. He'd blame her for letting it happen. She can hear him say it.

Of all the people round here or at school, why him?

Only he knows her too well, finds the test in the trash.

"How could you let it happen?"

Joanna flinches, waits for the blow.

"You think I'm going to hit you, don't you?"

He watches her.

"I might . . . or I might not. I haven't decided. Stupid, ignorant bitch . . ."

The blow, when it comes, is across her face, knocks the air out of her.

"Another fat, stupid child. You can't do anything right, can you?"

He hits her again.

"You better do something. Before anyone notices."

He has no idea it's not her baby.

He has no idea, either, that she's already planning every tiny step meticulously. That it was in hand, anyway, even without him knowing.

"Anything. I don't care. Just get rid of it. . . . Or I will."

39

I stare at Laura, then shake my head, because she's wrong. Rosie definitely wasn't pregnant. I distinctly remember Jo telling me.

"But Jo clearly told me that she wasn't. What was in the papers was just rumors. She was determined not to let it get to her."

"Another lie." We both say it.

Laura looks at me. "Why?"

I shrug. "Jo likes everything to be perfect." As I say it, I recognize how true it is. "The ways she dresses, her house, the husband she's always praising. Her teenage daughter? She hated that Rosie was even seeing Alex, let alone that she was pregnant with his child. She wouldn't want *that* being shouted about."

"But it was in the papers, Kate. Not all of them, but one or two printed horrible reports about how the wounds were mostly around her stomach. Jo couldn't have imagined she could keep it quiet. It would come out once the trial started. What's strange is she didn't confide in you."

"But there's a lot we didn't talk about, and I didn't want to upset her by always bringing up what was so painful for her. God, she lives with it in her head. She didn't need me constantly talking about it, too. And everyone knows, don't they, that the papers print as much fiction as fact?"

Laura's thoughtful. "If it wasn't all so tragic, it would be quite impressive. . . ." Then she says slowly, "Have you thought that just maybe . . . ? Those notes, Kate. Maybe whoever wrote them didn't know about Jo's still-born baby, but they knew about Rosie. Maybe the fetus is the second dead baby. . . ."

"So who's the third?"

Our eyes meet, and a wave of shock goes through me. Not Delphine . . .

On top of this, the unbelievable happens, as if the world has warped and slipped sideways. Out of nowhere, an alibi comes forward. I hear it on the radio as I'm driving. Neal was seen that evening. He couldn't have murdered Rosie. Then Alex is taken in again.

No. The word is loud in my head. I don't know why, but I know this is terribly wrong.

The necklace. It all comes down to the necklace. If they'd fallen out, there's no way Rosie would have been wearing it.

And Neal. His treatment of his daughters. Of Jo . . . the evidence on his laptop. The police have to charge him for all of that, surely. Or have they discovered something else?

After further questioning, this time Alex is charged. However, when he's bailed, there are too many lies and loose ends tangled together in my head. I ignore everyone's warnings. I call Dan and persuade him to give me Alex's address. Then I go to see him.

"What are you doing here?" Alex doesn't invite me in, just stands in his doorway, hostile, towering over me.

"I need to talk to you. Could I come in? Just for a few minutes?"

"Is this a setup? If Anderson has anything to do with this . . ." His voice is rough and full of menace.

I almost turn, leave him. Almost. Then take a deep breath, because I'm puzzled.

"I'm not here for them. I promise."

I try to forget that he's beaten someone up, that he's still accused of murder. I'm running on pure instinct, summoning every last bit of courage I can find, as, in silence, he stands back to let me in.

I follow him into the small, cottagey front room, which I could imagine would usually be cozy and comfortable. Though not now. It's a mess, as no doubt his head is.

"I don't normally live like this. This is all courtesy of the police," he says, on edge, looking around. "They don't tidy up after themselves. So what do you want?"

"I'm sorry." I hesitate, aware suddenly of how intrusive this is. "But you know I knew Rosie. Not as well as you, I realize that, but I can't believe you killed her," I tell him. "I know it's a police matter, but we need to work out who did it."

"I already told the police what happened that night. It was that bastard Neal." He sounds furious, and for a fleeting moment, the doubts are back. If he got that angry . . . could he have?

Telling myself to keep the faith.

"Well, it seems someone saw him that night. Drunk, passed out on the village green. They tried to wake him, but he was out of it."

A chance sighting, which changed everything. After I heard it on the radio, I called Laura, who filled me in.

Alex looks disbelieving. "You have to ask, don't you? Why this person didn't come forward before?"

"It was a guy who was cheating on his wife," I say quietly. "On his way home from an illicit meeting. He didn't want to give himself away . . . before." I pause, watching him take it in. "Only his wife found out."

Alex sighs and sits down, gesturing to me to do the same.

"I've told the police the truth." He rests his head in his hands. "It all went so wrong." When he looks up, his face is haunted. "We tried to keep it to ourselves, but you know, don't you, after the garbage the press printed? Rosie was pregnant."

"I've only just realized," I say truthfully. "Jo had no idea, though. She told me that what the papers printed was lies."

"Really?" He doesn't look convinced.

"Did you and Jo argue?"

He looks startled. "The week before, yes. She wouldn't let me see Rosie. She was doing her best to break us up."

"And you got angry?"

He nods slowly. "I lost it. I shouldn't have. She'd locked Rosie in her room. She was eighteen, for God's sake. What kind of mother does that?"

The kind of mother who lies. Who told Laura that Alex pestered them. That Rosie was done with him. Why?

"What about that last night? Rosie went to Poppy's, didn't she?"

"I met Rosie at about eight that evening. She'd been at

Poppy's house. Poppy said she'd cover for her, if anyone asked. She was good like that. She's a nice girl, for the record. Anyway . . . Rosie came here."

He goes on. "I cooked. She spent the rest of the evening here. We argued—again. She wanted us to cool things off—just till she went to university—because Joanna was being a nightmare about it. For her sister's sake, she said. I got really mad at her. I mean, her sister was going to have to cope without her at some point. I couldn't see the sense in dragging it out."

He sighs. "It wasn't a good evening. She was going to walk out of here, but I managed to persuade her not to. We made up. Then, at about eleven, her mother called to warn her. She was in a state. Said Neal had found out about us and was already on his way here. That he'd just hit her for no reason and was in a raging temper. I remember Rosie's face—white as a sheet. You could see how terrified she was." His face clouds over. "I've no idea how she knew where Rosie was."

Silent for a moment, he buries his face in his hands. "Joanna told her to get out of the house as fast as she could. That she couldn't come and get her, because he'd taken her keys. But to do it now, quickly, before Neal got here. Then she rang off."

His shoulders are rigid. "I told her to go back to Poppy's, because I knew she'd be safe there. I was going to confront Neal and have it out with him, once and for all."

His eyes are guilt stricken. "If only I'd gone with her . . . When Neal didn't show up, I went to Poppy's. What a man, leaving my pregnant girlfriend to go off on her own, knowing her psychotic father was on the loose. Only she never got there, did she? Her fucking father got to her first. . . ."

"But . . . this new alibi of his . . ." I'm confused.

Alex looks at me. "Don't you see? Neal bluffed, didn't he, Kate? After he'd done it, he dropped the car home, got the bottle he'd stashed in the back, wandered down to the green, and got smashed. How hard can it be to fake it? Cheating guy sees him on his way through. . . ." He shrugs.

Then my skin prickles. *What if Alex is lying? What if he didn't wait for Neal? What if, fed up with it all, he chased after Rosie, got into another row, and, in the heat of the moment, attacked her?*

"It has to be more substantial than that. The police would have checked the guy's story."

What if I'm wrong? If Alex is the murderer?

As Alex clasps his hands, a strange look flickers across his face. In the silence, uneasiness churns inside me. I glance at my watch, then get up.

"I have to go. I told Angus I wouldn't be long."

My throat's dry and the words stick there, but outwardly I compose myself, feeling my heart thudding as I head toward the door. Then, just as I go to open it, I feel his hand grab my arm.

Rosie

Joanna stays out of sight. It's lucky she's so good at hiding. Watches as I leave Poppy's house, waving to Poppy, then walk down the road, past all the other houses, happy. Happy I have a friend on my side, happy I have Alex, happy that I'll soon be away from here.

She knows I'm going to see him. It's eating away at her, in her stomach, crawling like maggots, making her sick inside. But she has to do this for Neal. Anyway, she reminds herself, she isn't Joanna anymore. A part of her has splintered away and become Kate.

She follows, stops round the corner from Alex's house, waiting, holding her breath in case I turn back or walk past or just stop, look over my shoulder. See her.

But I don't. Alex opens the door, and she watches his arms go around me, his head lean down, his lips on mine as we stand, lost in each other, in the moment. Then we're inside, the door closed behind us. Joanna swallows the bile in her throat. Knows she has to wait. Knows what she has to do next.

At home, the soft, sweet voice of the vodka bottle beckons. But though she's tempted, desperate even, for once she doesn't. Knows she can't. Thinks of later, when not only will she have a glass, but she'll drink it all. If she goes ahead, that is. Her doubts return, millions of little dust fairies all around her, until she takes a deep breath and blows them away.

Time plays tricks on her that evening. Ticks so, so slowly. It starts when Neal comes in. She hears his feet on the stairs, then in the bedroom, then back on the stairs.

"Where's supper?" He looks around the kitchen, then at the glass deliberately placed in front of her, with disgust.

She reaches inside and brings back Joanna. Fills her eyes with tears. She can do that so easily, just looking at him, with the ghosts of all those women standing around him, in her place.

"I forgot," she whispers. Adds a tremulous note for effect. Wobbles her lip. Cowers. "I'm sorry."

"You're pathetic." Thrown like a weapon.

"Shall I make something?"

"Don't bother. I'll find something myself."

She hears him open the fridge, knows that there's the slices of beef he likes, which she bought earlier. That he'll eat them and still be hungry, then sate his appetite with drink until he's passed out. She's counting on this. He has to.

But therein lies the beauty of her plan. She knows her husband so well. He eats all the beef, then pours a whiskey, then takes the bottle and turns on the television. She sips her water, breathes a cautious breath out.

Glances at her watch, which says only nine thirty, then hears more footsteps. Feels her insides flip over as the door is pushed open. Her hand goes to her mouth. Oh my God. She's forgotten Delphine. She always forgets Delphine.

Joanna thinks quickly. She can't let the fact that she's forgotten her own daughter spoil her plan. Not now. Quickly, quickly. Keep Delphine happy. *The first thing that comes to mind.*

"I'll cook pizza, honey."

Surprise flickers in Della's eyes that there's even pizza in the house. The "honey." We all know—in this house, how could we not?—there are enough calories in pizza to last you a week.

40

I panic, wrenching my arm free from Alex's grip.

"Stay away from me." My heart pounding as I reach for the doorknob.

But he refuses to back down and as the door opens, with one of his hands, he slams it shut.

"Kate . . . I'm sorry. I shouldn't have done that. I didn't kill her, I promise on my life. I have a temper. . . ."

In those seconds, as he looms over me, so close I feel the heat from his body, for the first time I truly know fear. Know he could kill me. Know there's no one I told I was coming here, because they'd talk me out of it.

I'm just waiting. Terrified.

Is this it?

But he releases his hold on the door, stepping back.

"I didn't kill her, I promise, on my life . . ."

He says it quietly, his final plea to me to believe him, as a picture of Rosie comes into my head. Her clear eyes, her hand on her necklace, her gentleness, the same perceptiveness that drew the horses to her. And as he opens the door to let me go, I know he's innocent.

* * *

In the meantime, I have to trust that the truth will come out, because Delphine preoccupies me. I ask no questions, offer no judgment, just let time and the horses work their magic on her, but noticing odd things for a girl of her age.

"She spends ages in her room," I whisper to Angus anxiously. "D'you think she's okay up there?"

"Probably. You don't know what she does at home, do you?"

"No . . . Maybe I'll check on her. Try and get her to come and watch the television with us."

Outside her door, I listen for a moment, uncertain if I can hear her talking or not. Then I knock.

"Delphine? Can I come in?"

There's silence; then the door opens suddenly. She moves noiselessly over to the bed and closes her notebook.

"Why don't you come downstairs? Join me and Angus. There's a TV program that's about to start."

She looks up, hopeful.

"Well, come on, then. Would you like a hot chocolate?"

"Am I allowed?"

"Of course you are. Grace lives on the stuff! Come on. I'll show you where it is. Then anytime you want to, you can help yourself."

It seems that this breakdown has sent Jo somewhere that defeats all her doctors. When I go to see her, there's only the faintest indication that she recognizes me, after which she's blank, staring at nothing, except she's not staring at all. Her eyes are unfocused; her body is frozen.

Even the mention of Delphine's name doesn't produce a flicker.

"It's like she's asleep with her eyes wide open," I tell Laura much later on, when she calls round on her way home. "What happens? Will she just come back, as it were, or will they give her drugs?"

"They probably already are," she says. "Poor Jo. This isn't going to be over quickly. Are you still okay with Delphine?"

"We're happy for her to stay. I couldn't bear to think of her anywhere else."

I couldn't do that, not to poor Delphine. Having settled, as far as I can tell, she deserves some stability in her life, which has already been far too troubled.

"There's Carol, of course. I called her earlier. She's more than happy to have Delphine there, but it means leaving school, her friends. . . . I've no idea what's best."

Given what's happened, is it harder to leave the familiar or easier to stay?

"Talk to her at some point," Laura says gently.

"I went to talk to Alex." I say it quietly.

Laura looks alarmed. "Kate . . . *please* . . . stay away from him."

"I had to, Laura. After everything I thought about him, I really don't believe he did it."

Laura sighs. "There's still a murder inquiry under way. And whatever you think, he's a suspect."

"He's innocent," I say firmly, noticing her eyebrows arch. It was the way he spoke as I left his house that convinced me he was telling the truth.

I didn't kill her, I promise, on my life . . .

"So if not him, who?" Laura asks.

"He's convinced it's Neal. Says that he faked being drunk, that the alibi isn't strong enough. . . ."

Laura screws up her face, thinking. "But that's wrong. This guy who saw him walked across the green just before eleven. Says he saw what he thought was a homeless man in the bushes, passed out. He didn't do anything. Obviously, he was in a hurry to meet his lady friend. But on the way back, Neal was still there, in exactly the same place. The guy tried to wake him, but he was snoring loudly and couldn't be roused. That's when he saw the whiskey bottle. Jo herself says that he crawled in, stinking of booze, early the next morning. There's an outside chance he was faking it, but honestly, I don't think he was."

"Then it has to be someone else," I say, just as I hear Delphine come downstairs. She's just back from school. "Are you okay, sweetie?"

"Can I make a drink?" Her face appears in the door frame, impassive.

"Of course you can. Call me if you need help."

I hear her fill the kettle and clatter around a bit, but then she comes back through, holding another of those white envelopes.

"I think this just came through your door."

I hesitate, then meet Laura's eyes as I keep my voice as normal as possible.

"Thank you."

Once she goes back in the kitchen, I open it and read the note to Laura.

Ask her about the necklace.

Then, as I put it down, something clicks into place.

Rosie

Without vodka to make them soften and blur into sleep, evenings are too torturously slow, Joanna thinks. It's so long since she's been sober, she's forgotten how slow.

Glances at her watch. Ten thirty. She hears Della upstairs in her room, doesn't go up there, see her sitting on her bed, writing silently. My only, lonely sister, who aches for someone to hold her close or smile warmly into her eyes.

Ten thirty-two. Joanna's restless. Is everything prepared?

Of course it is. She's Kate, remember? Practical and capable with those horses of hers, Kate can do this, too. Joanna knows she can. She closes her eyes, thinks of Kate's straight hair, her skin tanned from being outside, those awful, ugly clothes she always wears, those dreadful hands, her common sense. Understanding that tonight will serve her well. Hoping it's enough. She looks again. Ten forty-one. Gets her car keys, jingles them in her hands just as Della walks in, gets herself a glass of water.

"Mummy? Can I go to Harriet's house tomorrow?"

For a moment, Kate wonders why Joanna doesn't answer. Then remembers with a start, she is Joanna.

No. Just shakes her head.

She can't think about this now. The world exists only up until tonight. She can't think about tomorrow, not yet.

Ten forty-eight. Her heart starts to palpitate. She glances over at the phone. Why is Delphine still here? Watching her?

Bedtime. Mother Joanna voice.

She has to get Kate back. Closes her eyes again. Thinks of Kate's cool calm, her chunky thighs in her jodhpurs, hair that needs the attention of a good stylist. Breathes out again. It's okay. She's ready.

She picks up the phone. Calls me on Alex's phone. Speaks in such a caring way. Hears the shock in our voices. How does she know we're there? Together? Hears shock fade to suspicion, then fear, as she tells them Neal's on his way.

Forgets Della, halfway up the stairs, listening, wondering why her mother's lying about the car keys she's lost, which are in her hand; about her father, who isn't raging at all. He's just been drinking quietly, heavily, all evening. Or did she miss something?

But as Joanna-Kate leaves in a hurry, because now it's time for her to do this, she doesn't even notice Neal's gone. Has no idea why, at the last minute, she snatches up the knife.

The car is parked on the road. No gravel-drive noise. She drives slowly, with no lights, until she reaches the end of the lane. Not that her neighbors will notice. No one round here notices anything.

As she drives, her hands shake, fumble with the gear stick, turn signals, making her flustered. Makes herself take deep breaths. Summons the part of her she calls Kate. Sees Rosanna walking down the road. Back to that slut Poppy's, just as she guessed. And then it's easy.

I climb into the car, surprised. Joanna's jittery. It crosses my mind she's drunk, but then I know how terrified she is of my father. She drives until she feels my hand on her arm. Then she says, "Do you mind if we pull over? I'm not feeling too well. I need some air."

I'm used to Joanna not feeling well. Think nothing of it. She gets out and gulps the air like she's been suffocating; then she pulls on the coat that's in the back, says, "Such a beautiful night. We should walk."

She starts off up the lane, then turns, waits for me to follow. She tells me she doesn't want to go home yet. "Your father will be there. He'll be so angry. He's found out. We'll wait. He'll calm down. What will we do?" Then she says in a different voice, "It's a lovely night for walking in the woods."

I know then, she's mad. But I can't leave her here, my mad mother in the woods. So I follow Joanna as she keeps walking, every so often checking her watch. Remember, she has a plan.

And though I know that this is crazy, that Joanna's behavior is unnerving me, my response is involuntary, molded by my childhood, my synapses and neural pathways obedient to her will. As I was always going to, I do what she says.

Joanna-Kate doesn't remember the bank being this slippery or nearly losing her footing, having to clutch at branches to pull herself up here. But it's a secret, hidden, wild place—and so pretty when she came here in daylight. The trees are so tall, so black against the indigo sky, their jagged shapes carved against the moon.

"Look," she says to me. "Look up there. It's watching us." Then her eyes fill with panic. "Oh my God. It is . . . watching us."

I look up, try to see what she's frightened of. But there are only the trees like sentries, standing guard around us, beneath the moon, a benign friend.

At my side, she watches, tells me what a mess this all is, but how we can sort it out. That the baby will ruin everything, but there's another way, and if we put it behind us and start again, everything will be perfect.

And then it hits me. It's why she's so strange.

She knows I'm pregnant.

My heart flutters. "I'm keeping the baby." My voice is scared, shocked, resolute. "You can't stop me. It's my body, my baby."

"No," she cries. "That's not the answer. He mustn't know. Not ever. He'd kill me."

And there it is, in those few words. My existence, Della's, too, from the beginning, always second to him. Suddenly, I want to leave here. I know viscerally, on a primal level, that I'm not safe. Say in a calm voice that isn't calm at all, "Let's talk about it at home."

"Not yet," she says.

Soon.

She looks at my face, caught in the moonlight, like a ghost. Frowns. "We have to talk. . . . You can get rid of it, Rosanna. No one will know. I've found somewhere. We'll tell your father you're taking a course or staying with Carol." Carol, in a different, hateful kind of voice.

"I won't," I shout, furious, fearful, betrayed. *"I'm keeping it. It's my baby. Your grandchild,"* I scream at her.

But it's not Joanna's voice shouting back at me. She's a mad stranger, grabbing me, hurting me.

"You have to. It ruins everything. . . . No one will know. . . . You'll forget. It'll be over soon. Everything can go back to how it was. . . . Don't be selfish, Rosanna, always thinking of yourself, like a child. What about me?"

I try to pull away from her, but her rage is all-consuming, her strength inhuman, even though I fight back, punch at her, tear at her clothes, her hair.

"You have to," she mutters. *"Don't you see? It's the only way. You have to."*

I feel her shake me, then push me roughly, hard, her hand pulling my hair, smashing my head against a tree.

No . . . The world starts to spin, and suddenly, the stars are not just above. They're everywhere, all around me. I blink them away, then hold her eyes, see them flash as the moon catches them.

"I can't." For a second, I believe she's giving in. Her grip slackens, her head drops, but I'm wrong. The brute force born from a lifetime of anger, belittlement, and abuse, from being thwarted at every step, takes me by surprise. She shakes me, batters me repeatedly against the tree, cracking my head, my skin stinging as the bark cuts it, her rage a scream of vile words and hatred against her life, until I fall to the ground.

And as my legs crumple, my body sinking in slow motion, my eyes still locked on hers, so my head is the last part of me to hit, colliding, bouncing, splintering, against the rock.

Feel the blinding, excruciating agony of the knife that first time.

Then nothing.

In a moment of perfect stillness, the night on pause, she stares, not seeing, as I leave my body and float, watching her shocked face, hearing her gasp, stricken, her madness draining into the darkness. Oh God . . . What has she done?

I see her horror, because she didn't mean to kill me, just to make me understand that, as always, there are no choices, just necessities. Was that why she brought the knife? She drops to her knees. Makes this piercing, agonizing wounded-animal cry, doesn't know whose baby she's crying for.

Until something catches her eye. Alex's beautiful necklace, glittering in the moonlight. So beautiful, she can't leave it here. Reaching behind my neck to open the clasp.

Then panic seizes her. There's no going back. Not even in the darkest corner of her mind had she imagined it might come to this. What about the baby? The poor baby who couldn't live. Her baby's baby. She has to do something, to show how much she wishes it could have been different.

And slowly, it comes to her what that is.

Before she goes, she must cover her. In a rush, Joanna scoops up leaves, twigs, earth, whatever her trembling hands find, until my body slowly blends into the woods and disappears. Another sob wells up from the deepest part of her. What has she done? She can't leave me, not like this.

Joanna hunts around in the darkness for soft green moss, so pretty. So much more fitting for the daughter who'll always be perfect. Takes a deep breath. It wasn't what she planned, but it will still work. Neal won't be able to leave her now. It will be hard, but everything can go back to how it was.

Almost.

41

"Delphine? Did you write this?"

She turns to gaze at me with those pale eyes that hide everything. Then nods.

I hear a gasp of breath that's all mine. *"Why?"*

But she turns back to the jar of hot chocolate, measuring it out deliberately, silently.

"Delphine."

She turns round again, her eyes questioning.

"If you know something, you have to tell us."

But her look is blank, as though what she's done means nothing.

Laura chimes in. "It's okay, Kate." She catches my eye as she steps toward Delphine.

"It's too hard to talk about, isn't it?" Her voice is gentle.

There's a pause, and then, as she stirs her drink, the back of Delphine's head nods, barely perceptibly.

"Did Mummy or Daddy do something?"

This time, Delphine doesn't move.

"Is it easier if you show me?" Laura asks.

Delphine turns round again. Those pale eyes that have seen too much meet Laura's. She nods.

It's getting dark as we take my car and drive through the village. As we unlock the Andersons' house and let ourselves in, Delphine runs back out to the garage. When she returns minutes later, she's carrying a small leather purse, which she unzips, then tips into Laura's hand.

Laura picks up the necklace set with tiny colored beads, the one I've only ever seen on Rosie's neck. The one Alex gave her.

"Is this what I think it is?" Laura asks.

I nod.

"Is this Rosie's?" she asks Delphine.

"Yes."

"Did your mummy put it there?"

Again Delphine answers, "Yes."

She turns and goes out again. We follow, into the garage, where she goes to the shelves of her old books, where she pulls out a book with an overtly childish cover, then gives it to Laura.

It's like any other child's book of fairy tales, its cover beautifully painted with princesses and dragons from other worlds. Until Laura opens it.

Inside tells another story. In a hollowed-out compartment is an iPhone. Laura catches my eye, then looks at Delphine.

"Is this Mummy's?"

Delphine nods, then, without pausing, spins round, back outside, and through the side gate into the garden.

She runs across the grass, with Laura and me close behind her. Instinctively, I know where she's going, though I've no idea why. It's the apple tree, and when she reaches it, standing in the middle of the flower bed, she does the strangest thing. She leans forward and kisses it.

The three of us stand there for a moment, time suspended. Then Laura turns to me.

Her voice is urgent. "Can you get a spade?"

I dig for ages, as the light fades, while Delphine whirls around the garden, then sits on her swing, singing to herself. Eventually, some way down, the spade hits something.

Dropping to my knees, I stare closely at the earth as through a brief gap in the clouds, the last rays of sunlight catch dull metal.

"I've found something."

My heart in my mouth as my fingers carefully ease the knife from the ground.

Beside me, Laura gasps. "Leave it, Kate. We have to call the police."

"There's something else," I tell her.

It's just an ordinary plastic bag, heavily coated in soil, but as I pick it up, the stench is unbearable. Laura takes it, then starts to open it.

"Dear God."

Rosie

She doesn't need Kate now. It's just Joanna.

She needs to think. Wiping the knife before carefully putting it to one side, because she mustn't leave it here. Stripping off, like shedding a skin. Pulling on her gym gear, luckily, there in the bag in the back of the car. Hiding clothes stained with my blood and her tears. Her shoes. Then home. She needs to drink.

And on the way, it's so easy. She drops the holdall in someone's garbage bin, which will be emptied, its contents incinerated, before anyone knows it's there, because tomorrow's pickup day. Drives home and leaves the car on the road, tiptoes across the gravel and lets herself back in. No one will have missed her. No one will know.

Forgetting, as she always does, about Delphine.

And her reward is waiting in the fridge. The first glass she barely notices. She stops shaking after three glasses. Stops remembering after five. As the bottle empties, finds oblivion.

Until the next morning. Waking up. Head thumping, mouth gritty and dry. Remembers last night, meeting me, leading me into the woods, sick with horror as the rest of it comes back, too. That instead of killing my baby, she killed her own baby. If only she'd never brought the knife.

It was an accident, she tells herself. The most terrible, horrible accident, when she was just trying to help. She didn't mean for it to go wrong. And there's this other thing she has to do. Plant a tree. The apple tree. A tree of immortality and love. A mother's love. Her love.

And then comes the next part. The future. From here, she has to be so careful about what she says, what she does, what people see, every second of every minute of every day. Even more than before. Create her mask, behind which, behind the blankness in her eyes, you can't tell if there is a fairy princess or a psychopath. For as long as it takes for Neal to see how much he needs her.

Or it will all have been for nothing.

42

After, as the horror recedes slightly and the heat of another summer settles on us, I allow myself a glimpse of Jo's tangled world of shattered dreams and blurred boundaries, of the brutality and twisted logic that led her to believe that she could keep Rosie's secret and her own perfect world preserved forever.

I try to explain to Angus that you could liken what's happened to a rosebush, because however pretty it is to look at, however many blooms it has, if underneath the roots aren't strong or the soil's poor, it won't survive.

But he just looks at me, utterly incredulous. "Kate, she killed her own daughter, for Christ's sake."

I'm not sure Jo will ever leave this place she's found, with its blinding drugs and high-pitched walls that keep her safe. If she could even cope with the real world, least of all one that at last, because of Delphine, knows the truth. Maybe after killing Rosie, somewhere in the dark corridors of her labyrinthine mind, Jo sentenced herself to her own slow decline.

Rosie

It's easier than Joanna thinks it will be, even though her grief, shock, horror are all sickeningly real. As she's always said, when you want something enough, you pay a price.

Then, after all she's done for him, when he tells her quietly, with no threatening or bullying or harsh words, that he's still leaving her, that nothing will change that, she knows the light has dimmed, the passion has gone, feels a part of her die inside.

But even through her shock, her fear of being without him, she knows. She's always known. She can't let him be with someone else. Anything is better than that.

Humiliation, betrayal, even prison.

And in the end, because of what she discovers about him, it's so easy.

His arrest almost destroys her, but she clings on, won't let go, no matter how hard this is. In her twisted mind, she still has him.

For a while, she believes she can do this, but inside, what she's done tortures her. Every second of every minute of every day. Somewhere buried deep in her stone-cold heart, the small shred of decency and goodness that's somehow survived this long inches out and pitches her down the slope to madness.

And now, she's caught forever in her locked-down world, where no one will ever reach her.

43

What's happened makes me think about the lines we all etch into our lives, between right and wrong, good and bad, love and hate, a kind of moral compass, one that when her brain short-circuited, Jo lost forever as she crossed over into madness.

I still wonder how I didn't see. But as Laura puts it, we can use all our skills, our experience, observe body language, read between as many lines as we choose, but we see mostly what we want to see. And if someone wants to hide the truth, we may never know.

Trying Jo for murder may take some time, if it ever happens at all. Laura says there's an irony in that they've found the murderer, but all that's left is her body. And there are laws against taking someone to court who will just sit, not understanding, not seeing, not able to speak, catatonic, which is what she is now. But Jo's guilty, of deception, of emotionally abusing her children, of murder. Whether the law will ever call her to account for that, or whether locked away alone in her own hell, she's found her own way of atoning for her crime, she can never be free. But I don't think she ever has been.

All that may be, but even so, I knew her as a friend who was struggling, who needed me, just for a while. A damaged woman whose crimes were her obsessive love for her husband and her vulnerability. But more people are guilty. Laura's publisher flew her out to see Jo's parents, who would say nothing of any consequence, which, as I now know, means little. But they haven't been to see their daughter, which speaks volumes, nor do they show any concern. Behind the closed doors of Jo's childhood, anything could have happened. One day, if she's able to face it, maybe we'll know.

I'd thought Delphine would go to Carol's, but just before it was agreed, she took my hand and asked if she could stay with me and Angus. Even without everything she'd been through, her terrible secret, which she couldn't find a way to talk about, there was no way we could have said no.

I see Neal, just briefly, one last time. He comes over one evening, when Angus is home. We've talked about this, and Angus is prepared to be civil, though I know the personal cost to him. Really, he'd like to punch Neal's lights out, but the time for that has passed.

"Thank you," Neal says, meeting Angus's eyes first, then mine. "For taking care of Delphine. That's all I came to say."

It hurts to think that if it wasn't for us, if Carol also hadn't offered a home to Delphine, Delphine would have ended up in foster care. Not that it's of any real concern to Neal, who, because he could afford a good lawyer, paid a disproportionately small price for the abuse he inflicted. Who, with his newfound freedom and lack of interest in his daughter, doesn't actually care.

Now the sham of decency is on our doorstep, holding out his hand, a gesture of conciliation toward Angus, who sees through him.

"You shouldn't be here." Angus is openly hostile.

"I know. But you needn't worry. I came to tell you I'm leaving."

"You're a bastard, Anderson." Angus can't help himself.

I take my husband's arm. Neal shrugs, then turns to leave.

"Where will you go?" I blurt out the words.

He looks at me, holding my eyes, with the same knowing look I saw that evening he kissed me.

"Where I always said I'd go," he says softly.

At my side, Angus stiffens. Then, as Neal walks away, mutters, "Should have punched him."

"No," I tell him, reaching up and kissing his cheek. "You were wonderful."

"What did he mean just now?"

I watch Neal disappear out of sight.

"He's going back to Afghanistan."

When I ride Shilo through the woods that evening, I'm thinking of Rosie, then Alex and Delphine in the same instant, wondering if just maybe, in their shared loss, in some way they can help each other. Then I urge Shilo into a canter, listen to his hooves pounding, leaving my thoughts far behind.

I choose the same path I always take, up the slope to the clearing where Rosie died, where we pull up and just stand there. A rare peacefulness comes over me. The air is completely still, yet alive, so alive I can feel it on my skin, seeping into my soul, so that just for a moment, I myself, Shilo, the trees, everything, we're all one and the same.

I close my eyes, framing the thought in my head first, then my heart, before sending it out there.

Don't worry about Delphine. . . . I'll look after her. . . .

And wait. But there's nothing, not a flicker.

That's when I know Rosie's gone.

Rosie

What you don't know is that on the longest, blackest night, there is always a light. That the wind is myriad souls singing, passing from one world to the next, as they begin their journey to the stars.

Suddenly, my thoughts come in fragments. I know now that what needs nurturing isn't the blowsy, transient flower, but what's underneath, like people's hearts. But I know, also, the consequences of what happens if you leave a heart unloved, un-nurtured, unimportant, destined never to reach its potential.

Why? The word echoes around me, resounding through my soul. Why have children? I don't understand, when Joanna had choices. But like with everything, whether in this world or the next, there was a reason.

Then against the black, I see two far-off lights, pure, dazzling, untarnished, on a collision course. I watch them close until their paths touch, then flare brightly as one brilliant shooting star, before vanishing in opposite directions.

Once, I was my mother's perfect daughter. I could do

no wrong. Until she discovered that I wasn't perfect and nor was she, and it broke her.

Then I'm back at the beginning. It's coming to me; I'm starting to remember what's missing, who I've lost, who I'm waiting for.

And through the woods, I see her, with Alex's eyes, with the pale skin and the hair shining silver, like mine—because they are mine. She's running through the trees toward me, and as she gets closer, the love inside me wells up and overflows around us, enveloping her, drawing her close until at last she's here, with me. I reach my arms out, feel her melt into me, and the gaping emptiness is gone.

That's when time stops, the trees, the earth, the sky fading, slipping away, as it's the wind that comes for us, with its choir of voices, that most pure, blissful sound, soaring us higher, up into the heavens, into the stars, into the light.

READING GROUP GUIDE QUESTIONS

1. Does the idyllic village setting of the novel some-how make Rosie's murder more shocking?
2. In a small town, where you know most people, would a violent crime change the way you look at everyone?
3. After Rosie's body is found, is Kate's response understandable?
4. Discuss the different parenting styles described in the story.
5. Discuss how a parent's psychological flaws can damage a young person's development.
6. At what point does strict parenting become too controlling?
7. How well can we ever truly know someone?
8. Rosie's narrative tells her version of the truth. How believable do you think that is?
9. Discuss the ending of the novel. Do you think justice was served?

**From the acclaimed author of *The Bones of You*
comes a haunting and heartbreaking new
psychological thriller about a man thrust into
the middle of a murder investigation, forced to
confront the secrets of his ex-lover's past.**

"I was fourteen when I fell in love with a goddess . . ."

So begins the testimony of Noah Calaway, an ex-lawyer
with a sideline in armchair criminal psychology. Now
living an aimless life in an inherited cottage in the
English countryside, Noah is haunted by the memory of
the beguiling young woman who left him at the altar
sixteen years earlier. Then one day he receives a
troubling phone call. April, the woman he once loved,
lies in a coma, the victim of an apparent overdose—and
the lead suspect in a brutal murder. Deep in his bones,
Noah believes that April is innocent. Then again, he also
believed they would spend the rest of their lives
together.

While Noah searches for evidence that will clear April's
name, a teenager named Ella begins to sift through the
secrets of her own painful family history. The same age

as April was when Noah first met her, Ella harbors a revelation that could be the key to solving the murder. As the two stories converge, there are shocking consequences when at last, the truth emerges.

Or so everyone believes . . .

Set in a borderland where the past casts its shadow on the present, with a time-shifting narrative that will mesmerize and surprise, *The Beauty of the End* is both a masterpiece of suspense and a powerful rumination on lost love.

You think you know what it is to live. About those mo-ments seized, battles fought, love yearned for. But you don't. Not really, until it's slipping away from you. When your body no longer listens to you, but becomes a trap, inside which you can't move, can't breathe, can't reach out. No one can hear you. Not even the one person who could help you . . .

The memory is bittersweet, splinter-sharp. A transitory flash of long red hair damp from the mist; bone-chilling cold, the starkness of trees in winter. My heart quickening, as it always did. A girl I knew once, when the world was different, who filled my every waking thought, my dreams.

Nor can you know, we're like stars. At their brightest, most vibrant, before they die; a trail fading until the naked eye can't see it; the brilliant crescendo of a life that builds to silence.

Just as quickly it fades; a memory I've buried since I arrived here, years ago, when my Aunt Delilah died and left me her cottage. I'm questioning what's triggered it, glancing up from my desk just as the old black phone rings, past and present overlapping for a moment. It continues to ring, and though I'd rather not, I have to answer it.

Sliding my chair back, I get up and walk over to the windowsill. Feel behind the heaviness of the curtain to where it sits untouched. Unaware of the hope that flickers, like the flecks of dust stirred, caught in the dull glow of my reading light.

"Hello?"

"Hello? Noah? Is that you?"

I pause, startled, as fifteen years fall away. The clipped, precise tone is instantly recognizable, making my skin prickle, as I'm jolted back to the present, because the phone isn't part of the memory that's consumed me.

"Hello. Yes."

There's another brief silence before he speaks again, clearer this time. "It's Will."

I watch the moth that's taken refuge, camouflaged perfectly against the stone of the inglenook, as the fire I lit earlier sparks into life. My cottage has thick, stone walls that hold fast to the chill of winter.

He adds, "Thank Christ. I thought I'd got the wrong number."

Take the forest that's three-dimensional in the black depths of a still lake, each branch defined, every subtle shade perfectly mirrored, the sun looking out at you, so that if you stare for long enough, you forget. It's just a picture; hides the cold darkness that can close over you, that's silent.

Will and I were friends—once, a long time ago. But too much has happened, things that belong in the past.

As this, and much more, flashes through my head, common sense kicks in because I owe Will nothing. I'm about to put the phone down, when he says two words that alter everything.

"It's April."

Even now, my heart skips a beat at the sound of her name.

A moment, a few words, the single thought they provoke, can be devastating. Shatter what you've painstakingly constructed. Reveal who you really are.

"What about her?" I keep my voice neutral, my eyes fixing on the fireplace, on the moth's wings, twitching unevenly.

"There was an accident." He follows it up with, "She's in hospital. It's not looking good."

He speaks fast, impatient, his voice level, unemotional. I wonder if calling me is an inconvenience. And I'm sorry, of course I am. April and I were close, but it was a long time ago. Accidents happen every day. It's sad, but I've no idea why he's calling *me*.

There's only so long you can do this. Fake the pretense, dance to the piper's discordant tune. Hide an agonizing, unbearable truth that's been silent too long, that's hammering on the door, screaming, to be heard, for someone to listen.

"I'm not sure what happened, exactly. Look . . ." He hesitates. "I only called you because it'll be all over the papers. A guy was murdered—in Musgrove, of all places. Knifed to death in his car, parked behind the pub. The North Star—can you believe that?" He pauses again. "The thing is . . . Well, it looks as though she may have killed him."

I'm struggling to take in what he's saying, because the North Star was once our local hangout. There's a sick feeling in the pit of my stomach. Then I dismiss the possibility outright, because some knowledge is instinctive and I know this, with a certainty that's blinding, absolute. Will's wrong. I watch the moth launch itself into flight, its wings beating a slow undulating trail that circles the room twice, before battering itself at the closed window.

"That's impossible. She couldn't have."

Only no one comes, because no one knows, that you're bound and gagged, invisibly chained to a monster. There is no escape. There never can be, because wherever you go, he finds you. Won't let go of you.

"The police think there's evidence."

But as I know, it isn't always that simple. "The police could have missed something."

And what about hope? That eternal optimism of the human mind, as vital as blood and lungs and your beating heart, which carries you through suffering and heartbreak? Because when hope goes, you have nothing.

My jaw tightens. "When did it happen?"

"Last night. Late, after the pub . . ."

"Exactly," I flash back. "It's far too soon. They need to carry out forensic tests. They can't possibly know." I pause. "How did you find out?"

"They were seen together in the pub. The police found a woman's glove in his car, along with the murder weapon—and her phone. They traced it to her address, but by the time they got there, she'd taken an overdose." His voice is low. "They called an ambulance—then they called me. They must have found my number on her phone. Anyway, she's in the Princess Royal, near Tonbridge."

"Why's she there?" I ask stupidly.

"It's where she lives. Of course—I'm forgetting. You wouldn't know."

Suddenly your whole life is like a car crash, no brakes, gaining momentum, piling up behind you. Your mistakes, missed opportunities, all the time you've wasted, a twisted, rusting heap of scrap metal that can't be salvaged. Overwhelming you. Crushing you.

Even now, even though once, he loved her too, I hate that Will knows all this, how dispassionately he speaks, the condescension he barely conceals. That all these years later, he's still in touch with her when I'm not.

"She's hardly going to want to see me."

He hesitates. "She's not exactly up to seeing anyone. She hasn't come round, mate. She's on life support. God only knows what she took."

The *mate* is automatic, a throwback to our friendship—and out of place. But as I listen, I'm shocked, trying to absorb what he's saying, unable to picture April as someone who isn't vital and beautiful and brilliantly alive.

"The police are looking for witnesses. People who were in the pub, security cameras . . . If she's guilty, it won't be hard to prove," he says.

"*If* she is," I say pointedly.

"It's almost a foregone conclusion."

I used to think he was confident, not arrogant, but he really is so fucking arrogant. "Will. You know as well as I do. She wouldn't hurt anyone. She couldn't."

You can play the part for so long. Wear the mask, say what people expect you to say. Fight for as long as there is air in your lungs. Fly if you have wings.

But you can never be free from someone who won't let you go.

He makes a sound, a staccato laugh shot with cynicism. "When you haven't seen her for all these years, how can you possibly say that?"

He's a bastard, Will. Uses his surgeon's precision to dig the knife in, but he's forgetting, I knew her soul. I stay calm.

"The same way you know who you can trust."

He knows exactly what I'm saying. An uneasy silence falls between us.

"Fair enough." Will sounds dismissive. "I thought you should know, that's all."

"Fine. Hey, before you go, who was the guy?"

Will hesitates again. As he tells me, I watch the moth spiral into the flames.